# What Happens in the Ballroom

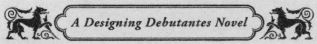

*A Designing Debutantes Novel*

# SABRINA JEFFRIES

## ZEBRA BOOKS
### KENSINGTON PUBLISHING CORP.
www.kensingtonbooks.com

ZEBRA BOOKS are published by

Kensington Publishing Corp.
119 West 40th Street
New York, NY 10018

All Kensington titles, imprints, and distributed lines are available at special quantity discounts for bulk purchases for sales promotion, premiums, fundraising, and educational or institutional use.

Special book excerpts or customized printings can also be created to fit specific needs. For details, write or phone the office of the Kensington Sales Manager: Kensington Publishing Corp., 119 West 40th Street, New York, NY 10018. Attn. Sales Department. Phone: 1-800-221-2647.

ZEBRA BOOKS and the Z logo Reg. U.S. Pat. & TM Off.

First Printing: April 2023
ISBN-13: 978-1-4201-5379-8
ISBN-13: 978-1-4201-5380-4 (eBook)

10 9 8 7 6 5 4 3 2 1

Printed in the United States of America

*For my husband, and soulmate, Rene, whom I love dearly.*
*Thanks for everything you do.*

# Chapter 1

*London*
*April 1812*

ᑕNathaniel Stanton, the Earl of Foxstead, stopped short, arrested by the sight of Mrs. Eliza Pierce headed toward him. How could he have forgotten how beautiful the widow was? It had scarcely been a year since they'd seen each other, and even then, only briefly while surrounded by friends and family.

Yet still she took his breath away.

Tonight, in that satin evening gown skimming her full form, with the squared bodice showing so much of her bosom, she looked as ravishing as a practiced courtesan, but with no heavy paint to mar her features. Her golden curls were caught up in a sort of band about her head, leaving one long tress to trail down her neck onto her nearly bared shoulder. He fancied that if he tugged that single curl, the rest would come tumbling down to her waist.

God help him. It had been too long since he'd had a woman. Unfortunately, this woman, of all women, would be the wrong one, since she already thought him a raging rakehell. Which made sense, given he'd been one for years before the war.

"Lord Foxstead, I'm surprised to see you here." Eliza smiled as she reached him, then held out her gloved hand. "I would never have taken you for a lover of amateur musical performances."

He took her hand. "Yet here I am, Mrs. Pierce."

She nodded in her usual serene fashion. "It's good of you to come. I couldn't persuade your friend the duke to do so."

"Of course not." Nathaniel squeezed her hand as firmly as he dared before releasing it. "Now that he has married your sister, he only sticks his nose out the door for his engineering projects."

"True." Her gay laugh poked at a part of him long hidden from the world. And from himself.

So did her eyes, which matched the blue of her gown so perfectly that he knew the fabric had been chosen for that purpose. His face must have shown his distraction, for his own sister cleared her throat.

"Forgive me, Mrs. Pierce," he told Eliza, "but may I introduce my sister, Lady Teresa Usborne? Tess has come to London for the Season."

Tess offered Eliza her hand. "It's lovely to meet you."

Eliza pressed Tess's hand. "I'm delighted to make your acquaintance." Then she broadened her gaze to include him. "And please accept my condolences on the death of your mother last autumn. I should have sent a note . . ."

When she trailed off, he said, "I'm sure you've had plenty to worry about yourself, especially with your sister's wedding. I hated to miss it."

"You were both still in mourning."

"It just ended," his sister said softly. Tess disliked any discussions of death. He couldn't exactly blame her, since they'd lost both their parents in the past three years. So, he wasn't surprised when she changed the subject. "I understand that you'll be performing this evening, Mrs. Pierce."

"Do call me Eliza, please." She lifted an eyebrow at Nathaniel. "Your brother always does. But yes, I'll be playing and singing."

"Both? You play an instrument?" He tried to hide his surprise. "I don't know why I didn't know that. Somehow, I've always missed hearing you exhibit."

"Samuel didn't like me performing for anyone but him," she said tightly. "Did he never even tell you I played?"

"No, actually." Another thing that surprised him. "I suppose you play the pianoforte."

"I do, but my instrument of choice this evening is the harp lute. I also play the regular harp and the harpsichord."

"Let me guess," he said. "You picked those three because your maiden name is Harper."

"My maiden name would have to be Harpist for that to work," she teased him. "Technically."

Tess laughed but he only stared at Eliza in bemusement. She had never teased him before. It gave him pause.

"You must be very talented," his sister said, "and not just in musical instruments. My brother has told me so much about you and your sisters and Elegant Occasions."

Despite being stained with scandal as the children of a divorced marquess and his adulterous wife, the Harper sisters had created a business that had become the most sought-after aid to throwing a successful social event. That was evidenced by the fact that tonight's musicale was being held in a marquess's mansion.

"Should I be flattered or insulted by what your brother told you of me?" Eliza asked his sister.

Tess chuckled. "Oh, flattered, to be sure. Nat has said nothing but good things."

"Nat?" Eliza turned her sparkling gaze on him. "Even Samuel never called you anything but Nathaniel."

He groaned. "Sadly, my family has used 'Nat' most of my life. I can't break them of the habit."

"We called him Natty when he was little," Tess said confidentially, clearly ignoring the glower he leveled on her. "Until he threatened to run away from home if we didn't stop." She smirked at him. "He was domineering even then."

"I'm not domineering," he drawled. "It's not 'domineering' when one's way is the only correct way."

Eliza laughed. "You sound like my new brother-in-law."

"He sounds like *me*, you mean."

"You're younger than he is, aren't you?" Eliza asked.

He arched an eyebrow. "Are you pretending to know my age, madam?"

"I know your age exactly. You're thirty-one. You and Samuel both started at Eton at the same age. Or so he told me."

"Close enough. I was actually a year younger than Sam. But he did speak the truth about us starting at Eton together." He frowned. "Although he knew I was a year younger. Can't imagine why he would tell you otherwise."

"In case you didn't notice," Eliza said dryly, "my late husband could be rather vain. He often pretended to be younger than he was."

"That doesn't surprise me." He paused, not wanting to talk about Sam. There was too much he'd have to conceal. "I just turned thirty."

She steadied a curious gaze on him. "How old do you think *I* am?"

"Good God, I wouldn't be foolish enough to guess," he said, ignoring his sister's skeptical glance. "I know you're the oldest of your sisters. But definitely much younger than I."

"I'm twenty-seven. Old enough to know you're flattering me. And why is that, I wonder?"

At that moment, as the silence stretched between them, his other companion for the evening entered the foyer looking worried as she approached Tess. "My lady, I searched everywhere in the coach, as did one of the footmen, and neither of us could find your shawl. Perhaps you left it at home?"

Before Nathaniel could reassure her, Tess said kindly, "No doubt. Don't you worry one moment about it."

"Eliza, may I present Mrs. Jocelin March," Nathaniel said. "She's staying with me and my sister at Foxstead Place for the Season."

Jocelin, blushing furiously, curtsied, and Eliza, always kind, offered Jocelin her hand. "How nice to meet you, Mrs. March."

The chit looked at the hand with a mix of embarrassment and intimidation before she took it. Nathaniel sighed. He was going to have to remind Jocelin once more that she belonged in society, even if she didn't feel as if she did. Even if there were . . . difficulties.

"Why don't you and Jocelin go find seats?" Nathaniel told Tess. "There's a matter I wish to discuss with Eliza."

With a nod, Tess took Jocelin off with her, since he'd already told his sister what he needed to talk to Eliza about. As soon as they were gone, Eliza stared after them, then lowered her voice. "Forgive me, but you must not be aware I'm in charge of this musicale. Can't whatever you want to discuss with me wait until it's over?"

He chuckled. "I'm certain you already have everything in readiness. Surely you can spare five minutes for your husband's oldest and dearest friend."

She eyed him askance. "Five minutes?"

"Or thereabouts. We can't stay afterward, because we

must rush home to relieve the poor maid looking after Jocelin's two-year-old son. As a bachelor, I didn't exactly have the . . . er . . . proper staff to handle a child."

"I can only imagine." Her lips twitched. "I'm sure her husband isn't up to the task, either."

"Forgive me, I forgot to mention she's a widow like you. Indeed, her husband served on the Peninsula as well, but not in the Twenty-eighth Regiment of Foot with me. I assume that Sam mentioned in his letters the man he was aide-de-camp for, Major General James Anson? Well, Jocelin is Anson's daughter." *Not too many details, my boy. That always gets you into trouble.*

Concern crossed her face. "Didn't the general die in the same battle as Samuel?"

Nathaniel nodded. "As did Jocelin's husband. Several regiments were involved in the Battle of Talavera."

"I'm aware," she said, her eyes misting. "I read everything I could about it."

"I was with the general when he died of his wounds a week after. He appointed me Jocelin's guardian before he perished, since by then he'd been told that her husband had died in battle, leaving her nothing." Damn, he had to tread carefully here. But it wasn't as if he were lying. More like stretching the truth as far as it would go. "Once she discovered she was bearing a child, everything became more complicated, as you might imagine."

"Oh, that poor woman!" Eliza said. "She seems awfully young to be dealing with so much."

"She's twenty. She was only sixteen when I met her. That's why I wanted to talk to you. I promised her father I'd make sure she found a good husband to take care of her, but I couldn't do much about it until now because of her pregnancy and her being in mourning, then us being in mourning. She lived with our mother until Mother died, and now she lives with Tess and Lord Usborne in Gloucestershire. But she can't do that forever."

"She and your sister do seem to get along," Eliza said cautiously.

"They do, but Linwood is too small for husband-hunting. And although she's my ward until twenty-one, she can't live with me."

"Obviously." She eyed him with interest. "Has she no other family? Of her own, I mean? I assume that the general or her mother had some, and perhaps even her late husband—"

"March was an orphan, so there's no family on his side." That lie came easily enough. "As for the general, his parents and only family died before he joined the army, and after that a wealthy gentleman for whom he'd done a great service purchased an officer's commission for him. He even fought in America for a time, which is how he met his wife."

"She was American?"

"Yes. She died in childbirth some time ago, as did her baby. Jocelin was their only surviving child." The part about the Ansons was all true, sadly enough. "It's not even possible to take Jocelin to live with her American relatives, given the tensions between our countries at present. Besides, once her mother married a British officer, her mother's family disowned her." The flash of sympathy crossing Eliza's face gave him hope that Elegant Occasions would take Jocelin on.

"That makes Mrs. March's situation even more tragic," Eliza said in a soothing voice.

*You have no idea.* "I'm glad you think so. Because I was

hoping that perhaps if I paid you and your sisters—paid Elegant Occasions—you might be able to . . . well . . ."

"Find her a 'good husband'?"

"Exactly. It is the sort of thing you and your sisters do, isn't it?"

A frown furrowed her brow. "Not quite. We could hardly engineer a début for a widow with a small child, even one with her titled connections."

"I'm not suggesting a début as such. But you could introduce her into certain circles, make sure that men looking for wives notice her. Because of her youth, she needs a chaperone, and I will not suffice. Tess does it at present, but she's not fond of London. So if you and your sisters could play that role for her—"

Someone called to Eliza from the door to the music room.

She glanced around and sighed. "I can't talk about this now. Why don't you bring Mrs. March to the town house tomorrow, and we'll discuss it while Verity is there? I'll see if Diana can't join us as well. Will that suit?"

"Of course. Thank you."

With a distracted smile, she hurried off.

He released a ragged breath. That had gone about as well as he could have hoped. At least he'd have a chance to convince the three sisters. And he would enjoy seeing them again, anyway. He'd always had a fondness for them, both before and after they'd married. Or rather, before two had married, if he included Eliza. From what he'd heard, Verity was still unattached.

Slipping into the music room, he took the seat his sister had apparently saved for him. She leaned close to whisper, "Well? Has your Eliza agreed to help with Jocelin's situation?"

"She's not *my* Eliza, by any means. But she did say she'd

meet with us tomorrow to discuss the matter. Give me a couple of hours with her then, and I'll talk her into it."

"I'm not so sure. That one has a mind of her own."

"Eliza? I suppose. But I've always thought of her as mild mannered, the sort who went along with what others said."

Although, if he were honest, he'd only had that perception from Sam, who'd claimed she lacked passion, not just in bed, but everywhere. She had no temper, Sam had said, which he'd seemed to think proved she didn't care enough about anything but her "precious sisters" to show the least bit of enthusiasm. Now that Nathaniel considered it, it smacked a bit of jealousy on Sam's part.

Of her sisters? That seemed far-fetched, didn't it?

"I doubt she's mild mannered when plans go awry," Tess said. "I daresay she can fight for what's needed when necessary. A woman can tell these things about another woman." She let out a breath. "Anyway, should I go along tomorrow, too? It might make Jocelin less nervous."

"There's no reason—she's my responsibility, and, in any case, you need time to yourself. It's not as if my accompanying a widow to Elegant Occasions would be considered scandalous. Even Eliza couldn't find fault with it."

"If you say so." With a veiled glance at Jocelin, who was busy untangling her shawl from the pins of her coiffure, his sister leaned closer. "You like her, don't you?"

"Jocelin?" he asked, deliberately misunderstanding her.

"Not Jocelin, you dolt. Mrs. Pierce."

Damn. The last thing he needed was Tess playing matchmaker. "I like her well enough. She was Sam's wife, after all." Whom he apparently wouldn't mind swiving.

Bloody hell. Being celibate for the last few years had clearly taken its toll. But that didn't matter. Until Jocelin was settled, he could not try seducing Eliza. He mustn't.

*Who are you trying to convince, old boy?*

He stared straight ahead. "I'll always regard her as a friend."

His sister snorted, obviously as skeptical as his conscience. "She's very pretty, and exactly the sort of woman you generally fancy."

He knew better than to respond to that. They sat a moment in silence.

When Tess apparently realized he didn't mean to answer, she released a breath. "You might consider bringing Jocelin's boy tomorrow as well. I daresay Mrs. Pierce would enjoy his shenanigans. She seems like the type, and it might ensure her help."

That wasn't a bad idea, actually. "You merely don't want him left with you and the servants. Why can't we keep a nursemaid on staff? I'm willing to pay for it."

"That child needs an army of nursemaids, I fear."

"He's just rambunctious. The way all boys are at his age."

"Suddenly you're an expert on children?" his sister asked.

Before he could retort, Eliza came to the podium and introduced the first lady to perform. He stifled a sigh. Now he would have to endure varying levels of execrable performances by young ladies with little talent.

Crossing his arms over his chest, he slumped in his chair.

"Do not embarrass me," his sister hissed.

"How on earth would I embarrass you?" he hissed back.

"The last time we went to something like this, you fell asleep and started snoring."

"I have never snored in my life."

"I beg to differ." Tess surprised him by turning to Jocelin. "When we were in the carriage on the way to London and my brother fell asleep, did he or did he not snore?"

Jocelin got that startled look of a rabbit transfixed by the sight of a human. "Uh . . . well . . ."

"It's all right, Jocelin. I know I snore. Occasionally." He smirked at Tess. "I only say otherwise to provoke my sister."

The music began, and he settled in. It was a bit better than he'd expected. He should have known that Eliza wouldn't put together anything ear-bleedingly bad. She and her sisters were consummate professionals. Which was odd, given that ladies weren't supposed to work. They had turned that expectation on its head.

Good for them. He hadn't managed to do that yet for himself, but he was certainly trying.

Over the next hour, they heard a decent sonata, an accomplished harp solo, and an insipid duet. He had just turned to his sister to ask how many bloody performances were listed in the program, anyway, when the voice of an angel came to his ears.

Sure that he was imagining it, he turned his head to find Eliza playing the harp lute as she sang one of Cherubino's arias from *The Marriage of Figaro*. It astounded him. Her voice was as pure a soprano as an opera singer's, and her skill on the instrument rivaled that of any player he'd seen before.

But he wondered if she knew that the part of Cherubino, particularly in this scene, was what they called in the theater a "breeches role," meant for an actress wearing breeches rather than an actor.

Mmm, Eliza in breeches. He could just picture it. He'd get to see her calves in nothing but stockings, her thighs and her rounded bottom molded in fabric instead of covered up by her gown and petticoats.

Of course, she would never wear breeches in a public venue like this. Only actresses dared do such things, and even then, only in the theater. It would be beyond scandalous, and Eliza wasn't the scandalous sort, at least according to her late husband.

But her expressive face as she sang and her cheeky understanding that the song was a droll commentary on how a boy became a man—made him rethink everything Sam had told him. No man with ears would believe Eliza lacked passion of any kind. So perhaps she wasn't quite who Sam had made her out to be.

Perhaps she was ready for a romantic entanglement.

Nathaniel groaned. This would already be a difficult few months, assuming that Elegant Occasions took Jocelin on. The last thing he needed to add to it was a flirtation with his best friend's widow.

Still, as she finished singing and playing to triumphant applause, he felt his old rakish urges, which hadn't troubled him in some time, reemerging. It might not have been part of his plan for the future, and it definitely wasn't wise, but one day soon he meant to have Eliza Harper Pierce in his bed.

However he could get her there.

# Chapter 2

As usual, Eliza was last to come down for breakfast. Morning was no friend of hers. She generally required two cups of coffee just to get dressed and out of her bedchamber. But today was worse because she'd scarcely had any sleep.

Last night in bed, she kept remembering how Lord Foxstead had devoured her with his eyes during her performance, as if he were a wolf picking out his dinner. She wasn't used to that sort of gaze from him. Having known him since before she and Samuel had married, she'd seen him level it on plenty of other women. But despite his reputation as a rakehell of the first water, he'd never used his flirtatious skills on her.

Until yesterday evening.

It had thrilled her. That, she hadn't expected, since she'd known full well he was only doing it to get something from her. But he'd looked good enough to dally with, even in half dress—a tailcoat of corbeau-colored wool, a figured waistcoat of cream silk, and breeches of sage-green linen.

Pausing outside the dining room, she collected her thoughts and prayed her lack of sleep didn't show. Diana might be the fashionist and Verity the temperamental artist, but Eliza moved behind the scenes to pay the bills, handle the various tradesmen accounts, and unruffle feathers for tradesmen and clients alike. It required a methodical attention to detail and a talent for figuring out other people's motives and emotions, not to mention a calm demeanor. That was why she saved all her true feelings for her music.

Apparently, so did Lord Foxstead. Because the fire in his gorgeous raven eyes as she'd sung last night had ignited her in places she'd long thought dead.

Now she must smooth her features into serenity and pray that the mask would hide her chaotic emotions. At least Rosy, Diana's sister-in-law who would be filling Diana's shoes soon, was on her honeymoon trip. And Diana didn't usually come over until later, so Eliza only had to deal with Verity.

Adopting an air of competence and confidence, she swept into the dining room and headed straight for the sideboard. "Good morning."

"You look fetching today," her sister said. "That parrot-green shade is so becoming on you. Isn't that your new walking gown? Weren't you saving it for some special affair?"

Eliza filled her bowl with porridge. "I thought I'd try it out, see if it feels constraining when I wear it all day."

Verity laughed. "So it has nothing to do with the fact that Lord Foxstead will be here shortly."

"Certainly not." Eliza met Verity's gaze with what she hoped was a steady look. "Why should it? And how did you know he was coming, anyway?"

"He sent a note saying he'd arrive at noon."

Her heart began to race.

*Stop that!* She chided her incorrigible heart. *Lord Foxstead isn't the sort of man you want, and you know it!* A pity that her body wasn't listening.

Meanwhile, Verity sipped her tea, dressed in her white

spotted muslin and fussy morning cap, looking for all the world like a prim miss. Appearances were deceiving with that one, to be sure.

"Did you happen to see the Phantom Fellow at the musicale?" Verity asked.

"Is that what we're calling him these days?"

"That's what *I've* been calling him," Verity said.

"It's an apt description," Eliza said, "considering he generally disappears before any of the rest of us spot him."

"You caught a glimpse of him once. At that large affair in Eaton."

"Barely. You are right about the man. He does his best not to be seen." Eliza eyed her sister closely. "Except by you."

"I just happen to notice him. Everyone else assumes he's someone they don't know. I only wish I could learn his name."

"Why? So you can have a little flirtation with him?"

"Don't be silly. I've no interest in him that way." Verity set down her teacup. "Although I did hear that you and the earl talked privately at the musicale last night. And that he appeared quite enraptured by your performance later."

Oh, dear. So Eliza hadn't imagined it. Had he, perhaps, really meant it?

Ridiculous.

She shot Verity a dark look as she took a seat at the table. "You must have good spies in that household."

"I have good spies everywhere," Verity said with a gleam in her green eyes. She got up to place another shirred egg on her plate. "Of course, when they speculated he might have an interest in you . . ."

"What nonsense." She only wished it wasn't. "He merely wants something from me—from us. That's the only reason he paid me any heed. You'll recognize that once I reveal why he's coming here today."

"Because he wishes to hire us?" Verity grinned. "Unless he's coming to propose to you."

"Right." She snorted. "I'm exactly the sort of wife an earl needs—a widow drenched in scandal, who's approaching thirty and has no dowry."

"You are nowhere near thirty yet. And he's a *wealthy* earl, so he doesn't need a dowry. Also, as Geoffrey's good friend, Foxstead may just yearn to join our cozy little family."

Eliza laughed outright. "He's never yearned for that before, and he was Samuel's good friend long before the man proposed to me. Besides, since when does a rich man want *less* wealth?" She busied herself with stirring her porridge. "Eventually he'll require an heir and a spare, so he'd do better to find a young virgin of unimpeachable virtue, with enough instruction from her hapless mama to look the other way while he dallies with a mistress."

"I will inform him of your suggestions for his future wife. I'm sure he will appreciate the advice."

Eliza snorted. "How amusing you are this morning. But he isn't our prospective client, though he's paying for the one who is." She explained everything Lord Foxstead had told her the previous night.

Verity paused in the midst of buttering her toast. "What did you think of his ward?"

"She's a veritable babe in the woods—I can hardly believe she's as old as twenty. Still, I find it curious that her father appointed a known scapegrace like Lord Foxstead as her guardian."

"Since Mrs. March was his commander's daughter, with no friends or family in England aside from her child . . ." Verity put down her toast. "And if his lordship's own mother and sister champion her, too . . ."

"I know. And we could use the funds. Still, how did she end up with a two-year-old if her late husband was on the Peninsula?"

Verity shrugged. "Perhaps Mr. March was on leave for some reason. Why? Are you saying *Lord Foxstead* is the boy's father?"

"It's possible, isn't it? I remember the exact date when Lord Foxstead returned from the war and visited me to inform me of Samuel's death, two and a half years ago. Isn't it possible that his next visit was to the young Widow March to tell her of the death of *her* husband? And perhaps he found a widow who wasn't grieving all that much? It would be easy enough to fudge the child's age a few months either way to cover up the earl's involvement."

"You're forgetting that Mrs. March might have been with her husband on the Peninsula."

"The army doesn't send women to war, Verity. Not yet, anyway."

"Don't they? Who nurses the wounded and washes all the men's uniforms?" Verity refilled her teacup. "I hardly think the men do it. You never hear about a washerman, after all. And male chefs notwithstanding, I doubt army cooks are as good at making scarce provisions palatable as a wife would be."

Eliza frowned as Verity's supposition hit home. Samuel had told her that officers were never allowed to bring their wives with them. Then again, she had long ago lost faith in Samuel's slippery grip on the truth.

"Is she pretty?" Verity asked. "Lord Foxstead likes them pretty, from what I've heard."

"She's the sort of shy waif any lord would fancy as his wife—all bouncing black curls and impossibly long lashes and demure green eyes." Not to mention that unlike Verity, who was slender, and Eliza, whose curves could be a bit too ample, Jocelin March had the perfect figure somewhere in the middle. "Oh," Eliza added, "and he calls her by her Christian name."

"Geoffrey calls *me* by my Christian name, but that doesn't mean I'm his mistress."

"I should hope not. Our sister would box his ears if our brother-in-law even considered it. Besides, he seems madly in love with her."

"True." Verity waved her butter knife at Eliza in a very unmannerly fashion. In their youth, their governess had tried unsuccessfully to rid her of the gesture. "So, did this young woman friend of Lord Foxstead's call *him* by his Christian name?"

Nathaniel. Such a nice name. "I don't think so. I can't remember. But you know how he is. He tries to seduce every attractive female he meets."

Verity arched her eyebrows high. "Is that what he did once he had you alone at the musicale?"

"Don't be absurd. He hardly had time to do *that*," she said defensively. *More's the pity.* Deciding to parry gossip with more gossip, she said, "Should I believe Geoffrey when he said Lord Foxstead made advances to you and Diana and even Rosy last year during the Season?"

"Advances!" Verity laughed. "Because he danced with all of us? That's ridiculous. Consider the source, for goodness' sake. Geoffrey didn't want any man looking at his future wife—or dallying with his sister—so he tried to make Lord Foxstead out to be some fiendish fellow on the prowl."

"When I first knew him, before I married, he was precisely that. Even after I married, he was known for his dalliances. Are you saying he made no advances to you? That you have no interest in him whatsoever?" Why did she feel compelled to find that out? Why should she care if Verity was setting her cap for Lord Foxstead?

"Don't be absurd. Although I will concede he's rather stunning. Even better looking than your late husband."

Who'd been quite the handsomest man Eliza had ever met . . . until he'd introduced her to his friend.

She tamped down a feeling of disloyalty. With the earl's Titus-cropped black hair, striking features, and devil-may-care smile, Lord Foxstead would put any other gentleman to shame. Even the new scar on his cheek, which he must have received during his two years in the infantry, only served to give his face character.

"But there isn't a scintilla of attraction between us," Verity went on. "When he danced with me at Almack's last year—before his mother died and he had to leave London— we spent the entire time talking about you."

"Me?" Eliza ignored the silly flutter in her chest. "Why-ever for?"

"He wanted to know how you were handling Samuel's death."

That deflated her. "Oh. That was rather kind of him."

She had to admit Lord Foxstead *could* be kind when the situation warranted. After he'd returned to England to take up his title and come to tell her of Samuel's death, he'd said he didn't want her to hear of it from the papers. Some-how the newly minted earl had broken the news to her in a more compassionate manner than she'd ever guessed him capable of.

"What did you tell him?" Eliza stirred her porridge. "About how I was handling Samuel's death, I mean."

"That you seemed fine." Verity searched her face. "That you always seem fine. Unlike me, who can't hide my roil-ing emotions from one minute to the next."

Eliza stifled a grin. "You do have a somewhat mercurial temperament."

"I take after Mama, unfortunately." Her sister sighed. "Which is why I shall never marry. Men do not handle mercurial temperaments well."

Reaching over to pat Verity's hand, Eliza said, "Please don't consider Papa and your foolish former fiancé as typical men. Some men—nicer men—would handle your temperament just fine."

"I doubt Lord Foxstead would be one of them. Though I wouldn't mind attempting to handle *him*, if you know what I mean."

When Verity followed that statement with a waggle of her eyebrows, Eliza couldn't help but laugh. "For an unmarried lady, you certainly have a salacious turn of mind." She rose to fetch some candied apple for her porridge. "Anyway, I'd feel awful if we *didn't* take Mrs. March as a client. The woman truly does need help, if not to find a husband, then to get her away from Lord Foxstead before she is publicly ruined."

"You know," Verity said, "it's possible he just wants her properly prepared for society so *he* can marry her. That's assuming there was never any scandalous relationship between them, and her son isn't his. Besides, you are the one always urging us to accept the wealthiest clients, the ones of highest rank."

"True. Sadly, we haven't married dukes like our dear sister, so we don't have the luxury of ignoring the prospect of a fine fee, no matter how much we prefer the more deserving clients."

"They are so much easier to deal with," Verity said. "But we have none of those at present."

"And Rosy's husband isn't rich. Not to mention that my late husband waltzed off to war on a whim without so much as leaving me provided for, and you, my dear, keep insisting you don't intend to marry. If not for the house Grandmama left me, there would be no Elegant Occasions, and you and Diana would still be living with Papa."

They both shuddered.

Eliza sighed. "So if we are to remain comfortable into our old age, assuming neither of us marries, then the business requires wealthy and titled clients."

"Lord Foxstead meets both criteria. Which is why we should accept Mrs. March."

"Precisely." Even if Eliza would want to thrash the earl every time he flirted with other women. "But I think while they are here today, we should observe them to see if there is any hint of impropriety between the two."

"Oh, I quite agree. We absolutely must get to the truth of their association, if we can. We've only been successful to date because our clients believe us above reproach, despite our parents' scandalous behavior."

"Exactly." And if Mrs. March did prove to be in thrall to Lord Foxstead, who was taking advantage of her youth, Eliza would help the woman escape him before her future was destroyed. "I'm glad we're in agreement on that score."

Eliza set that subject aside, since they had another to deal with. "Speaking of our parents' 'behavior,' when was the last time you dealt with either of them?"

"Well, I rarely see Mama, but with Papa sometimes coming to the occasions we plan for clients, I do see him a bit more. He was at that ball last week that we had charge of."

"I know. I missed talking to him, thank heaven, since I was busy doing hair and then helping you with the food."

Verity eyed her skeptically. "I didn't need the help. You just avoid him when you can. He *is* still our father, you know."

"Who refused to give my husband my dowry, which

indirectly affected *me* financially. Then he tried to strong-arm me into marrying a friend of his after Samuel died. Some father he is."

"You're usually the tolerant one of us three."

Eliza tipped up her chin. "He doesn't deserve my tolerance." For more reasons than she wanted to go into. "Besides, you saw how he acted toward Mama at Diana's wedding."

"Mama wasn't exactly cordial, either. Although I suppose they behaved as well as could be expected for sworn enemies."

"That's what worries me." Eliza set her bowl down at her seat but didn't sit. Instead, she began to pace. "Assuming everything goes well at the birth, Diana wants us to handle the baby's christening, which Geoffrey will pay for, of course. She's also eager to have a house party as part of it, if she can talk Geoffrey into it. But you know perfectly well Mama and Papa will both expect to be at the christening, with their respective new spouses, no less. Can you imagine them all under the same roof for several *days*?"

"Unfortunately, I can. We'd need mops for the bloodletting."

"And cotton in guests' ears for the screaming."

As if conjured up by their discussion, a small boy in a blue skeleton suit ran into the room and cried, "Toes!"

"Fingers!" Verity responded, always ready for a game, even with a child.

Eliza smiled at the towheaded lad, whose ruddy cheeks were matched by equally ruddy lips. "And what is *your* name, young man?" she asked, though she had a pretty good idea whose child he might be, given whom they were expecting to arrive any moment.

"Jimmy." He rocked back and forth from foot to foot, his brow creased in thought. "When Mama mad . . ." He puffed out his chest and yelled, "James! William! March!"

She and Verity laughed.

"Is your mama mad often?" Eliza asked, instantly charmed.

"Mama not mad," he answered, shaking his head. "Jimmy good boy."

"I can tell," Eliza said.

He shot her a look of pure mischief. "James William March ba-a-d boy."

Mrs. March rushed into the room. "He most certainly is."

Eliza's butler, Norris, came in, looking flustered. "Mrs. William March, Master James March, and Lord Foxstead, madam," he announced.

Mrs. March curtsied to Eliza and Verity, a blush rising over her cheeks. "I'm so sorry. Please forgive us." She bent to look at her son, who'd crawled under the table to escape her. "James Wi— *Jimmy*, come out here right now!"

To Eliza's surprise, he did. "Toes, Mama!"

"You can't just demand food at other people's houses, lad," Lord Foxstead said mildly as he entered the room.

"Ohhh, *toast,*" Eliza and Verity said in unison.

"We have toast." Eliza hurried over to the sideboard. "How much would you like, Jimmy?"

The boy stared down at his hands as if trying to sort that out on his fingers. Then he held up all ten. "This many!"

Lord Foxstead strode over to the sideboard. "You're not getting ten slices of toast, you little rascal. Two will do you nicely." He pointed to the tongs in Eliza's hand. "May I?"

"Of course," Eliza said. When his hand brushed hers as he took the tongs, her legs wobbled a bit. Stupid legs.

Clearly, it had been too long since she'd been around a man who tempted her. And heavens, but Lord Foxstead was even more attractive in his iron-gray morning coat than he'd been in more formal attire last night. Either way, the earl filled out a coat very well.

"If you had to judge from how much Jimmy eats," Lord

Foxstead said conversationally, "you'd think we never fed the boy."

"He really doesn't need more toast, my lord," Mrs. March put in.

Lord Foxstead smiled down at Jimmy. "A lad like you always needs toast, don't you, Jimmy?"

"Toes!"

With a laugh, the earl brought the plate to the table, then lifted Jimmy up to sit on a chair. Jimmy's nose was at table level.

"Let me get a cushion," Eliza said.

But before she could walk off, Lord Foxstead took a seat on the chair next to Jimmy's and hauled him onto his lap. Then he groaned. "You're right about the toast, Jocelin," the earl said as Jimmy squirmed a bit. "This lad will soon weigh as much as a pony if we don't pull on the reins."

With the two males sitting so close, Eliza was able to look for resemblances. She thought she saw some, but she was probably imagining what little she did see. It certainly wasn't enough to justify thinking that the earl was the lad's father. She honestly hoped he wasn't. She hated to think Lord Foxstead, rakehell or no, would stoop so low as to seduce a woman he had pledged to help.

Then again, he *had* been Samuel's worst influence back in the day.

When Jimmy reached for the plate, Lord Foxstead said, "Whoa, there, Jimmy. It hasn't even been buttered yet."

Jimmy shook his head and scowled. "No butter. No like butter."

"But surely—" Lord Foxstead began.

"No like butter!" Jimmy cried.

"Very well. Have at it then," the earl said and put the plate within Jimmy's reach. "No butter for you."

The lad devoured the two slices, scattering crumbs all

over Lord Foxstead's white trousers, waistcoat, and cravat. The man didn't even seem to notice. Or care.

But *someone* did. In that moment, Eliza caught the look on Mrs. March's face as the young woman regarded the earl. Pure hero worship shone in her eyes. Oh dear.

Time to figure out if Eliza's fears were correct. Because if they were, she and Verity would have to change strategies.

*So* you *can have him?*

She banished that thought to the wilderness of her mind, to be studied later. "Now that little Jimmy is done eating, perhaps Verity could take him to the garden? Surely he'd enjoy that."

"Good idea." Lord Foxstead set the boy down on the floor. "And that will make it easier to talk."

Verity instantly sprang up and took the child's hand. "Jimmy, do you like fish? Would you like to see the gold-fish pond?"

"Fish!" Jimmy said. He seemed to have only one level of speech—emphatic.

Jimmy and Verity both trooped happily off. Not many children were that easily led. Then again, Jimmy probably went off with nursery maids and family members like Lord Foxstead's sister all the time. But if so, why was he here?

As if reading her mind, the earl said, "We've had some trouble finding—and especially *keeping*—the right nursery maid for Jimmy. I'm not quite sure why."

"Clearly, you haven't been around many boys his age, or you'd know they are adventurous and hard to manage," Eliza said. "Besides which, they're prone to stumbling into things they shouldn't . . . like mud puddles and stinging bees and snapping dogs."

"I certainly never was." Lord Foxstead's voice turned steely. "I was never allowed to be. But I would not want that for young Jimmy." He stiffened. "How would you know what little boys are like, anyway?"

"First, my father has three small stepsons I see occasionally, and second, I volunteer at the Foundling Hospital. I've dealt with plenty of boys." She turned to Mrs. March. "The Foundling Hospital is always looking for posts for the young ladies they sponsor, so if you'll permit it, I can probably find a nursery maid for Jimmy who is more likely to stick around, if only out of gratitude for the post."

"Thank you, but he doesn't need a nursery maid. All the ones who've come have been . . . well . . . mean. I can look after him well enough myself."

This wouldn't work unless Eliza could put Mrs. March at ease. "I'm sure that's true, but you'll be busy preparing for your introduction into society. The Season is taxing, and someone will have to look after Jimmy while you're at balls and such. Assuming that his lordship is willing to pay for a nursery maid." If he was, that would tell Eliza quite a bit.

"I-I hadn't thought of that," Mrs. March said in a small voice. "Jimmy's a good child, you know. He just has a great deal of energy in situations like these. He wants to see and do everything at once."

"Of course." She made her voice soothing. "That's to be expected of any boy his age."

"He's over two years old," Mrs. March said defensively.

That gave Eliza pause. If Jimmy was indeed that age, Lord Foxstead had probably not sired him. "In any case, the boy could use someone to take him outdoors and keep him entertained while you hunt a husband."

"Oh." Mrs. March looked defeated. "I can find a nursery maid myself if someone will just tell me how it's done—whom I should look for and such."

"What she means is if someone more discerning than I could find one," Lord Foxstead told Eliza dryly. He turned to Mrs. March. "Perhaps Mrs. Pierce could give us a list of young ladies who need work, and you and I could interview them together. Would that suit?"

Mrs. March beamed at him. "That would be wonderful, my lord."

With difficulty, Eliza hid her reaction to the pair's exchange. It wasn't Mrs. March's words that disturbed her. It was the clear adoration in her expressive eyes. That could make their efforts to help the young lady problematic.

*And you're jealous.*

Nonsense. She wasn't the jealous type. Besides, hadn't she already decided that the Earl of Foxstead was not for her?

"I shall happily provide Lord Foxstead with a list of prospective nursery maids." Eliza broadened her gaze to include the earl. "Now that we've settled that, let's retire to the drawing room upstairs."

As they decamped, she paid close attention to how his lordship behaved with Mrs. March. He seemed solicitous of her, but no more than any gentleman would be to a young lady. And when the widow took a seat on the settee and flashed him a hopeful look, he chose a chair instead, though he could easily have sat beside her.

Or perhaps Eliza was reading too much into where they sat because she didn't want him to be attached to Mrs. March for her own selfish reasons.

Putting that thought aside, she chose to sit next to Mrs. March herself. "Now, let's talk about what you hope to attain—besides gaining a husband, of course. It would help if you could also tell me how you prefer that we at Elegant Occasions go about getting what you want."

"Very well," Lord Foxstead said, ignoring the fact that she'd been addressing Mrs. March. "Obviously, we need Jocelin to attend several social affairs where she can meet gentlemen of good reputation and standing."

When Mrs. March dropped her gaze in clear consternation, Eliza sighed. Could Lord Foxstead really be that oblivious to Mrs. March's feelings for him?

Apparently so, for he went on in that vein. "A widower with children would suit, I'd imagine, since he might more easily accept Jimmy. Some men prefer not to raise other men's children."

"But not all," Eliza pointed out. "Papa married Sarah precisely because she'd borne her late husband's sons." She glanced at Mrs. March, hoping to provoke a response. "My father needs an heir, you see."

The woman didn't even look up. But then she whispered, "Don't all titled gentlemen need heirs?"

"Any landed gentleman does, yes. What's more, they'll be encouraged by the fact that you gave your husband a son."

*Unlike I, who gave mine nothing at all, not even a decent dowry.* But Samuel should have expected the latter, given what he knew of her father, not to mention the fact that they'd eloped.

Eliza took out her notebook and pencil to keep from dwelling on that. "Have you any preference as to the sort of gentleman you hope to attract, Mrs. March?"

When the woman frowned, the earl said hastily, "Someone relatively rich, I should think."

With the lift of one brow, Eliza stared him down. "The last I checked, Lord Foxstead, your name is not Mrs. March."

That startled a laugh out of his ward.

Lord Foxstead narrowed his gaze on Eliza. "The last *I* checked, the one who pays the bills also makes the rules."

"That did not work for your duke friend last year, sir, so I doubt it will work for you," she said tartly. "And you lack the advantage of being related to the young lady whose introduction into society you wish us to engineer."

Eliza waited, practically daring him to claim Jocelin as his mistress.

He searched her face, as if looking for a weakness to exploit. Then he shrugged. "Fine. I will keep quiet until we discuss your fee."

"Excellent choice." Eliza turned to Mrs. March. "Now, my dear, do you have a type of gentleman you prefer?"

The woman looked down at her hands. "So long as he's kind and good, I don't care what he looks like or how rich he is." When the earl cleared his throat, Mrs. March added, "I'm sorry, my lord, but wealth really doesn't matter to me."

"Never mind him," Eliza said archly. "Much like my father, Lord Foxstead likes to be in charge of everything. And much like Mama, I like men who don't."

"Obviously your mama didn't always prefer that," Lord Foxstead quipped, "or she wouldn't have married your father in the first place."

He had a point. She couldn't remember when Mama had started resisting Papa's commands, but her mother hadn't been so bold when Eliza was a child. Perhaps Mama had grown tired of Papa's stubborn insistence on getting his own way through the years. Just as Eliza had grown tired of Samuel's.

She buried that thought. "What I'm trying to say is you should let Mrs. March give her own opinions. Her choice of husband concerns her more than you."

Eliza patted the poor young woman's hand. When she looked startled and jerked her hand away, Eliza sighed. Mrs. March seemed very skittish around her. Perhaps she'd noticed the way Lord Foxstead had flirted with Eliza.

Now *that* was a reason that made sense. It also meant they wouldn't get far in their discussion as long as he was here.

Fortunately, just at that moment, Eliza heard Jimmy approaching from the hall. The lad was hard to miss since he seemed to have only one pace—running. He darted through the door and headed straight for Mrs. March. "Mama, Mama, come see! Big goldfish!"

Though Mrs. March brightened at the sight of her child, Verity looked a bit harried. "He's quite . . . boisterous, isn't he?" Verity said.

"Sometimes." Mrs. March leapt up to take his hand. She looked to Lord Foxstead as if for permission to leave, and Eliza took that for a sign, too.

Eliza rose. "Verity, why don't you take Mrs. March and Jimmy across to the square so he can run a bit? I need to discuss the . . . er . . . fee with Lord Foxstead."

Curiosity shone in every line of Verity's face as she nodded. "Come along, troops. We'll take some toast left over from breakfast and feed the pigeons."

"Toes!" Jimmy cried and tugged his laughing mother toward the door.

Eliza waited until they'd gone, then rose to pull the door to, though not entirely closed.

Lord Foxstead stood to watch her with all the wariness of a cornered stallion. "I take it you mean to discuss more than the fee."

"How astute you are."

She expected him to ask what. Instead, he strolled to the window and looked out. "I remember the last time I was in this room. You were more . . . subdued."

"Of course. You'd just told me my husband was dead."

"I mean, before I told you." He faced her with a brooding expression. "You wore a yellow gown with a white dimity apron and sat on that settee gazing warily at me. Until I informed you of Samuel's passing. Then I feared you might faint."

"I've never fainted in my life, sir." And she couldn't believe he'd noticed what she was wearing.

"You certainly don't look prone to fainting spells today. You look like a woman preparing for battle." He crossed his arms over his chest. "You know, I always thought of you as the mild-mannered one."

"Of what?"

"Elegant Occasions. Diana is the sharp-tongued one, Verity is the impassioned one, and you're the mild-mannered one."

That startled her, then annoyed her. "Why? Because I keep a rein on my temper? Because I don't always speak my mind like Diana, or blather my emotions like Verity? Because I keep my own counsel? That doesn't mean I'm a milksop."

"I didn't say you were a—"

"You can't put us in neat little boxes, you know. We're more complicated than that. People in general are more complicated than that."

"Forgive me," he said quietly. "I meant no insult."

She caught herself. He didn't realize why she was angry at him, of course. And he wouldn't unless she told him. "There's a reason I'm less even tempered today than you apparently perceive me to be."

He approached her with a guarded gaze. "Oh?"

"I'm concerned about the true nature of your relationship to Mrs. March. So before we continue this discussion, I demand that you tell me exactly what it is."

# Chapter 3

The bottom dropped out of Nathaniel's stomach. Bloody hell. Had she guessed the truth about Jocelin? Had he given it away somehow?

Trying to buy time to figure it out, he said, "I'm not sure I understand."

Her frown deepened. "I need to know if Mrs. March is—or ever was—your mistress and if Jimmy is your son. Because if they're your secret family, then we need to rethink your plan to introduce her into society. I mean, it couldn't . . ." She petered out as she apparently took in his stunned expression.

The accusation differed so markedly from what he'd been expecting that at first he could only gape at her. Then he found his voice. "Why the devil would you assume . . . No! Of course not!" He shoved his hand through his hair. "Jocelin isn't my mistress. I don't bed children."

"Jocelin is hardly a child."

"To me, she is. When I first met her, she was sixteen and newly married. She was only seventeen when Jimmy was sired, and, I should add, not by me. I do not rob cradles, madam. How could you think it?"

"How could I *not* think it?" She strode up to him, her

fine blue eyes sparking with every step. "For one thing, how could Mrs. March have found herself in the family way when her husband was on the Peninsula? You said Jimmy is two, so he had to have been conceived in England around the time you returned, a few months shy of two years and nine months ago."

Damn. He hadn't realized what Eliza might presuppose. Others might, too, so he'd best make the truth clearer. Or as much truth as he dared let her see. "Mrs. March was abroad with her husband. I thought you knew that."

She stared at him. "But wives do not generally . . . Samuel said wives of officers do not—"

"If he said that, he lied. Yes, there's a quota for the rank and file—only a few wives are allowed to go—but any *officer* can bring his wife abroad if he chooses. Most don't. It's a hard life. Sam probably knew you would wish to go, so to avoid an argument he told you that you couldn't."

Her lips tightened into a thin line. "That sounds like him."

"Jocelin was raised in the regiment, but only because her mother died in childbirth when Jocelin was six, and there was no one else to take her. So she joined her father, and he hired another officer's wife to look after her when he couldn't. It's why she's always so nervous in polite society. She feels more comfortable among soldiers." That was mostly true.

Eliza seemed to chew on that a moment. Then her gaze darted to him accusingly. "But didn't the Battle of Talavera take place in July of 1809? Even if Jimmy was conceived right before it, he'd be older than two by now."

"And he is. He was born at Amberly, my estate, in February 1810, having been conceived in May 1809. While Jocelin was abroad. With her husband. In another regiment."

"How do *you* know when the boy was conceived?"

"She told me, of course."

"And he was born at *your* estate?" she asked with raised eyebrow.

Of course the damned woman would fix on that. "My mother was still alive then and residing there." He glared at her. "Any more impertinent questions?"

"Impertinent! I assure you that any questions I ask will pale to the vile gossip that will be spoken about her if there's even a hint that she's your mistress. Others may also notice she's extremely uncomfortable around me and adoring of you. Clearly, she's in love with you and resentful of this whole process where you are planning to banish her from your life by marrying her off."

Only with an effort did he resist the urge to laugh in her face. The woman was so far off the mark, and he couldn't even tell her why. "Jocelin is not in love with me or any nonsense like that. Nor do I plan to banish her from my life. She and Jimmy have become part of my family and now always will be, even when she comes of age and I'm no longer her guardian. And if I was seeking a mistress, I wouldn't choose the daughter of a man I respected and admired, a man who begged me on his deathbed to be her guardian!"

As he turned to walk away, he thought better of it and pivoted back to face her. "Clearly, you regard me as even more of a scoundrel than I thought and my whole family as suspect! Even if my mother had ignored the possibility of Jocelin being my mistress, do you really think my very respectable *sister* would give succor to any mistress of mine? Or to my supposed bastard child? Good God! She'd sooner cut out my tongue."

Her implacable expression reminded him that Sam had said she could occasionally be stubborn.

But then, so could he. "Don't let Tess's amiable personality fool you—she's a proper woman, and her husband is a pillar of their community. She would never jeopardize her own standing for some illegitimate family of mine."

Crossing her arms over her ample bosom, she asked, "Then why the sudden need to marry off Mrs. March?"

"I told you—I promised her father I'd do so. Besides, my sister and brother-in-law hope to have children of their own soon. When that occurs, they don't want poor Jimmy to feel as if he's playing second fiddle to Tess's own children."

Which would almost certainly happen if Tess and her husband ever learned the truth about Jocelin.

"Very well." Eliza cocked her head. "So Jocelin isn't your mistress. But Verity suggested this might all be a ruse to get Jocelin properly prepared for a future as your wife."

He scoffed at her. "Don't you think I'd tell you if I wanted that? If I intended to marry her, I would say that plainly. What reason would there be to hide it?"

"Because you wish to see if she can become what you need her to be as your countess," she said, tipping up her chin.

This got worse by the moment. "Where the devil do you and your sister get these notions? I don't want to marry Jocelin, and I certainly don't want to screw her." The minute the words left his mouth, he wished he could yank them back. "Pardon my vulgarity."

To his surprise, she didn't even look outraged, as Tess would have. If anything, she looked faintly amused. "No need to apologize. I'm used to dealing with the ladies of the Filmore Farm for Fallen Females. I've heard plenty of vulgar language, I assure you."

"Have you, now?" Possessed by an urge to shake her calm, he added, "I daresay you've learned a great deal more than just vulgar language from them." When she blushed, taking him by surprise, he found himself wondering what her learning might include.

And what could make a widow blush.

He forced that idea from his head before it took him into dangerous waters. "What gave you this maggoty idea about me and Jocelin, anyway?"

She met his gaze steadily. "The way you behave toward Jimmy. The way Mrs. March behaves toward you."

"Ah, yes, your assumption that she's in love with me." He raised his eyes heavenward. "I'm quite sure you're wrong."

"Then you're even more oblivious to her feelings than I thought," she said, her voice gentler now. "Every time she sees your kindness to Jimmy, she gets this worshipful expression on her face. It's clear she's only here to please you."

That was true, though not for the reasons Eliza thought. A pity he dared not enlighten her. "I doubt Jocelin thinks of me as anything more than a guardian. Indeed, I hope you're wrong about her. I would not wish to hurt her."

"Then at the very least, you should pay better attention to what she says and how she acts. If you have no intention of marrying her now—"

"Or ever," he put in.

"Then you need to tell her that plainly."

"I will, I assure you. Because I could no more marry Jocelin than marry Tess. Every part of me recoils from the idea." Realizing how strong that must sound, he drew in a calming breath. "But I'm still not entirely convinced you're right. I've never seen any evidence of . . . of worshipful looks from young Jocelin."

Then again, he hadn't really been paying attention. He'd had too much on his mind, what with trying to get Amberly working properly again and engaging new tenant farmers for that purpose. If Jocelin was mooning after him, if the girl had expectations, he must end that at once.

As if by some diabolical plan, voices outside in the hall showed that Jocelin, Verity, and Jimmy were approaching. In a flash, he thought of what to do to determine once and for all whether the young woman was in love with him, as Eliza claimed.

With no time to warn Eliza, he drew her into his arms and kissed her as hard as he dared. She stiffened a little, obviously surprised, but to his amazement, she kissed him back.

In that moment, he forgot entirely what he'd meant to accomplish. He forgot who he was, where he was, and why he absolutely shouldn't have taken Eliza in his arms. All he knew was her lips were more supple than he'd imagined, and her full curves against him tempted him to caress them right then and there.

Which was sheer madness, of course. As was kissing her, which he couldn't seem to stop doing. Engulfed by the scent of her perfume—something light and fruity—he nibbled her lips, stroked them with his own. When he deepened the kiss, plunging his tongue into her mouth, she gave a positively wicked moan that enticed him to slip his hands down to her bottom and bring her flush against him. Her response was to grab his head and hold him close.

So much for mild-mannered. Eliza aroused was any man's carnal dream. But even as he thought it, he felt her withdrawing just before something hit the floor with a resounding crash.

He turned to see Jocelin frozen in the doorway, with a cup of tea in one hand and her other hand suspended in air. At her feet, a small plate of cakes had shattered on the threshold. And her devastated expression plainly showed how she felt about seeing him kiss another woman.

Damn it all to hell. Eliza was right.

* * *

Eliza moved away from Lord Foxstead, intent upon doing what she must to somehow erase what the poor woman had just witnessed. "Mrs. March . . ."

Clearly, the young lady refused to stay for that, because she turned on her heel and hurried from the room, leaving Verity to drag Jimmy back when he wanted to pick up the porcelain shards of the saucer.

"Jimmy fix it!" he cried.

"No, Jimmy. It's not your fault. Mrs. Pierce will fix it, all right?" Her face beet red, Verity glanced at Eliza. "I'll . . . uh . . . take Jimmy and get a footman to clean this up."

"Leave the mess for now, if you would, but do take Jimmy to his mother," Eliza said. "And close the door, Verity, if you please. I need a few more words alone with Lord Foxstead."

The minute the door closed, she whirled on him. "You are not to do that ever again!"

"I only wanted to see if—"

"I know why you did it. And I'm sure you noticed poor Mrs. March's reaction."

He sighed. "Sadly, I did."

"But I will not be used to torment the young lady. And furthermore—"

"No need for 'furthermore,'" he said hastily. "I apologize. I was wrong to have done it in front of her, and I sincerely beg your forgiveness."

She eyed him with blatant suspicion. "You've never admitted you were wrong before."

"It's a skill I'm attempting to learn," he drawled. "One *can* change, you know."

"But one rarely does." Samuel certainly never had. "Unless one has a strong motive to do so."

"And I do."

Crossing her arms over her chest, she said, "Oh? By all means, surprise me."

"It's personal. And private." When she opened her mouth to protest, he added, "But I was genuinely shocked to see Jocelin's reaction. Until that moment, I truly hadn't believed she had set her cap for me."

Despite Eliza's misgivings, his expression of heartfelt contrition deflated all her anger. "I would protest that her feelings had been obvious even to me, who'd just met her, but I've dealt with plenty of gentlemen blind to the emotions of the women closest to them, so I know it occurs frequently."

His gaze on her narrowed. "I don't know whether to be gratified that you've accepted my apology or insulted that you think me an ignorant dolt who couldn't see what was right in front of me."

She fought a smile as she turned and walked away. "Perhaps you should settle on something in the middle."

He was silent so long she wondered if he'd heard her.

Then he followed her. "I wasn't so ignorant that I couldn't tell you were fully participating in our kiss, despite your objections afterward."

So he'd noticed that, had he? And he would probably also see through any of her attempts to protest his impressions. "Be that as it may, if Elegant Occasions is to continue being regarded as reputable, I have an image to uphold." Facing him again, she forced sternness into her tone. "So you must never kiss me again in front of my sister—in front of anyone."

His lovely eyes gleamed at her. "Does that mean I can kiss you if no one's around?"

Why, the devil was flirting with her, of all things! She fought to ignore the thrill coursing through her and said what she was sure would put him off. "Only if you're courting me, Lord Foxstead."

"I think you've known me long enough to call me Nathaniel." With a rogue's smile, he stepped closer. "And perhaps I am."

"Am what?" she asked, sounding far too breathy.

"Courting you."

A bitter laugh escaped her. "Liar. A man like you doesn't court a woman like me."

He looked genuinely perplexed. "As far as I can tell, we're of similar rank and position."

"Except for my family being dogged by scandal and my not being an innocent."

"Damn it, you're right," he said sarcastically. "You have nothing to commend you. I'll just have to settle for making you my mistress."

Even knowing he was joking didn't quite take out the sting. "Being a mistress sounds so permanent," she quipped. "Even if you gave me carte blanche, it would hardly be worth it. I suppose I could handle a quick tumble, but anything more would be too much for my busy schedule." She smiled. "Besides, you couldn't afford me."

"Couldn't I?" His voice rumbled with the promise of dark and sinful pleasures.

So when he pulled her close and kissed her again, she let him. Because this kiss wasn't engineered for anyone else's benefit. And because she was startled to find that he, of all people, made her long to be with a man for the first time in years. To be with him in particular.

This kiss was rougher than before, more elemental. His mouth drank of hers with deep, steady forays of his tongue. He smelled of citrus and tasted of coffee, making her hunger and thirst for him. And he held her so tightly she could feel the rising bulge in his trousers.

The fact she could arouse him intoxicated her. Alarmed her.

She clutched at his arms, meaning to push him away, but instead she held him closer, just so she could have his hard chest pressing against her breasts, making thcm throb with need and heat. She knew, without his saying a word, that being bedded by him would be an experience far beyond her own.

That made him dangerous. Regretfully, she drew back, wondering if she dared let Lord Foxstead bed her.

He must have wondered the same, for he released her, murmuring, "I believe you're right. You may very well be too rich a dish for my blood."

As he may be for hers. The only man she'd married had eventually turned her into someone she didn't even recognizc. By the time Samuel had said he was going off to war, he'd twisted her into such knots that she'd almost felt relief when he'd left. She refuscd to let any man do that to her again.

But that didn't necessarily mean she had to deny herself a mere flirtation, did it? Perhaps even a small affair? It didn't have to lead to anything. It would be better if it didn't.

While Nathaniel headed for the door, she smoothed her skirts and touched her coiffure to make sure his ardent kisses hadn't dislodged any hair pins. But she couldn't still the pounding of her pulse and the delicious excitement left from just his hard body pressed to hers.

Deftly avoiding the pieces of shattered porcelain and

crumbled cakes, he paused with his hand on the door handle. "It's a pity, though. You have a body made for temptation. I would dearly love to show you—" He broke off. "Ah, but if you do not wish it, it's not to be. And a quick tumble would never be enough for me."

After opening the door, he paused. "I regret that we must leave before Diana arrives, but I think it best that I take Jocelin and Jimmy home. I need to have a long talk with my ward, and the lad probably needs a nap." With a wary expression, he added, "Assuming it's acceptable with you and your sisters, I should like to return tomorrow and try this discussion again. I still prefer to hire Elegant Occasions. But I will understand if you would rather not take Jocelin on."

She stared at him, considering. Even if she wanted to refuse his patronage, she shouldn't. They always needed funds, especially if they wanted enough to keep up their regular payments to the charities they supported. Besides, without Elegant Occasions, Mrs. March would have a hard time finding a husband, particularly if she continued to yearn so visibly for Lord Foxstead. Eliza's conscience wouldn't let her abandon the young woman and her little boy.

Perhaps it was the devastated look on Mrs. March's face when she'd seen them kissing or perhaps it was just her charming son, always demanding toast. But Eliza simply couldn't refuse either of them.

Fighting for calm, she put on her best "mild-mannered" expression. "Then I'll see the three of you tomorrow," she said softly.

To her surprise, relief washed over his face. And with a terse nod, he was gone.

She stayed in the drawing room, knowing that was perverse of her. But she simply couldn't face Mrs. March right now. She'd be fine tomorrow, back to being sensible Eliza. And if tonight she indulged her fantasies a bit, imagining how being in Nathaniel's bed would feel, who could blame her?

Imaginary swiving was probably better than the real thing, after all.

# Chapter 4

Nathaniel couldn't help noticing how infinitely kind Verity had been to them as they'd taken their leave. He also noticed that Eliza absented herself from the process.

He couldn't blame her, given the situation. Still, after they were in the carriage with Jimmy, Nathaniel allowed himself the small pleasure of replaying his and Eliza's kisses.

He'd wanted to see if Sam had told the truth about his wife. Clearly, the man had not. Still, Nathaniel hadn't expected the kisses to be so impressive. If he could have, he would have kept kissing her—would have done more than that, too. He would have filled his hands—and then his mouth—with those bountiful breasts, eager to hear Eliza moaning in the throes of pleasure.

A quick tumble, indeed. He wanted to show her he could be better than that. Feeling a thickness in his trousers, he shifted on the seat and tore his attention from the surprising Eliza Pierce.

He had to stop stalling. He had to figure out how to ask Jocelin about her true feelings for him, damn it. And he couldn't think of anything he wanted to do less.

"Lord Foxstead!"

Only then did he realize Jocelin had spoken his name more than once. "What is it, my dear girl?"

She had continued to use his title from the moment they'd met, and he had encouraged it, feeling it was appropriate for the difference in their ages. But he'd called her by her Christian name from the beginning. Because he knew more about her than he dared tell her. Than he dared tell anyone.

"I need to know, my lord . . ." She hesitated to glance down at Jimmy, who giggled as he bounced up and down on the carriage seat. "Do you find looking after me and Jimmy a hardship? Because I'm willing to earn my own keep, you know. I could go into service or . . . or work in a London shop. I mean, if I could figure out what to do with Jimmy while I'm working—"

"You are not going into service or any of that." He shuddered at the very thought. The general would haunt him, to be sure. "You and Jimmy aren't a hardship, for God's sake. You are as important to me as your father was." He wished he could tell her why. But no one—not even she—could ever know. Besides, he'd sworn an oath to General Anson not to tell her.

"Yes," Jocelin said, "but when you promised Papa you'd find me a husband, you weren't counting on Jimmy's surprise appearance."

"It doesn't matter. I am happy to have you both in my life."

She stared down at her hands as she worried one of the ties of her pelisse. "Will you be so happy once you wed Mrs. Pierce?"

Damn. Time to have the conversation he'd been dreading since she'd seen him and Eliza kissing.

"Mrs. Pierce and I are a long way from a wedding. One

kiss does not a marriage make." Two kisses didn't, either. But it could damned well make an affair. If she was amenable.

"Even so, you will one day marry *someone*, if only to sire an heir. And then you'll have to figure out what to do with me and Jimmy, if I haven't managed to find a husband."

"You *will* find a husband," he asserted, "because that's what Elegant Occasions does, and they've never failed a young lady before."

"But are you sure we should even attempt this, my lord?" she asked. "Engage this . . . this business on my behalf?"

"I know what I'm doing."

"What if Mrs. Pierce should find out that Jimmy is a bas—is illegitimate?" She nodded toward her son, who thankfully was absorbed in gazing out the window at some shop they were passing.

"I'll make sure she doesn't," Nathaniel said, "and anyway I doubt that it would bother her. After weathering her parents' scandalous divorce successfully, she is not going to be concerned about Jimmy's parentage. Besides which, she and Verity clearly like the lad. They would do nothing to hurt him. Or *you*. They're not that sort of women. And the fact that she and her sisters are championing you will allay anyone else's suspicions as to his birth."

Assuming that he'd allayed Eliza's about *him*.

"Look, soldiers!" Jimmy cried, then added with quiet reverence, "Soldiers."

Nathaniel got a lump in his throat. A pity he wasn't Jimmy's father. The lad would never have to worry about being loved, and no one would dare malign him as the son of an earl, bastard or no.

Jocelin was quiet.

Unfortunately, Nathaniel would have to press a little harder before he abandoned this uncomfortable discussion. Jocelin's unambiguous reaction to his sharing a kiss with

Eliza—and Eliza's own questions—made it clear that the house of cards he'd built around Jocelin and Jimmy could fall easily if he wasn't careful, exposing them all to pain and heartache. He must keep that from occurring.

"I'm sorry you had to witness the kiss between me and Mrs. Pierce—I had no idea it would upset you so."

She met his gaze, her gaze shuttered. "It didn't upset me. I just . . . tripped over the threshold coming into the room."

"Jocelin, dear girl—"

"I am not a girl anymore! The existence of Jimmy should prove that." She smoothed her skirts. "It did not upset me." Her expression of wounded pride belied her words. "Why would it? Mrs. Pierce seems like a nice woman, quite appropriate for a man like you who ought to be looking for a suitable wife, given your age."

Nathaniel had to bite his tongue to keep from saying he wasn't so old as all that. Let Jocelin keep her dignity. She'd had few enough chances to do so heretofore.

"Despite being ancient," he quipped, "I'm not yet in search of a wife. One thing at a time." There was too much to deal with in his life just now. "Besides, Eliza has been in my circle for years. She's more of a good friend than someone I'd court."

*Liar.* She mostly had been until last night, especially after the hours he and Sam had spent talking about family.

But now he wondered if he could even trust what Sam had told him. Had she changed entirely while they were at war because of her experiences helping to run Elegant Occasions? Or had he simply never seen her as she was?

"You did not kiss her the way a man kisses a friend," Jocelin said, with a hint of resentment in her tone.

How could he deny that? It had probably been obvious to anyone who'd witnessed the kiss. The truth of the matter was that his . . . attraction to Eliza might have sharpened as a result of her performance at the musicale, but it had been bubbling up here and there ever since he'd told her of Sam's death.

Before then, she'd either been Sam's wife and thus forbidden, or he'd been at war or in mourning and not in a position to marry.

Well, that wasn't quite true. He could have courted her last year during the brief period between mourning his father's death and mourning his mother's. His friend Geoffrey, the Duke of Grenwood, had courted Diana and won her, too. Nathaniel could certainly have courted Eliza. Instead, he'd danced with everyone in their circle *but* her.

And why? For a whole host of reasons still viable now.

One, the secrets of his parents' marriage nearly destroyed his family, and he wasn't about to let them destroy him and any future wife. But he seemed to have a problem keeping quiet about things with Eliza.

Nor was that the only secret he'd have to keep from her. She already knew he was responsible for Sam going to war in the first place, but she didn't know he was also responsible for why Sam became Anson's aide-de-camp. Knowing that might send Eliza fleeing him.

Then there was his duty to his title. Eliza would want to be in the city all the time because of Elegant Occasions, but he was determined to do his best by Amberly. It might take a while to get it running efficiently under an estate manager, since the combined deaths of his parents had left it foundering until he'd returned.

All of that was nothing to Jocelin's situation, which he'd also have to keep quiet.

He groaned. Therefore, there'd be no courting of Eliza. At least not yet. She, too, obviously saw the foolishness of them courting, so he would bow to her cooler head in that respect. But he wasn't ready to give up the chance of having her in his bed. Because the mere thought of it had his heart racing.

Perhaps after Jocelin's situation was settled, after he and Eliza had satisfied the needs of their physical attraction, they could talk again about courtship.

And if she still did not wish that? If she never wished to remarry?

He would simply have to accept it. He'd already yearned for so many things in his life that he'd never received. He'd just have to add that to the list.


Eliza left the drawing room as soon as she heard Diana arrive. Devil take it! She should have caught Verity in time to beg her silence.

Too late. The moment she joined her sisters in their private parlor overlooking the square, it was clear what they'd been discussing because both jumped when she entered, then laughed when she groaned.

Eliza attempted to ignore them. She walked straight to Diana and sat down in her usual spot on the sofa next to her, then put her hand on Diana's growing belly, something Diana understandably only allowed her husband and sisters to do. "And how is my little nephew this morning?"

"Niece," Diana protested. "I'll have you know we are planning on a long line of heirs to Elegant Occasions."

"We?" Eliza eyed her skeptically. "*Geoffrey* is planning on that?"

"All right, so I haven't mentioned the possibility, but he'll agree, I'm sure."

Verity scoffed at them both. "It's not as if either of you can choose the child's sex. The baby will be who it will be. Now, enough about children. I had to deal with Jimmy all morning, and adorable as he is, he ran me off my feet."

"Which is why you're standing instead of sitting?" Eliza teased.

Verity scrutinized Eliza from her spot near the window. "I'm standing because I'm dying to know if Lord Foxstead is as good at kissing as he should be after all his years of catting around."

"I shan't dignify that with an answer." Besides, it was private, and Eliza didn't want to share it with her sisters.

"Ooh, aren't *you* high in the instep." Verity plopped down on the cushion-filled chair opposite them.

"Leave her be," Diana said. "If she doesn't want to talk about it, she should keep it to herself."

"Thank you," Eliza said with a gracious nod at her younger sister.

A troubled frown crossed Diana's brow. "But do be careful. Lord Foxstead has flirted with all of us, so a kiss may very well mean nothing to him."

"I'm quite aware," Eliza answered. Even *two* kisses might mean nothing to a man with his reputation.

"To be honest," Diana went on, "I thought for sure he had his sights set on Verity."

"So did I," Eliza said. "Or on his ward, Mrs. March."

"That reminds me," Verity said, "it occurred to me after we spoke of the possibility of Jimmy being Lord Foxstead's son that he didn't even know Jimmy disliked butter. Doesn't that seem like something a father would know?"

Diana shook her head. "Our own father barely saw us before we were seven. He certainly was never aware of our food preferences. Only our nursery maids—and perhaps Mama—knew that."

"I'll grant you, Papa wasn't much involved with any of us, including Mama," Verity said. "But Mrs. March lived with Lord Foxstead and his mother for a time. One would think they all ate together, especially if they didn't have a nursery maid." Verity tapped her chin. "I do wonder, however, how she ended up living with his mother and then his sister if she was Lord Foxstead's mistress."

Eliza grimaced. She'd never been good at eating crow. "Well, as a matter of fact he cleared up the whole business about . . . er . . . where Mrs. March was while her husband was abroad."

"Was she with Lieutenant March?" Verity asked, then laughed. "She told me. I managed to ask her delicately about her husband when we were at the park. She didn't say much, but she managed to get *that* out." Her eyes twinkled. "So much for women not going to war."

"In any case," Eliza said loftily, "I seem to have been mistaken about his feelings for Mrs. March."

"I should say so, given that kiss." Verity looked at Diana. "You should have seen exactly *how* he was kissing her."

"Oh?" Diana asked, her curiosity obviously rekindled.

Verity lowered her voice. "He had his hands on her bottom and she had hers in his hair."

"Well, well," Diana said. "Then I guess we can conclude his kissing has been much perfected by his 'catting around.'"

She and Verity laughed.

Eliza glared at them both. "It's not as if I'm some delicate flower who's never been touched by a man, you know. I've been married, for pity's sake. If I want to put my hands in a man's hair, I can do so perfectly well."

Verity sobered. "Diana's right about him, though. Do take care, dear sister. He may be testing me and you to see which of us would suit his intention to find a wife."

"He's certainly taking his time about it if that's his intention," Diana said.

"His mother died," Verity said. "That's all. But he's not getting any younger. He's already thirty-one."

"Thirty." When they lifted their eyebrows at Eliza, she

could have kicked herself. She stared at them defiantly. "He's thirty. Samuel said thirty-one, but he lied."

"What a shock," Diana muttered.

"My point is," Verity went on, "his parents are both dead, his sister is married, and he needs an heir. So if he has any sense, he's looking for a wife. I mean, what else was he doing when he danced with all of us last year?"

"Not all of us," Eliza muttered. "Not me." It had gnawed at her ever since. What was so wrong with her that he wouldn't even dance with her?

"Wait a minute." Diana straightened with her eyes alight. "Has he *ever* danced with you?"

"No. Or at least not since we were young and Samuel was courting me. Lord Foxstead had a reputation even then." She added defensively, "What of it?"

"What of it? Don't you see? It's like the little boy who kisses all the girls except one. Invariably, the one he *doesn't* kiss is the one he likes."

"That's ridiculous," Eliza said, trying to ignore the apt analogy. "The earl is *not* a seven-year-old." And the last thing she needed right now was excuses for why he hadn't wanted her. "He seems to have no trouble with kissing me as long as it's private. It's dancing with me in public he has a problem with."

"Oh, pish," Verity said. "He wouldn't be so rude as to kiss you in public. Even Geoffrey never did that until Diana married him. Besides, being in a room with the door open is hardly private. Only imagine how much more he'll wish to dance with you now that he has kissed you."

"My dear Verity, it's more the reverse," Diana said. "A dance leads to a kiss, which leads to an embrace, which leads to—" She smirked at Verity. "But no, I can't tell you that since you're still an innocent."

Verity threw a cushion at her.

Eliza rose. "You're both children sometimes, I swear."

"Wait!" Verity said and grabbed Eliza by her skirts. "We have to discuss what to do about Mrs. March."

"Yes," Diana chimed in. "I know nothing about her."

With a sigh, Eliza resumed her seat.

Diana patted her knee. "But before we leave the topic of Lord Foxstead, I want to say, most sincerely, that you deserved better than Samuel, and now perhaps you'll get it."

"With Nathaniel? I hardly see—"

"You're calling him *Nathaniel* now?" Verity grinned over at Diana. "Oh, she's in trouble for certain. No one calls Lord Foxstead Nathaniel."

"I didn't even know it was his Christian name," Diana said. "I've never heard Geoffrey use it."

"His family uses it," Eliza said defensively. "They call him Nat. Notice he did not give me leave to call him *that*."

"Yes, but he didn't give Mrs. March leave to call him anything but Lord Foxstead," Verity pointed out. "So you're already ahead of the game."

"Speaking of Mrs. March," Diana said, "I'm sorry I arrived too late to assess her for myself, but what's she like? Pretty? Awkward? Lacking in social graces?"

"A bit awkward, yes," Eliza said.

"But more shy than anything," Verity added.

"The way Rosy was 'shy'?" Diana asked with clear sarcasm.

Eliza sighed. "No. Actually shy. Painfully so." She turned to Verity. "Did she say much to you while you were with her and Jimmy?"

"Hardly a word. And you know I'm generally good at getting ladies to talk if they're timid." Verity flashed her sisters a rueful smile. "When they see that I will say just about anything, it makes them comfortable enough to at least voice a small opinion or two."

"To say the least." Diana glanced at Eliza. "Remember how reticent Miss Paskell was when we first met her?"

"How could I not?" Eliza chuckled. "Verity turned her into a copy of herself, even before the young lady married a marquess. And now the woman is as endlessly entertaining as Verity."

Verity rose and took a couple of dramatic bows. "Thank you, thank you. She's my masterpiece. We're still friends, you know."

"We know!" Diana and Eliza said in unison.

Then they both laughed. Eliza relaxed a bit. Sometimes it was just good to talk with the women who understood her best. As long as they weren't interfering in her romantic entanglements.

Eliza smiled at Verity. "We'll charge *you* with getting Mrs. March to open up."

"I might be able to help with that when I do her gown appraisal and supervise her fittings," Diana said. "That inevitably invites confidences from the young ladies. And if she looks as pretty as you say, I might not have to do much in the way of altering her style."

"It will help if we can keep her son from distracting her too often," Verity put in. "I'll admit she was a bit more forthcoming talking about him. And being outdoors seemed to relax her, even when she had to run after the child."

"That reminds me," Eliza said, taking out her notebook. "I promised I'd find a nursemaid for Jimmy. I can do that today, pay a visit to the Foundling Hospital."

"Good idea," Diana said.

"But getting back to our plans for her," Verity said, with a wary look at Eliza. "I do think we must suggest that Lord Foxstead not accompany her too much to society affairs. Otherwise, we risk people making the same assumptions about the two of them as Eliza did. Diana and Geoffrey can go or Eliza or even Lord Foxstead's sister, if Lady Usborne is amenable."

"And Eliza should be the one to tell him about our decision," Diana pointed out. "He won't get angry at *her.*" She grinned. "Not if he's already had his hands on her bottom."

"Verity is exaggerating about that," Eliza muttered.

"Or if he does have to accompany Jocelin for some reason," Diana went on, "they should be kept apart." She lifted a brow at Eliza. "Another task we should assign to Eliza—that of keeping him entertained, since he likes her so much."

"I'm not too sure of *that*, either." Eliza paused. "Although I do agree they should be kept apart, mostly because I think she's madly in love with him."

"Really?" Diana said. "That's unfortunate. For *her*, I mean, since he obviously doesn't feel the same and hasn't seen fit to explain that."

"Actually . . ." Eliza drew in a steadying breath, knowing that her sisters were going to pounce all over what she was about to say, but only too aware it had to be said. "Apparently, the fool was oblivious to her feelings until he saw her face right after she witnessed us kissing. By the way, *that's* why he kissed me. To determine whether I'd been right when I'd told him how she felt about him."

"Oh, of course, that explains it," Verity said, with a roll of her eyes. "The kiss had nothing to do with the way he follows you with his gaze when you leave a room or asks how *you're* doing while he's dancing with *me*—"

"He did that with me, too!" Diana told Verity. "Talked about Eliza while we were dancing, I mean."

"Now you're just bamming me for fun," Eliza said, trying not to read too much into that interesting revelation.

Diana thrust out her chin. "I swear I'm not. The only time I ever danced with him, he wanted to know if Samuel's death had lain you low. When I told him of course it had, he seemed perturbed to hear it, then changed the subject."

Eliza shook her head. "Why does he care? And why did he never ask *me*?"

"I don't know." Diana stared at her. "I did tell him the right thing, didn't I? You were pretty low at the time. Weren't you?"

Eliza stiffened. "I was at first . . . until I found out the man had left nothing for me to live on and had a number of gambling debts besides. Which, of course, I blame on his time spent with Lord Foxstead."

"I wouldn't be so hasty to blame the earl if I were you." Verity darted a glance at Eliza. "I overheard Samuel ask Papa for money to pay a gambling debt once, and I gathered it wasn't the first time. Of course, that was before we left home, and Samuel went to war."

Eliza arched one eyebrow. "And it doesn't disprove the earl's influence."

"True," Diana said, "but it's not as if Lord Foxstead *made* your husband play cards past the point where he could no longer afford it."

Diana was right. Still, this discussion of Eliza's marriage to Samuel and her history, such as it was, with Nathaniel was all too much for her. Eliza jumped to her feet and planted her hands on her hips. "Are we going to talk about our new client and how we should proceed? Or should I just go for a walk until the two of you finish dissecting my life?"

Her sisters sighed in unison. Then Verity made a face. "We'll behave. Though sometimes you're no fun at all."

Samuel had started saying that, too, toward the end of their marriage. She'd always thought it unfair. But what if he'd been right? What if she *had* been the dull creature he'd made her out to be? Or at least had become that after they'd married? Lord, she hoped Nathaniel didn't see her that way.

She sat back down and smoothed her skirts. It didn't matter if he did. Because she might let him lie with her, but she would never let him marry her. She wasn't going through any of that again, no matter how fine Nathaniel looked in his coats. She'd learned her lesson with Samuel.

# Chapter 5

When Nathaniel and Jocelin arrived at the house in Grosvenor Square the next day, he was surprised to have Norris show them into the garden.

"The duchess and her sisters shall be with you shortly, my lord," Norris said. "Would you or the miss like some tea, sir?"

"That would be wonderful, thank you, Norris."

As soon as Norris left, Jocelin whispered, "The duchess? I-I cannot meet a duchess! What will I say? How do I act?"

"It's fine, dear gir—dear lady." The words felt funny coming out of his mouth. She was barely more than a child to him. But he must acknowledge that a female in her situation could most certainly be considered a woman. "One of the ladies of Elegant Occasions married a duke last year. But though she is now a duchess, you'd never guess it by her behavior. She doesn't stand on ceremony, and you will like her, I swear."

"A-All right. If you say so." She glanced over at the goldfish pond. "I do hope Jimmy doesn't prove too much for Lady Usborne today."

"I'm sure she'll be fine. I took a look at the list of names of young misses that Eliza sent over, and we have already arranged a whole schedule of nursemaids to interview tomorrow. Tess can make do until then."

"But—"

"Don't worry, Jocelin. Why don't you take a seat on the bench there and try to relax? It's a beautiful day, and spring is at hand. You might as well enjoy it."

He'd only been in the Pierce garden a handful of times. Once Sam had married, he'd preferred to go to Nathaniel's bachelor town house rather than have Nathaniel at his own home. It had taken their time on the battlefield for Nathaniel to figure out that, while Sam liked having an earl's heir for a friend, entertaining him in a family setting made him nervous.

For the first time he wondered if it had something to do with Eliza. Had she not wanted Nathaniel there because of his reputation? Or what seemed more likely the more Nathaniel knew Eliza—had *Sam* not wanted him there for the same reason? Had the damned arse been afraid that Nathaniel would try to seduce his wife? It was an enraging thought, though more likely than he'd considered before. He wanted to know the answer, but he wasn't sure whom to ask about it.

Probably not Eliza, and definitely not in front of Jocelin.

Who now took a seat on the bench. Nathaniel preferred to stand. And roam. There wasn't much room for it, but he did anyway. He noticed a corner with a profusion of some bright flower and a painted birdhouse tucked away in its midst.

Rounding the goldfish pond, he walked over to examine it. Shaped like a triangle, the birdhouse had two sides that formed an overhanging roof painted a pretty sky blue, and a third side that acted as a platform for the house part, which contained arched openings for the birds. Little flowers were painted along the bottom of the house, with the ledge thrusting outward, completing the effect. The remains of various seeds were scattered along the ledge.

"The birdhouse is mine," Eliza said from behind him. "I like the birds coming around, so I feed them."

He turned to look at her, noticing that Diana had come out with her. Jocelin had already risen, and Diana was urging Jocelin to sit again. That left him free to return his attention to Eliza, who was holding a bag of seeds.

"What sort of birds do you get?" he asked.

"Finches, robins, and doves, mostly, but the occasional nightingale and blackbird, too. My favorite in the spring is the nightingale, of course." She scattered seeds on the birdhouse's ledge. "Her song is so lovely and varied."

"Like recognizes like," he muttered under his breath.

"What?"

"Nothing. Just thinking aloud."

Of course she enjoyed birdsong. Eliza's voice had the pure resonance of a nightingale's, and today she even resembled a dove in some respects—all lace-adorned bosom and a white muslin gown with a short train that almost looked like feathers trailing behind her. A dove-white apron completed the effect.

"I confess that my sisters hate my feeding them," she said. "The robins and blackbirds can be especially loud, and the nightingales sing too much for Diana and Verity during the very season of year when we come in exhausted before dawn. But the birds don't bother me since I can't ever go to bed right away anyway, so I like lying there listening to them."

"Which explains why Geoffrey calls you a night bird."

She rolled her eyes. "He just prefers that everyone rise at dawn like he and Diana."

That reminded him—Diana needed to be introduced. He

turned toward the bench, and Eliza placed a hand on his arm.

When his gaze shot to her, she murmured, "Let them talk a minute and get to know each other."

"But I must introduce Diana."

"I already did, while you were examining the bird-house."

"Ah. I merely thought . . . well . . . Jocelin was nervous about meeting a duchess."

"She doesn't look it. Meanwhile, I send her into a fright every time." Eliza lowered her voice. "The poor woman doesn't like me, does she?"

He sighed. "I'm sure she would if not for who you are. To me, I mean. I should never have given into the impulse to let her see me kiss you yesterday."

"I regret that it happened, too."

"You misunderstand me. I don't regret the kisses. I just wish we could have indulged in them privately." Where he could have embraced her and touched her breasts and had his very wicked way with her.

What was wrong with him? Jocelin had to be his first responsibility, so why was he risking alienating the very person who could get her settled in society? "Those kisses were all I could think of last night," he admitted.

Because clearly, he'd lost his damned mind.

"Says the rakehell with the notorious reputation," she countered.

That chafed a bit. "Not anymore."

"The rakehell part or the notorious reputation part?"

"The first. Once one has a notorious reputation, one can't get rid of it easily."

She smiled. "As my parents have repeatedly demonstrated."

"But truthfully, it's been some time since I've actually behaved like a rakehell."

"I'm simply supposed to take your word for it?"

"You have to do what makes you comfortable." He stole the bag of seed from her, taking care to run his finger across her palm as he did so. "And I have to do the same." He scattered some seeds over the ledge as he fought to quell his racing heart. "After all, I still have a rakehell's skills, which I can use very well. Do you doubt me?"

"No, indeed. You were very . . . skilled yesterday." She cocked her head. "The question is how many women you use those skills with."

"None in quite some years. Until you, anyway." Taking her hand, he closed her fingers around the bag of seed and held it there, marveling at how delicate a hand she had. "I know you probably don't believe it, but it's true."

War had changed him, no doubt about it. He'd seen too many women used and abused on the Peninsula not to be affected. His mother's revelations had also taken a toll.

When Eliza finally slipped her hand from his, looking flustered and heated, he glanced over to see that Diana and Jocelin were gone. "We should go in." He couldn't believe Jocelin had left without saying a word to him.

"Not just now," Eliza said.

He narrowed his gaze on her. "I beg your pardon?"

"She and Diana have gone up to the fitting room so they can try some gowns on her to determine what styles she looks best in." She tilted her head up. "So unless you wish to see Mrs. March in various stages of undress . . ."

"God, no."

That seemed to please her, which definitely pleased him.

She thrust the bag of seeds in her apron pocket. "Then why don't you and I discuss the plan for Jocelin that my sisters and I have developed? If you approve, I can spell out how much the fee would be."

So they were back to business affairs. Fine. That was probably best. "I don't care how much it is. I'll pay it regardless."

"Really?" She eyed him skeptically. "So, a hundred thousand pounds sounds right to you?"

His mouth dropped open. "A hundred thousand pou—"

Her peal of laughter cut off his outraged response. Trying to suppress a smile, she said, "In other words, you *do* care how much it is."

"I have money, you little minx, and I'm willing to spend it to get Jocelin well situated," he snapped. It was the least he could do for her under the circumstances. "But that doesn't mean I'm insane."

"Thank goodness." Her eyes twinkled. "I wouldn't wish to go into business with a madman."

Shaking his head, he flashed her a rueful smile. "What is the actual fee you're proposing?"

She named a more reasonable figure, which was less than he'd been expecting.

"That sounds acceptable."

"I can provide you with an estimated amount for each item or service we intend to provide. Just give me until tomorrow."

He gave a dismissive wave of his hand. "I don't need the details. I know none of you would cheat me."

"Oh, you do, do you? Clearly, you and Geoffrey are cut of a different cloth."

He shrugged. "That's because I was raised in the aristocracy while he was used to watching every penny. I suppose that's what happens when you discover at his age that you've unexpectedly inherited a dukedom and all that goes with it. Old habits die hard, as they say."

"True." She gestured to the bench. "Why don't we take

a seat while we discuss everything my sisters and I have planned?"

"We could go inside and sit in the morning room."

She hurried ahead of him to the bench. "I prefer the outdoors."

"But that's not why you don't wish to go in." He chuckled. "You think being in the garden where your sisters can look out and see us will keep me from trying to kiss you."

"Won't it?" She sat down and spread her skirts around her in an obvious attempt to relegate him to the other end of the bench.

Clearly, she didn't know him very well. Lifting a handful of her muslin skirts, he sat down close to her, then spread her skirts over his knee.

That seemed to flummox her. "A gentleman doesn't commandeer a lady's skirts, sir."

"I'm not a gentleman," he told her.

She frowned. "Weren't you just telling me you're not a rakehell anymore?"

"I'm not a rakehell, either." He hardened his voice. "I'm a soldier. And a soldier commandeers whatever he needs to win."

"To win what?" she asked lightly.

"You."

*Damn, man, that's the last thing you need to be doing— trying to* win *her.*

Her shocked expression mirrored his very thought. Then he watched as the color rose in her cheeks, turning them a lovely pink. He would have kissed her right then if he'd dared, but he truly didn't want to embarrass her in front of her entire household. Bad enough he'd already done so in front of Verity and Jocelin.

He smiled. "But I'm willing to wait until we're alone. Really alone."

"Are you?" She relaxed, then cast him a decidedly minxish smile. "Then so am I."

His blood ran fierce and hot . . . for half a second. "Because you'll make sure we never are?"

"Because, sir, it will take being alone for us to have any sort of . . . satisfying encounter."

It was his turn to be shocked. But before he could demand to know when and where, she pulled her skirts off his knee and added, "Today, however, we need to discuss your ward. So we'd best both keep our minds—and bodies—on the task at hand."

He shifted to face her on the bench, pressing his knee deliberately against hers. "I can do two things at once, you know. As, I imagine, can you."

"At the moment, I prefer to do only the one."

She folded her hands primly in her lap. He tried not to be distracted by the idea of what lay beneath those white skirts of hers.

"Here's what we propose for the first event," she continued, like a schoolmistress reciting a lesson. "We chose what we believe will be an easy one: a benefit for the Foundling Hospital in the form of a fete in Richmond hosted by friends of ours—the Crowders."

"What sort of fete? One like Prinny's last year at Carlton House where there was dancing and supper? Or one like a village fete with acrobats and swings?"

"No acrobats and swings, I'm afraid, nor babbling brooks running down the supper tables."

"Ah."

When he said nothing more, she asked, "You didn't approve of the prince's elaborate supper?"

"It was a shameless extravagance, and one the nation shouldn't have had to fund."

"I quite agree. Though I'm rather surprised you do."

"Soldier, remember?" he said grimly. "There were too many times our men did without food or necessary ammunition because of cost. The prince's 120,000-pound affair could have funded our entire regiment for the whole war."

She eyed him quizzically as if trying to figure him out.

He couldn't have that. "Besides," he said, falling back on the lighter tone of a rakehell, "they ran out of iced champagne far too early. And the bands were abominable."

"Well," she said, "this fete is on the first of May, so it will mostly include quaint customs for May Day like maypoles and games and mummery. Oh, and the guests will also select a May queen."

"Whose idea was that?"

"Mine, actually. I saw some pictures in a book of old-fashioned May Day celebrations and thought it would be fun."

"It's imaginative," he said. She'd never struck him as that sort, although now that he thought about it, it made sense, given her love of music.

She brightened. "I did leave most of the décor to Verity, since it's her strong suit, but I chose the orchestra myself. It will be playing pieces that evoke spring." Once going, she seemed eager to tell him all. "Diana is already planning on dressing Jocelin in a gown with a profusion of embroidered flowers, and I mean to dress her hair accordingly. There will also be a delicious dinner outdoors, with Verity supervising the food. Since the guests represent a wide range of supporters of the charity, Jocelin will have the opportunity to meet a variety of people. What do you think?"

He stared at her. "Actually, that sounds . . . perfect. Assuming we're able to hire a nursemaid from the Foundling Hospital, Jocelin will be delighted to be part of helping the institution, and since my mother was a supporter, I might know a number of people to whom I can introduce Jocelin."

Eliza looked briefly uncomfortable, but he didn't dwell on that, sure that she was merely worrying about all the particulars.

Meanwhile, he was excited. What a relief to see that his instincts about Elegant Occasions were spot on. Leaning forward, he asked, "What other events do you have in mind for her?"

She spent the next half hour laying out a dizzying list of activities. First, lessons with dance and etiquette instructors, to be followed by various small parties and dinners that were nonetheless to be held at some of the finest homes. Then concerts and trips to museums and such, designed to allow the various gentlemen Jocelin had met to court her under more sedate circumstances.

"By the time all of that is done," he drawled, "she will surely have found a worthy gentleman or two. And once again, in all these situations, I'll be able to introduce her to men I know who—"

"About that," Eliza interrupted, that same expression of discomfort crossing her face. "We've decided . . . *determined*, really, that it would be best if you did *not* accompany Jocelin to events. That she should attend them with us and not with . . . *you*."

He stared at her, hardly able to speak. Then he scowled. "That will never happen."

"Why not?"

"You've seen how nervous she gets around people of our class. I won't abandon her in her hour of need. And I can be useful, damn it. I know gentlemen from all walks of life." He crossed his arms over his chest. "Besides, what if some fellow should get her alone and try to have his way with her? I promised her father I'd protect her."

"That is what you hired us for, remember?" Somehow, her voice became both soft and resolute, like satin over steel. "To protect her, introduce her around, *and* put her at ease. I'm sure the three of us can do a better job of that than you can alone."

He scoffed at her.

Big mistake. Raising her brows high, she rose as if to leave. "This is ridiculous. My sisters actually expected you to be open-minded enough to see the wisdom of absenting yourself from Jocelin's events, but I told them you were too stubborn and hidebound for that."

He jumped to his feet. "Hidebound! I am *not* hidebound." His father had been hidebound, especially when it came to Nathaniel. But *he* was not any such thing.

Eliza shrugged. "Suit yourself. I will simply inform my sisters that you refused to stay away from Mrs. March."

"See here, you can't tell them any such nonsense! I didn't refuse to do anything. You know as well as I do I have no romantic interest in Jocelin." He didn't want Eliza returning to *that* assumption, after all.

"All the same, I must tell them that you insist upon being around." She sighed, almost dramatically. That gave him pause until she added, "I can't guarantee they'll decide it's worth the risk."

"Risk! What risk?"

"That she's unable to find a husband because she is so clearly standing around yearning for *you*. No man wants to marry a woman who's visibly in love with someone else."

Damn. He hadn't considered that. "Is it . . . really *that* 'visible'? To the extent that people would notice?"

"*I* certainly did. And every emotion Jocelin feels is always writ large across her face. She is an open book."

"While you are a very closed book," he grumbled.

At last he'd rattled her. "What's that supposed to mean?"

He stepped closer. "It means that after Sam's death, you buried yourself with him. You allowed your sisters to handle most of Elegant Occasions' events while you hid away here doing the books and paying bills."

"I was in mourning! Ladies aren't allowed to attend social events in mourning."

"Not then. After that. I looked around for you at every affair we both attended, wanting to ask you to dance, and each time you were gone home or in back or talking at length to some important person. I even headed your way when we were at Almack's, but you were having none of that, oh no. You disappeared and went God knows where."

She huffed out a breath. "I did no such thing. Or rather, I didn't do it intentionally."

When she started to turn away, he stepped in front of her. "Verity told me you were speaking to the orchestra leader or some such. She said you had to catch him during the period that the orchestra wasn't playing."

"You are ridiculous. If you had wished to dance with me, you had plenty of chances." She planted her hands on her hips. "And for your information, I haven't 'buried' myself anywhere. I've been taking the time to find my bearings."

"He died three years ago this summer," Nathaniel said grimly. "If you'd taken that long to find your 'bearings' while captaining a ship, the ship would have run aground."

"I don't have time for this," she stated and stepped around him.

He blocked her again. "Hear me out. I've been meaning to discuss this with you, so we could get past it. I know why you've had mixed feelings about me ever since I returned." He sucked in a bracing breath. "Because you blame me for Sam's death."

She gaped at him. "Why on earth would I do that?"

"Because he wouldn't have gone to war if not for me."

"He went to war to do his patriotic duty." She added cynically, "And to cover himself in glory, no doubt."

"Perhaps that was part of it, but it wasn't the main reason." His stomach churned. Could she really not have known?

"Oh, I'm sure he was also mortified by the burgeoning scandal surrounding Mama and Papa's divorce. Samuel never liked having his good name tainted . . . except when he eloped with me." Betrayal showed in her face. "That was apparently fine."

"Is that what you thought? That he joined to escape the scandal?"

"Mostly. I didn't entirely blame him. If I could have escaped it myself, I would have."

"He never said one word about the scandal to me. Sam went to war because I dared him to. You know he could never ignore a dare."

# Chapter 6

Eliza could only stare at him. Surely he was joking. But he wasn't wearing his joking face. "What are you talking about?"

"You really didn't know?"

"That you dared him to go to war? Of course not!"

"Damn," he muttered under his breath. "He said he told you."

She stared about the garden unseeing. "He lied." Tears gathered in her throat. She willed them back. "He did that a great deal." He used to blame her for it when she caught him in one, said she'd forced him to lie. Only later had she left his spell long enough to realize how wrong that was, but by then he was abroad.

"I'm sorry." Nathaniel looked truly distraught.

She knew the feeling. Anyone close to Samuel inevitably discovered how very much he lied. Then again . . . "Why would you dare him, anyway?" It certainly showed a want of good judgment.

"Because I was stupid." With a shake of his head, Nathaniel turned to pace the tiled walkway beside the pond. "It started when we were at the club one night. We'd both been drinking. He was reading a newspaper that detailed how the Battle of Eylau had gone, and he raged about how idiotic the Russian strategy had been." He glanced at her. "He liked to do that, you know—second-guess military strategies."

"I'm aware. The first time he did it with me, before we were married, I assumed he came from a military family." She sighed. "But the truth was, his father always lauded some cousin who was a general, and that irked Samuel. He was convinced that if his father had only bought him a commission, he would have been a general, too."

"Yes, I heard that from him more times than I could count. He said it so feelingly, I thought he might be right." His voice turned bitter. "Until I ended up serving in a war with him."

She swallowed. "The dare, Nathaniel. Pray, continue."

"Right." He stared down into the pond. "By then, I'd had enough. He was railing against the Russians for not beating Napoleon at his own game, and I picked up the newspaper to get fodder to fight him on his nonsense when I read that the battle hadn't been won by either side. Napoleon gained only a little ground, at tremendous loss of life, and the Russians held them back, suffering the same loss of life. The press deemed the whole battle pointless. So I started laughing."

"Oh, dear," she said, bad memories flooding in. "Samuel hated being mocked."

"Yes, he did. When he demanded to know what I found so humorous, I told him no one could have won that battle, not even God himself, and certainly not him. Even if he could ever *be* a general, which he couldn't."

She caught her breath. Early in their marriage, she'd had such arguments with Samuel. She knew how they inevitably ended.

"He got angry, of course, and said he could work his way up the ranks in a matter of months if he chose. And I said he'd have to join the army first, which he didn't have the resolve to do."

A shudder swept her. She could see the scene in her mind so readily—Samuel stomping about and Nathaniel mocking him. It would have been like pouring gunpowder on a fire.

"He said I was wrong. That he would go out right then to join the army. I was sure he was . . ."

"Lying?"

"More like exaggerating. Or . . ."

"Bravado."

"Yes," Nathaniel said. "So I dared him to do it. When that gave him pause, I told him I'd pay for his damned commission myself."

"You didn't," she said in a hushed whisper.

He scrubbed a hand over his face. "I was certain he'd never take me up on it. It was all swagger and drunken ravings to me."

"Yet the next day he went right out and joined, didn't he?"

"Yes, he did. Refused my offer to pay for his commission, too."

Right. Instead, he'd used the money they were supposed to live on to buy one. He had his pride, after all. "Still, you ended up paying for your own commission. Why go with him at all? You didn't have to go just because he did."

"It didn't seem right to dare him into serving if I wasn't willing to serve, too. Believe me, taunting him into serving in the war isn't something I'm proud of. Besides, with his gift for bombast, I was afraid he'd say something to the wrong people and get his arse kicked." His sudden grin did something to her insides. "If you'll excuse my vulgarity, madam."

She shook her head. "You and your vulgarities, I swear. You're as bad as Geoffrey."

"I beg your pardon?" He struck a lofty pose. "Geoffrey will say anything to anyone."

"Sometimes, yes. But he's not nearly as bad as my late husband, who was always full of bluster and boasting. Full of himself, to be honest."

Nathaniel sighed. "I had hoped you never saw that side of him. That he was a better person with you. Men sometimes are."

"Only the liars and the frauds, the ones who live two lives. But not good men like . . . like Geoffrey, for example. And you. Sometimes."

"Sometimes, eh?" Nathaniel stared off at the birdhouse. "You give me too much credit. After all, I was the one who sent your husband to war."

"He sent himself, and then you ran after him to protect him from himself. However did you put up with his arrogance for two years?"

He flashed her a rueful glance. "I was young and stupid and arrogant, too."

"Still are. Arrogant, I mean."

Smiling faintly, he said, "Not as much as I was then, I hope. The war knocked some of it out of me, and General Anson knocked out the rest." He added in quiet reverence, "He was the best man I ever knew."

Awareness dawned. "And that's why you're doing all this for Jocelin?"

He hesitated just long enough to give her pause. "Mostly." Then he quickly added, "So you never knew about the dare?"

"That can't possibly surprise you. He wasn't about to tell me he was abandoning his wife because you dared him to join the army. That would have made him look less than heroic." When Nathaniel appeared suddenly uncomfortable, she added, "And I'm sure you occasionally saw him in that capacity, too."

"I did. But I never thought you were aware of his true nature. All these years I've felt so guilty for taking your husband from you—"

"You didn't take him. He took himself." She laid her hand on his arm. "So I hope this absolves you of your guilt."

He stared down at her hand. Then he grabbed it and gripped it in both of his. "What it does is shatter my foolish assumption that you buried yourself in the grave with Sam. You saw him more clearly than anyone, didn't you?"

"Not at first. But eventually, yes." It had taken her longer not to blame herself for falling for Samuel's facile charms and marrying him.

She wasn't daft enough to tell Nathaniel that, however, and expose her vulnerability to *him*, too. Bad enough that she desired him desperately.

Instead, she covered his two hands with her other one. "As for burying myself, I wouldn't call it that, exactly. It was more like staying where I knew it was safe—with my sisters."

"Does that mean you're ready to venture out of their arms?"

"I don't know." She gazed up at him with a lifted brow. "Are you ready to convince me to do so?" Oh, Lord, what was she thinking, to say something so *blatantly* flirtatious?

It seemed to surprise him, too, but the sudden gleam in his eyes gave her his answer. With determined purpose, he pulled her down the walkway into the morning room. Once inside, he looked about, apparently wanting to be sure they were alone. Then he pressed her up against the wall, his gaze burning into hers before he took her mouth with his.

His ravening kiss thrilled her. Especially when he began to caress one of her breasts so expertly that it heated her . . . from skin to blood to bone. His tongue delved silkily in her mouth while his thumb stroked her nipple through her gown with a delicacy she would never have expected of any man. What a masterful motion!

There was no denying his rakehell skills, to be sure.

With a moan, she caught his shoulders to keep him from moving away. Now he had both hands on her breasts and was kneading them to wonderful effect. She thought she might swoon!

Or tear off her clothes.

"God," he whispered in her ear, "I could go mad not being able to touch your naked body."

"I could go mad not having you do so," she admitted. "But we can't indulge our impulses here, Nathaniel."

He leaned his head back to stare out the door into the hall, then flashed her a fierce, confident, and yes, arrogant smile. "No one is around at present, dearling. We can do whatever the hell we want. Although perhaps we should find a less risky place to do it. We can easily be seen from the hall."

"Thankfully, it's always darker in here in the afternoon," she murmured, "especially when there's no fire in the hearth. But we should sit in the wingback chairs. I've stayed hidden in them before."

Arching one brow, he looped his hand about her waist. "To do this?"

"No! I am no seductress, sir."

He led her to one of the chairs, then took a seat and pulled her into his lap. "You could have fooled me," he growled.

His hands worked at removing her fichu to expose the tops of her breasts. All he had to do was shove her gown down enough to free one, and he had part of her exposed.

The glint in his eyes showed his approval. So did the rise of his . . . member beneath her bottom. "Ah," he said, thumbing her nipple again. "Your skin is so soft. You're every bit as luscious as I imagined."

She could hardly breathe. "You actually imagined me like this?" she asked, wishing she could already be undressed and beneath him. Right now. In this room.

What madness.

"I've 'imagined' and envisaged and dreamed—shall I go on?" He bent his head. "Let's just say I've considered doing this a great deal since yesterday." He nuzzled her breast. "Your scent alone incites me to riot."

"It's a perfume I make myself . . . mostly of orange blossoms." She was babbling, for pity's sake, though her voice sounded as throaty as a seductress's.

Then he caught her nipple in his mouth and sucked it with such perfection she thought she'd lose her mind. Or her virtue. Not that a widow's virtue mattered all that much.

"You excel at this," she said, digging her fingers into his arms. This was better than anything Samuel had managed. In the bedchamber, his skills had been surprisingly lackluster. Or so she'd deduced from how the Fallen Females described lovemaking. "But you ought to. You've . . . oh, Lord . . . had plenty of practice. I suppose."

"Plenty." He rubbed her other nipple into a fine point through her gown. "Enough to know that a body like yours should be . . ." He managed to wrestle that side of her gown down. Then he gazed upon both breasts with pure pleasure in his eyes. "Treasured. Worshipped."

To her delight, he proceeded to worship her breasts with mouth and tongue and even teeth, tugging the nipples lightly until she thought she might explode. "Lord, Nathaniel . . . that is . . . amazing."

"Oh, dearling, we are just . . . getting started." When she squirmed on his lap, he groaned, and his flesh hardened even more beneath her. "If you keep doing that, I swear I'll need more than just a taste of you."

She felt his hand inching her skirts up, sliding between

her legs to where she was already desperate for his touch. "We can't. Not. Here."

As if to reinforce her fears, a voice sounded down the hall. "Eliza, where are you?" It was Diana.

Verity's voice sounded next. "She's got to be here somewhere. I don't see her in the garden. Although maybe they're out of sight of the windows."

"They? Do you think she's still talking to Lord Foxstead?"

"Damn," he muttered under his breath and finally halted his caresses.

Frustrated by the abrupt end to their enjoyments, Eliza nonetheless tugged at her bodice, desperate to get it back up and in place. "My fichu," she hissed. "Where is it? What did you do with it?"

He felt around on the floor beside the chair. "I've got it!" he whispered and shoved a strip of lacy fabric into her hand.

She scarcely had time to loop it about her neck and tuck it into her bodice before she heard her sisters in the hall. "Shh." She pressed her finger to his lips. "You stay here until I've led them away."

Grabbing her hand before she could pull it free, he kissed her palm. When he released her, she strode out into the hall, curling her fingers up about the kiss as if somehow that could hold it there.

"Did I hear you calling me?" she asked.

Her sisters eyed her suspiciously. "Where is Lord Foxstead?" Diana asked, her gaze fixed on Eliza's bosom.

"Last I saw him, he was in the garden. I assume he's still out there." She hated lying to her sisters, but if they guessed what she'd been up to, she'd never hear the end of it.

And it was equally likely Nathaniel might find himself at the mercy of Geoffrey's fists. Eliza's brother-in-law had a pernicious determination to protect not just his wife but her sisters.

Verity seemed to be struggling to hold back laughter. "Is that . . . a lace doily you're wearing . . . about your neck?"

She glanced down and stifled a groan. "Of course not. It's my fichu."

Diana lifted a brow. "It's not one I've ever seen you wear, and it's certainly not the one you were wearing earlier."

"Well, I spilled some tea on that one. So I had to change it out for this one. It's new. I . . . er . . . bought it last week." Oh Lord, she was so bad at subterfuge.

Verity and Diana exchanged knowing glances. They knew just how bad at it she was.

"So," she said brightly, "where is Jocelin? How goes the fashion discussion?"

"It went well," Diana answered. "As soon as the maid is done helping her dress, we want to leave for the dressmaker's. We came looking for you and Lord Foxstead to find out if you both wanted to go and how much of a fee he's willing to pay for our services."

"All of it, he says." Eliza took them both by the arms to steer them back upstairs. "I was just heading to the drawing room to write down everything for his approval. Now that you've got some idea how much the dressmaking will cost, we should finish up the estimated costs so I can make sure he means what he says before we leave."

"Well, I hope he shows himself before then." Verity smirked at her. "Though I can't imagine where he's gone."

"Nor can I," Eliza said, and meant it. "He may have left altogether. I told him what we decided about his not being around when we take Jocelin to events, and he seemed amenable."

Diana released a breath. "That's good. All she talked about during our fashion assessment was Lord Foxstead this and Lord Foxstead that. We simply must keep them separate. And surely, he'd rather be doing anything other than escorting four women about London."

"Unless he's just trying to get under Eliza's skirts," Verity said.

"Oh, Lord," Eliza muttered, and released them. As both her sisters laughed their way up the stairs, she fell behind just far enough to peek back at the entrance to the morning room.

She spotted Nathaniel sneaking out of the other garden door. With a secretive smile, he touched his finger to his lips. Then he was gone.

Good heavens, she was in such trouble. He was rakish charisma personified. He and her late husband were alike in that, although, as far as she knew, Samuel had always been faithful to her.

That was why she must keep her guard up even more with Nathaniel. Clearly, she had a weakness for such fellows. But this time she knew better than to fall for one. She had no intention of finding herself married to another man who would charm her into ignoring his gambling and drinking . . . or browbeat her into accepting his will in all things.

Elegant Occasions had taught her that her opinions had worth. And she would never again forget that.

# Chapter 7

Nathaniel wasn't terribly surprised to see Jocelin and the Harper sisters appear startled when they entered the establishment of the dressmaker, Mrs. Ludgate, to find him waiting there.

As the others strolled right into Mrs. Ludgate's fitting rooms, Eliza took him aside. "I thought we agreed you wouldn't accompany Jocelin."

"*We* never agreed to anything. We got distracted instead." When she glowered at him, he held up his hand. "But I am happy to agree to your requirement—for events and only events. Even in that situation, I am not allowing Jocelin to go back and forth from Foxstead Place alone at all hours of the night. If you and your sisters cannot accompany her in your carriage to my town house, then I expect you to send one of your footmen to fetch me so I can do so."

"That's a bit extreme, don't you think? You could merely send one of *your* footmen with her when your coachman delivers her in the morning."

He knew he was overreacting a bit, but he couldn't help it. He had to keep her safe, and letting her out of his sight worried him. "Perhaps. But Jocelin isn't used to the city. This is her first time in London, and I won't risk having a footman fall asleep in your carriage and some footpad leap inside to assault her."

"The lady used to walk among soldiers in an armed camp, for pity's sake. Surely, she would know to scream or alert the coachman or footman somehow."

"You do realize that with a general for a father, she was as safe in that camp as she is in the countryside here. No one would have dared to harm her." Well, that wasn't entirely true. One of her "protectors" had sneaked past all their cautions and seduced her, anyway. Sadly, or perhaps not so sadly, her seducer had died in battle.

"I thought you said she and her husband were in a different regiment than her father's."

He stifled a groan. His lies were already coming back to haunt him. "They were. I'm speaking mostly of her when she lived with her father, before she married. She did marry young, after all. The members of our regiment conspired to protect her, and her father made sure she knew where it was unsafe to go. Her husband did the same. But London is a different world."

"You aren't giving her credit for having any brains or courage or sense of self-preservation," Eliza snapped. "What about during battles? Didn't she help with the wounded?"

"She did not. Her father—and her husband—sent her to the back of the lines with the other women, where they knew she would be safe. She was seventeen when they died, for pity's sake. Indeed, since she followed their directions implicitly, I'm giving her plenty of credit for both brains and a sense of self-preservation. As for courage, I think *any* woman who suffers in childbirth has courage to spare."

She blinked. "That is very enlightened of you."

He cast her a wry smile. "It's all due to my mother. When

I was sowing my wild oats, she despaired of me, so she didn't see the fruits of her education. I'm happy I had a chance to be with her before her death to assure her that the man she despaired of was gone."

"But is he really?" She lowered her voice to a whisper, though no one was in the waiting room but them. "You just now nearly seduced me in our morning room."

"Not 'nearly' enough, my sweet," he quipped, then cursed himself for falling back into old habits with her.

Hadn't he already deemed her forbidden to him? Unacceptable at present? Especially since she and her sisters had taken Jocelin on. What was to keep them from ending their involvement the minute he stepped over the line with Eliza?

Diana poked her head out of the dressing room. "Are you coming, Eliza? I want your opinion about something."

"Give me a few more minutes," Eliza said before turning back to him. "I have to go. As to Jocelin's comings and goings, we will make sure to carry her to and fro if that's what you require. So you might as well leave. We don't need you to charge it to your credit, since Mrs. Ludgate knows we'll always pay her and make sure the client reimburses us."

He wouldn't have guessed that, but it made sense, given their reputation. Still, he'd thought he would have to leave his name and direction at least. "Did you never have anyone drag their feet about paying?"

"Occasionally. But between my butler Norris's connections from the army and Diana's various stratagems for ensuring that they honored their commitments, we rarely had to worry in the past. And now that she's married to Geoffrey . . . well, as you might imagine, we never do anymore."

A bark of laughter escaped him. "Of course you don't. Grenwood and I nearly came to blows over my dancing with Rosy. I can only imagine what he'd do to anyone who crossed Diana."

She clearly fought a smile. "Geoffrey can be . . . shall we say . . . difficult when it comes to my sister."

"Right." He'd encountered that, too, when Geoffrey had nearly taken off his head over his dancing with Diana.

Something in the corner of his eye caught his attention, and he looked over to find Jocelin emerging from the back rooms, led by Diana.

"Since you wouldn't come to us, Eliza," Diana said, "we decided we'd come to you."

Good God. He'd rarely seen Jocelin in anything but day gowns, and even when she did dress for evening, her attire was quite modest. There were no balls in Linwood—the village was tiny—and she'd generally preferred to stay with Jimmy rather than consign him to a harried servant.

So to see her garbed for evening in *London* took him aback. The gown of rose-colored silk was cut low enough he could see the tops of her breasts, for God's sake! He had to resist the urge to demand they put her back into virginal white and give her a chin-high fichu, so no inappropriate gentlemen would try to paw at her.

At Diana's instigation, Jocelin turned and then swished her dress, her face alight. "Can you imagine what they'd all think to see me like this in the camp?"

He forced a smile. "You would stun every soldier into silence."

"They're used to seeing me in the plainest, most practical wool or cotton. But this . . ." She swept her hands down the silk. "This makes me almost beautiful."

"You *are* beautiful. The gown only allows that to show."

She flashed him a hopeful look. "Do you really think so?"

Damn. She could read into any innocent statement a promise of marriage. Torn between the need to stoke her confidence and the need to dispel her idea that he would ever even consider marrying her, he settled for a brotherly expression. "Of course." He made his tone kind. "You will turn every man's head at any affair you attend."

The disappointment in her face broke his heart. That was something else Eliza had been right about. Jocelin's emotions *were* writ large in her expressions, and if he attended events with her, or at least was nearby at such affairs, he'd be risking her very future.

Bloody hell. He wished he'd been paying better attention to her in recent weeks. He still prayed it was a mere infatuation, much like the one she'd had for her seducer, but if it wasn't, he would have to deal decisively with that problem, and that in itself would be difficult.

"It's a very becoming gown, Mrs. March," Eliza said, obviously trying to smooth things over. "And on you, it's even more attractive. You have the perfect form for it."

"Thank you," Jocelin murmured, though she now avoided both his gaze and Eliza's.

He sighed.

"Come, my dear," Diana said gently, as if sensing Jocelin's feelings. "We've got plenty more gowns and other things to order."

"Oh, but I don't wish to spend *too* much of the earl's—"

"Your father would want it, dear girl," he broke in. This time his use of the word "girl" was deliberate.

She stiffened. "Very well. If his lordship doesn't mind the cost, then I am happy to do as he wishes."

Nathaniel stifled a groan as she turned and hurried back into the fitting rooms.

"She'll be fine," Eliza said under her breath. "Young women are resilient. You must simply give her time."

"Time is not our friend." If anyone uncovered Jocelin's

secret, marriage would be out of the question for her. He had to find her a husband before then.

He caught Eliza regarding him oddly and figured he'd best distract her. "Meanwhile, I wouldn't mind seeing *you* in that dress," he murmured. "And then rapidly out of it."

"You'd have to get me out of it before anyone saw me in it." Her gaze turned wistful. "I would look awful in that gown."

"That's impossible. You couldn't look awful if you tried."

She laughed. "You are better at buttering up a woman than even Samuel was, and that's saying something."

"Don't compare me to him," he said instinctively.

Her gaze shot to him. "Why not?"

"Just . . . don't." He had worked hard to change who he'd been before the war, and he refused to take up that mantle again. He looked steadily at her. "I would never give you a compliment I didn't mean. And I mean this one: You look lovely no matter what you wear."

"That's a flattering . . . a *kind* remark, but Jocelin and I have wildly different body shapes. She is tall and curvy, so that gown flatters her. Meanwhile, a gown of that cut would emphasize that I'm short and rather too buxom."

"Is there such a thing?"

She smiled and shook her head. "For gowns? Oh, yes."

"Ah." Deliberately, he raked his gaze down her gorgeous frame. "I don't care about gowns. I know what I like in a woman, and buxom definitely qualifies. So does your coloring and your taste and . . ." He caught himself before he could reveal just how much she could affect him. "You've got everything, Eliza. Don't let anyone tell you differently."

"What makes you think they have?" she asked rather archly.

"You haven't remarried, have you? I actually expected you to have done so by now."

"I've not remarried by choice." She took a breath as if to steady her nerves. "Samuel ruined me for other men. I dare not risk ending up in the same situation I was in before. Now I know that marriage is not for me, and that suits me just fine."

No doubt she meant that to be a warning of sorts. God, how could he not have noticed how deeply Samuel's reckless behavior had affected Eliza? What kind of man could Nathaniel have been to have ignored that?

The kind who'd been too absorbed in his own problems. Who'd thought drinking and wenching would settle his restlessness. It never had. And now he wondered why he'd expected it to.

"I don't believe you," he said softly. "You would make some caring man of character a wonderful wife. Please don't let Samuel rob you of that."

"Some *other* man, you mean." When he frowned, trying to think how to answer, she added, "And that's fine by me. I have no need of a husband." She cast him a coy smile. "But I might have need of a lover."

The remark caught him by surprise.

Before he could answer, however, she said, "I must go. I'm sure I'll see you in the coming days."

Then she swept into the fitting rooms, head held high, and left him with his blood in a frenzy and his jaw on the floor.

This was going to be a very long Season if he didn't take control of his needs. Because he could not marry her and would not start an affair he had no intention of finishing. Not yet, at least.

So he'd just have to stay away from her. That was the only solution to his dilemma.

# Chapter 8

Two weeks. Could it really have been that long since Nathaniel had shown Eliza how enchanting his rakish skills could be? Since Eliza had given Nathaniel her parting sally?

Sadly, yes. And she'd felt every second.

At first, she'd thought it would take him a mere day to respond to her remark. But days passed, then a week, then two. And nothing happened. If anything, he'd become more formal around her, as if recognizing how wise it was for them *not* to be involved.

Not that they'd had any chances to be alone together. True to his word, he had let Elegant Occasions handle the few small events they'd arranged to help Jocelin get acclimated. Whenever there were lessons to be done—etiquette or otherwise—her sisters were around, and he was careful not to sit near Eliza . . . if he were even there.

So there'd been no sly whispers, no dry remarks. He hadn't once found an excuse to pull her away from her sisters for another kiss-and-caress session or cajole her to meet him late one night.

Well, she'd waited long enough for him to make the next overture. Clearly, he wasn't going to take her up on her "offer." Her bold words must have scared him off.

Fine. If that were the case, then a pox on him. She didn't

need him anyway. There were plenty of men in society who'd fight for the chance to be her lover.

A pity none of them appealed to her.

Now, as Eliza arrived at Foxstead Place at one PM to pick up Jocelin, she tried not to think about whether she'd see him. She resisted the urge to check her turban to make sure it was straight or pinch color into her cheeks or even to straighten her gloves.

Her sisters had sent her here alone to ensure she kept Nathaniel from attending the charity fete at the Crowders' Richmond mansion. But if she couldn't, she'd promised to keep him away from Jocelin herself. They thought they were being so clever, throwing her and Nathaniel together, but she knew keeping him entertained would be a misery when he'd made it clear he would prefer *not* to spend time alone with her.

Still, she could not let them down. Or Jocelin, for that matter. She'd grown fond of the young lady, despite everything.

When she entered Nathaniel's expansive town house, three times the size of hers, she got a pleasant surprise when a certain small boy ran into the foyer to tug at her skirts.

"Missis Pears!" he cried. "Jimmy miss you!"

She ruffled his hair. "I missed you, too, sweetie."

A couple of weeks ago, she'd volunteered to watch Jimmy while Nathaniel and Jocelin had been interviewing possible nursemaids. They'd had a delightful day, eating pears and banging on her pianoforte and singing. That's when the lad had begun calling her Mrs. Pears. It was close enough to her real name that she hadn't bothered to correct him.

She honestly didn't know *why* Verity had complained about him. Jimmy was a little dear. Her time with him was the only experience that made her question her determination not to marry.

Then she reminded herself how Samuel and her father and even Verity's despicable former fiancé had behaved toward the women in their lives, and she renewed her resolve. She got to see children at the Foundling Hospital. Surely that was enough.

"I'm sorry, Mrs. Pierce," his nursery maid said as she ran up to them. "The little fellow got away from me. It won't happen again."

"Don't worry about it, Molly," Eliza said with a smile. "I'm told you're doing an excellent job. And this one leads everyone a merry dance."

"Except you," a male voice put in.

He *was* here.

She smiled as coolly as she was capable of when her hands were clammy and her heart thundered in her ears. "Lord Foxstead. I should know by now that wherever Jimmy is, you can't be far behind."

Then she fixed on his attire, wondering where he was going. His bottle-green coat and brown-striped linen waistcoat, along with his yellow, tight-fitting, nankeen trousers and kid gloves, took her by surprise. He wasn't usually so colorful. Besides which, he had a cornflower in his lapel.

But when the footman stepped forward to hand him his top hat, and she spotted the bunch of lavender in his hatband, she knew what he was up to.

Oh dear. She lifted her gaze to his. "Please tell me you are headed to a village green somewhere to celebrate May Day with friends."

Looking chagrined, he stepped close to say in a low voice, "I know what you said, and I was willing to do it your way until—"

"Isn't it wonderful, Mrs. Pierce?" Jocelin said breathlessly as she approached. "Lord Foxstead is going with us after all. He insisted he wasn't, but he changed his mind just yesterday."

Eliza lifted an eyebrow at him. Changed his mind, had he? She was going to change his mind back by giving him a piece of *hers*! But that might be hard to do. How could she chide him when Jocelin looked so pleased?

Jimmy tugged at Jocelin's skirts. "Jimmy go, Mama. Jimmy go!"

Jocelin bent to lift him in her arms. Thankfully, she was already wearing the scarlet cloak they'd picked out so carefully. It wouldn't do for her to get her new gown of sky-blue silk smudged before she even reached her first big event of the Season.

"You can't go, dearest," Jocelin told Jimmy with obvious concern. "You have to stay here with Molly."

"Jimmy go! Jimmy go!" he chanted, thrusting out his petulant lower lip.

Before Molly could even step in, Nathaniel hauled the boy out of Jocelin's arms and into his. "Trust me," he said in a laughing voice that stopped the boy's pouting, "you'll enjoy being here with Molly more. You can play with those big wooden soldiers I bought you yesterday. Doesn't that sound like fun?"

Jimmy blinked, then broke into a grin. "Soldiers!"

Soldiers like his late father, the poor dear. It made a lump stick in her throat. So did watching Nathaniel with the boy. All Nathaniel's bewildering changes of mood evened out as he dealt with Jimmy. He could speak to the child on his own level without blinking an eye.

She wasn't sure why, but it gave her hope. She winced. That she and Nathaniel could have an affair. That was all she'd meant.

"I daresay they don't have toy soldiers at the place where

we're going," Nathaniel continued. "Just a bunch of boring old people like me and your mama and Mrs. Pierce talking about dull things."

"Speak for yourself," Eliza said with a lift of her chin. "I'm not the least bit boring, I'll have you know. Jimmy and I had great fun the day I watched him, didn't we, Jimmy?"

"Uh-huh," he said with a bob of his chubby chin. "Missis Pears not boring."

Nathaniel's eyes, deep and dark and mysterious, met hers. "I take it back," he said in that rumbling tone that made her blood rumble in answer. "Although Mrs. Pierce does have a tendency to frustrate a person at times, she couldn't be boring if she tried."

Eliza resisted the urge to see if Nathaniel's words had upset Jocelin. Meanwhile, Jimmy looked from him to Eliza, clearly unsure what was going on.

Molly swiftly seized the opportunity to take Jimmy in her arms. "Let's go find those soldiers, shall we?"

Jimmy clapped his hands. "Soldiers!"

And off they went, with Jimmy whooping.

When Eliza finally gathered the courage to glance at Jocelin, she was watching her child. Certainly no one could fault the young woman for *that*.

"Jocelin," Nathaniel said. "Why don't you go on to the carriage? I need to speak to Mrs. Pierce alone for a moment."

Jocelin nodded and headed for the door.

"Don't forget not to put your hood over your hair!" Eliza called after her.

The young lady laughed. "After you worked so hard teaching my lady's maid how to do it up for today? Not a chance!"

As soon as she was gone, Nathaniel crossed his arms over his chest. "I understand you are planning on introducing Jocelin to some army officers at this affair."

"I am," she said, bewildered by his harsh tone. "The Crowders' son is about to leave for the Peninsula with a cavalry brigade, and Major Quinn is a distant cousin of mine on temporary leave from his regiment. When I mentioned that they'd be attending the event, Jocelin begged me to introduce her to them. She was very excited by the prospect."

He glowered at her. "I told you I wanted her to meet wealthy gentlemen of good reputation and standing."

"That's not what *she* wants. And I have to respect her wishes. *She* is our client, after all. You are merely her guardian."

"Merely!" He looked away, a muscle jerking in his jaw. "I did not risk my life to get her safely back to England only to see her returned to the fray!"

He had risked his life for Jocelin? He must have owed her father a great deal. "You're making several assumptions," she said calmly. "First of all, she may not like either man once she meets them. Second, if she does take a fancy to one of them, she could choose to remain in England after marriage the way most wives do. She does have a child now. Why would she risk Jimmy's life to go?"

"Because she grew up in it, and it's all she knows. I had a hard time getting her to return to England. Even after Talavera, she wanted to stay to nurse her father back to health. He begged me to take her back here with me once it was possible to leave, but we couldn't leave at once, so . . . By the time we could, he was dead, and her grief made her compliant enough that I could insist on her returning with me. Otherwise, I think she would have stayed without me."

"Heavens, and bear a child in the camp? Would she really have done that? Alone?"

"She didn't even know she was pregnant yet, remember? Besides, widows are snapped up in the army if they decide not to return to England. Every unmarried man wants a wife to clean and cook for him and share his bed. I once saw a woman mourn her husband for five hours before accepting another man's proposal of marriage. Why any woman would *want* to stay with a regiment in Spain is beyond me, but some do."

"Good Lord. And they raise children there, too, I suppose."

"Some of them, yes."

"But would Jocelin have wanted that?" Eliza asked.

"I honestly don't know." For the first time ever, he appeared flustered. "At first, she seemed happy with the life she had here. But she's young. She grew restless. She wants a husband, and who can blame her?" He searched her face. "Not every woman is like you."

"Not every woman had a husband like Samuel."

He nodded. "My point is, she got so excited about the possibility of marrying an army officer that I fear she might actually do it, if only so she can live in the camps again."

"And you think preventing her from meeting any officers will change her mind about it? That's rather presumptuous of you. She will like who she likes."

"But *my* duty is to her late father, and he would never have wanted her to have such a husband if it meant she returned to the war."

"It doesn't matter what he wanted for her, and it certainly doesn't matter what *you* want for her. She's a grown woman. She can make her own choices. So if your purpose in going today is to ruin her chances with two possible suitors she might prefer—"

"It isn't. I simply want to be able to assess them, to see what they're looking for in a wife."

"You could do that independently of the Richmond May Day affair."

He conceded that point with a nod. "But I can't necessarily observe how they behave around her. That's why I'm going. Once the men have talked with me and Jocelin, and I'm satisfied they won't try to carry her back to the Peninsula with them, I will withdraw."

"Can I really trust you to do that? You've already broken your word once."

He looked irate. "How have I done so?"

"You promised to stay away. Now, you're not."

"Oh, *that*. You'll admit I have good reason."

"I'll admit no such thing," she said. "That remains to be seen."

Should she tell him of her promise to her sisters? That if she couldn't keep him from going, then *she* had to keep him entertained? No, best not to. He would assume she was trying to get him alone to seduce him or something of that ilk.

And she wasn't. Truly.

Lord, she was such a liar.

"I have one other purpose in going." He avoided her gaze. "Jocelin has a substantial dowry, and I'd hate to see it go to some fortune-hunting officer. I want to make sure that neither would be marrying her only for her fortune."

"A *fortune*? The devil you say!" She gaped at him. "And when were you going to tell me . . . and . . . and my sisters this?"

With a shrug, he met her gaze. "When you stopped thinking I have some private, intimate relationship with her." He drew in a heavy breath. "As her guardian, I happen to be in charge of her inheritance, which was substantial enough to provide her with the funds for the dowry, although I still would want her to find a good husband and not just a fortune hunter."

Biting back the harsh words that leapt to her tongue, Eliza forced a smile. "I see. And I suppose you've been supporting her and her son all this time, so that her inheritance didn't have to be appropriated for that purpose."

"I have," he said, bristling. "As you might guess, Jocelin doesn't cost much to feed and clothe."

"Except for all the new gowns for her introduction to society. Not to mention, our fee for helping her with that." She lowered her voice. "So, in essence, she *is* your mistress, just not one whom you happen to bed."

He stiffened. "Surely by now you can tell she is *not* my—" He caught himself when he noticed the butler straining to hear.

"I know," she murmured. "She may still be mooning after you, but it's painfully obvious you aren't doing the same."

He relaxed a fraction. "I'm not even sure she's mooning after me anymore. I think we had two things in common— the army and her father—and the more time passed without him around and without us being in a regiment, the more she let go of me, too. Which is good."

"Perhaps. She does still seem to talk to you more freely in general than to anyone else."

"Does she? Then think of her as more of a sister to me. Or a niece or daughter or any other sort of female relation you can name."

She tapped her chin. "I wonder what that makes Jimmy. Nephew? Great-nephew?" Her voice trembled with suppressed laughter. "Grandson?"

"Devil take it, no. I'm not *that* old, for God's sake. I would have had to sire Jocelin at . . . at the age of ten."

She burst into laughter. "I'm teasing you, Nathaniel. Is it that hard to tell?"

"It is, actually," he grumbled. "You didn't used to tease me. It will take me a while to accustom myself to it."

She shook her head. "You're hopeless. I've never seen a rakehell so wary of women."

"Not a rakehell."

"A soldier, forgive me. Though I still say you aren't giving Jocelin a chance to choose for herself. If she prefers someone from the army—"

"Enough, minx. We can't stand here discussing it all day." He waved a footman over, who handed him a handsome bouquet that Nathaniel then held out to her. "For you."

That brought her up short. She hadn't been expecting *that,* to be sure, not after the way he'd avoided being alone with her and his testiness over her introducing Jocelin to officers.

Her first reaction was to melt and take them. Then she wanted to kick herself. Men *knew* how some women reacted to flowers. Samuel had given her enough roses to fill a hothouse, because he'd figured out that she adored them. But it had never done a thing to change the fact that they couldn't afford that luxury. Or that he lied to her sometimes.

Still, Nathaniel hadn't exactly lied to her. He was just reneging on a promise. Hardly the same. Right?

"I already have violets adorning my turban," she said warily. "Lots of them."

"Ah, but those are silk. It's not the same." He thrust his bouquet closer. "These are real blooms. For May Day."

"And you say you're no longer a rakehell." She wanted to strangle him. She wanted to kiss him.

Reluctantly, she took the bouquet and sniffed it. The arrangement of sweet William, lilies, daphne, and jasmine smelled heavenly, each type of flower melding with the others to create a rich scent.

"Am I forgiven for insisting on going along?" he asked smugly.

Oh, he was a clever fellow, rakehell *or* soldier. "Do

you swear you won't interfere during her encounters with gentlemen?"

"I swear. *Now* do you forgive me?"

"Just because you made a promise not to interfere, and you gave me a bouquet? Hardly. First, your promises are clearly not reliable. And second, if you had truly wished to buy my forgiveness, you should have presented me with a troubadour to serenade me." She smelled the bouquet again and fought a smile. "But this will do, I suppose. For now."

"Then I will accept your provisional forgiveness . . . for now. Next time I'll bring an entire orchestra to serenade you. Lord knows I couldn't do it. I sing like a frog." He offered her his arm. "Shall we?"

She hesitated. Her sisters were going to wring her neck for letting him come along—and they'd definitely hold her feet to the fire regarding her promise. Nor was she entirely sure he wouldn't muck things up for Jocelin.

At the same time, he was clearly going to go whether she "let" him or not, and if she didn't forgive him, he was liable to do it behind their backs. So it was better if she were with him to ensure he *did* keep his word. "Very well."

She took his arm with one hand while she held his flowers in the other, and they headed out for the carriage.

The bouquet was quite an impressive selection, she had to admit. "You certainly marshaled your defenses quickly if you had these already put together for my arrival."

"There's a rather extensive garden behind Foxstead Place. And my housekeeper knows exactly how to gather an arrangement that suits my needs."

"Oh, I daresay she does, given your reputation with women," she said archly. "Indeed, I'm surprised your garden can keep up."

"Pax, dearling," he said as they went down the front steps. "I swear this is the last time I will show up unannounced for an occasion of yours. I will also do my best not to be anywhere near Jocelin while we're in Richmond . . . except to assess your officer friends."

She sighed. "You are just like Geoffrey. He's always surprising us with a change to our plans. Sometimes I swear he does it just for his own amusement."

"First of all, of course I'm like him. He *is* my friend, after all." He grinned. "And it *is* amusing to watch you three ladies scramble to adjust."

"Take care, Lord Foxstead," she said as they neared the carriage. "Or I will make you go in your phaeton to Richmond."

"Make me! How would you manage that?" he joked. "Not that I would mind taking the phaeton. Jocelin rather enjoys riding alone in a carriage if the scenery is pleasant." His eyes twinkled at her. "And I would gladly drive those country roads at a manic pace as long as I had you at my side."

"You knew what I meant," she said, trying not to laugh. "I would stay with her in the carriage, and you—"

"Would be bereft." He laid his free hand over his heart. "It is hardly the same to race around in a phaeton by oneself. I would definitely need an audience to admire my driving ability."

"Oh, Lord," she muttered. "What you need is a keeper."

"Are you volunteering for the position?"

Her gaze shot to him. Was he teasing? Flirting? After spending the last two weeks being formal with her, he couldn't be serious. "No woman on earth would be able to 'keep' you anywhere you didn't want to be."

He laid his hand over hers with a serious look. "You'd be surprised."

"Nothing about you would surprise me," she said in a low tone as they reached the carriage.

Waving the groom away, he opened the door to her carriage. "How odd," he murmured. "Everything about *you* surprises me."

Dying to know what he meant, she would have asked, but he was already handing her in and Jocelin was clearly listening.

Eliza took her seat next to the young lady, trying not to notice how Nathaniel's tight trousers showed the muscular flex of his calves when he climbed in and sat down opposite them. But she couldn't ignore the way he instantly took charge by calling out to her coachman to drive on.

That was one more reason not to encourage any advances he *might* make today. She didn't need another husband, and she didn't want a lover who took over her life again. So it was probably best to let sleeping rakehells lie.

If she could.

# Chapter 9

Nathaniel settled back against the seat and watched as Eliza proceeded to ignore him. He couldn't blame her. He *had* broken his promise. But he'd had good reason, knowing the worth his fellow officers would attach to a woman like Jocelin. And the risks involved if they pursued her.

First of all, there was a slim possibility one of them might have spent time with her "husband's" regiment. If so, they might deduce that the man was fictitious. No one must ever guess that, or Jocelin's reputation would be shattered and Jimmy's future as well.

Second, he couldn't risk one of them sweeping her off her feet and carrying her back to the Peninsula. What about Jimmy? The lad couldn't go to war.

Third, what if the officer only cared about her dowry? That could not happen. Nathaniel wouldn't let it.

The trick was going to be playing the concerned guardian and guiding Jocelin's answers without causing Eliza to get suspicious again. Her suspicions about him and Jocelin might be groundless, but they could lead to more damaging misgivings.

He must prevent that at all costs.

But watching Eliza with Jocelin made him wish he dared confide in Eliza. Despite her concerns about Jocelin's connection to him, whenever Eliza dealt with the girl, her tone was gentle and reassuring. It showed her to be a good person, better than he'd realized.

On the surface at least. He'd learned not to trust people much in the past few years. And given what Sam had apparently put her through . . .

No, best to keep his own counsel.

"Now," Eliza said to Jocelin, "tell me what you are to do when you're introduced to the Crowders."

Jocelin sat up straight. "I'm to say how pleased I am to make their acquaintance and how lovely a home they have," Jocelin recited, like a parrot mimicking its master.

"And what else?" Eliza asked.

Jocelin seemed caught by surprise. "I . . . I . . . Oh! I forgot to curtsy first."

Eliza smiled. "Very good. I'm sure you would have remembered in the moment."

"Why does she have to curtsy to Mrs. Crowder?" Nathaniel demanded. "Jocelin is the daughter of a decorated army general. Last I heard, Mrs. Crowder was just the wife of a cit."

"Ah, but not merely 'a cit' anymore," Eliza said. "Mr. Crowder was recently knighted for his service to the crown, so he's Sir Bartholomew Crowder now, and his wife is Lady Crowder."

Nathaniel cocked his head. "You don't say. What service did he provide?"

"His company discovered an enhancement to Baker rifles that makes them far more efficient and effective. Or so I'm told."

"Wait. We're going to the home of *that* Crowder? If I'd known, I would have insisted on going along just to meet *him*."

"And that's precisely why Jocelin must curtsy to *Lady* Crowder, whose husband is a knight. Whereas—"

"—my father, important as he was in the army," Jocelin cut in, "rose through the ranks. He became an officer because of providing a service to an English lord who purchased his first commission for him. But he has no real standing of his own in English society."

"And your husband?" Eliza prodded.

Jocelin blinked, and Nathaniel could swear his heart stopped. Then she said, "He, too, rose through the ranks to become a lieutenant. Neither Papa nor my dear Lieutenant March had family or connections." She looked at Nathaniel triumphantly. "Which is why I must curtsy to Lady Crowder."

"Good God, Eliza, you've turned her into one of us." Which he wasn't so sure was a good thing.

Back when he and Sam acted like arses in London, Nathaniel would have termed the Crowders "mushrooms," who had no business mimicking their betters. It shamed him even to think of it now. But the war had taught him—*Anson* had taught him—that a man could make something of himself and become twice as important to the world as some pompous earl's son.

Eliza was staring at him. "Do you intend to question everything Jocelin and I discuss on our way to Richmond? Because you did promise you wouldn't interfere."

"'During her encounters with gentlemen' is what I said." When Eliza scowled, he added hastily, "But I won't interfere again, I swear. I'll be silent as the grave now."

She looked skeptical but apparently chose to take him at his word, for she returned to instructing Jocelin or whatever it was she was doing. "Do you feel comfortable with curtseying?"

Jocelin nodded. "We practiced it often enough that I

think I'll remember where my feet are supposed to be and how low I'm to bend."

"Fortunately, you're possessed of a natural grace and elegance that will profit you well. In your gown, with your hair just so, you look positively ethereal."

A soft blush spread over Jocelin's cheeks. God, those officers were going to be almost as smitten with the chit as he was with Eliza.

Smitten? He wasn't smitten, for God's sake. It was pure lust that drove him to Eliza. She didn't look ethereal in the least. In her low-cut green gown and her purple and green turban bedecked with peacock feathers, she looked like a lushly made Siren of the Sea . . . his Mermaid of the May.

No, she wasn't his. She couldn't be. Unless it was as his mistress, which he began to think was a fine idea. He'd fought his attraction for two weeks, and what had it got him? Difficult days and sleepless nights.

No more. That first night he'd seen her at the musicale, he'd said he wanted her in his bed. Well, he did. The very thought made him . . .

Oh, damn. Thank God both ladies were now more intent on looking out at the beautiful scenery of Richmond. Otherwise, they might notice that he'd placed his hat on his lap.

Jocelin turned on the seat to face Eliza. "But I'm still confused about when to curtsey while we're outdoors. I know when I'm walking, I'm merely supposed to bow slightly to acknowledge someone I know. But if I'm outside, but not walking—"

"Curtsey if you're standing with people and can do so easily. Otherwise, if you're walking down a pathway, for example, and you encounter Lord Foxstead or any other gentlemen to whom you've been introduced, you simply give a quick bow of your head."

"Yes, my lady."

"No, not 'my lady,' remember? 'Madam.'"

Jocelin swallowed. "Right. Because you took your husband's name instead of keeping your rank."

"Not just for that reason. If you see Verity, you may call her Lady Verity, but do not use 'my lady' throughout the conversation. Only servants do that."

The young woman sighed and stared down at her hands. "There are so many rules to remember."

"More than you will ever need. But this is a friendly crowd. They won't be insulted by any oversight of etiquette. That's why it's such a good situation for practicing what you've learned."

"And I'll be there if you need support," Nathaniel put in.

Jocelin eyed him askance. "Begging your pardon, sir, but I think Eliza will be of more use for that."

Nathaniel winced. *Just stab a dagger through my heart, young lady, will you?* And when had she started calling Eliza by her Christian name? Under the circumstances, that was decidedly odd.

But all he said was, "Undoubtedly."

Eliza looked as if she were hiding a smile. "Do keep in mind, though, that you'll mostly be with the duchess." When Jocelin got a panicked look on her face, Eliza added hastily, "Diana, that is."

"Oh, right." Jocelin smiled shyly. "I forget she's a duchess. She seems so . . . normal."

"She'll be happy to hear that," Eliza said with a chuckle. "No one regards Diana as normal in the least, not even us. Anyway, since Diana and Geoffrey will be attending as guests, they will accompany you."

"Everywhere?" Jocelin said, with a hopeful look.

"Everywhere you wish them to. Verity and I have much to do in our respective areas. So, after I introduce you to the officers, it will be time for me to get to work. But you can always ask one of the staff to fetch us if you need us."

"I shall keep that in mind."

"Now, let's go over your manners at table."

Jocelin nodded. "No eating with a knife. Also, I'm to put my gloves in my lap as soon as I sit down, and I'm not to use a knife and fork on my bread, which is to be broken."

Caught by surprise, Nathaniel glanced from Jocelin to Eliza. "Will we be sitting down to dinner?"

"Yes," Eliza answered. "Sort of. It will be al fresco, since the weather is fine, and the hours are longer. Everyone can view the beauties of the outdoor gardens better, not to mention the cavorting of youths about the maypole."

"There's to be a Jack in the Green and Morris dancers and all sorts of fun," Jocelin said excitedly, reminding him she was still young enough to enjoy such sylvan pleasures in the company of other young people. Clearly, he should have brought her to London sooner.

Eliza glanced out the window. "Oh, dear, we're nearly there. So let's return to our overview of etiquette rules. When you are asked to dance and you accept, which hand do you hold forth for the gentleman to take?"

"My left."

"And what do you do about your gloves?"

"I-I don't do anything."

Eliza broke into a smile. "That was a trick question, and you answered it correctly. Gloves are kept on except during dinner."

"And except if a man holds his hand out for you to shake," Nathaniel put in.

When Jocelin got another panicked expression on her face, Eliza said, "Stop that, Lord Foxstead! We haven't even covered that—it's very complicated, and it probably won't come up today, anyway."

"There's so many rules for hands and gloves," Jocelin said forlornly. "However did you learn them all?"

"Our governess rapped my knuckles if I did the wrong thing." Eliza gave a rueful shake of her head. "I rarely did it twice, I assure you."

A wide-eyed Jocelin thrust her hands in her cloak pockets.

Nathaniel laughed. "Eliza's not going to rap your knuckles, trust me."

"No, but I might rap *yours*," Eliza said, tipping up her chin in challenge. "We've only gone over half the things I wanted to cover again, thanks to you and your interruptions."

"You're not going to rap my knuckles, either," he quipped. "It would ruin my gloves. We can't have that, can we?"

Jocelin gazed out the window with despair on her face. "I-I can't do this. I knew I couldn't. He always said I'd be abysmal at . . . going into proper society."

"He who? Who would dare to say such an awful thing to you?" Eliza asked, clearly outraged.

Nathaniel and Jocelin exchanged a glance. "Jocelin's husband," Nathaniel answered. "He wasn't a very . . . nice man."

"I know a bit about that myself," Eliza muttered, not quite under her breath. "And now we're here." Eliza half turned toward Jocelin. "Look at me, my dear." When Jocelin did so, Eliza said, "You are adorable, and you've got the rules down pat, for the most part. Think of how long it takes a new army recruit to learn the rules of regimental life. You've had all of two weeks to learn the rules of high society, and you have done so admirably."

Jocelin swallowed hard. "Do you really think so?"

"I know so. Besides, you've already met a number of people who will be here. You liked our friend Miss Crowder, didn't you?"

Jocelin bobbed her head.

"Well, she's very much looking forward to seeing you again, and introducing her brother to you. I believe I already told you he's in the cavalry."

Nathaniel snorted.

That startled a smile out of Jocelin. "Lord Foxstead doesn't like men in the cavalry. He says they too often bully the infantry just because they think they're better than foot soldiers."

Eliza, that minx, lifted an eyebrow at him. "Then why didn't you buy a commission in the cavalry, Lord Foxstead? Lord knows you ride well enough."

"How do you know I ride well?"

"I've seen you ride plenty of times."

Not to his knowledge. He would have to explore that a bit further at another time. But not now, with Jocelin listening. "As it happens, the Twenty-Eighth Regiment of Foot was connected to my home in Gloucestershire, so that's why I joined them. It made sense to do so at the time."

"They were probably also the only regiment with openings for officers," Jocelin said helpfully. "And they moved you up quickly. You did make captain the next year, did you not? By purchase."

"I did. And I remained a captain until I sold my commission the following year. I'm not ashamed of it, if that's what you were hinting at. I acquitted myself like an officer and a gentleman, which is about all a man can do on the battlefield, dear girl."

Jocelin withdrew a bit into herself once more. "I was not hinting at anything. And you mustn't call me 'dear girl.' It's very inappropriate. Am I right, Eliza?"

"*Very* inappropriate," Eliza said, her eyes twinkling at him. "I daresay his calling you that would ruin everything."

"Enough, both of you." He picked up his top hat as a servant hurried forward to put down the step. "If you think to fright me into leaving, think again. I'm staying here until the bitter end, and nothing you say will prevent it."

By God, he would do what was right by Jocelin, whether she wanted it or not. He owed that much and more to the general.

Nathaniel would *not* shirk his duty. He would damned well pay attention to what was going on and not be so blinded by other concerns that he didn't see what was happening before his very eyes.

Not this time.

# Chapter 10

$C$An hour later, Eliza watched as Jocelin, Nathaniel, and the Harper ladies' friend Isolde Crowder walked down the hill to view the area where dinner was to be served. It contained a number of tables being set by footmen next to a few tents where the food would be dished out before being served. The tables faced a small stage for the opera singer who was performing, and next to that, a maypole, which as of yet was not in use. That would come later, when the orchestra, placed to the side of the tables, began playing the proper music.

Verity came up beside Eliza. "What do you think?"

"Oh, you have outdone yourself this time. The carved and painted flowers atop the maypole? Where on earth did you find such a thing?"

She shrugged. "Someone was tearing down an old theater, and they were going to throw the thing away. A perfectly good maypole! I asked for it at once, then cleaned it up and painted it. It looks as good as new, doesn't it?"

"It does. And I like how you continued the theme on the tables with those fanciful centerpieces."

"Those are also from the torn-down theater. Although the candelabras are Lady Crowder's." Verity frowned. "It's hard to think of her as *Lady* Crowder now. I'm so used to calling her Mrs. Crowder."

"Well, she's a good-hearted woman. If you slip up once in a while, she won't mind."

"I'm not so sure about that." Verity fell silent a moment, surveying the area below. "I meant to tell you that you did an excellent job with Jocelin's hair. The way you intertwined the ribbons with her braids and those little bunches of silk flowers forming a sort of crown? Next time I actually attend an event, promise me you'll do my hair like that."

"I will do whatever you wish, sweetie. But don't let me keep you—I know you have matters to attend to in the kitchens."

Verity hadn't yet noticed Nathaniel, and Eliza hoped she never did.

"Wait—is that Lord *Foxstead*?" Verity hissed.

Too late. Nathaniel, Jocelin, and Isolde were slowly mounting the hill, headed straight for them.

"Weren't you supposed to banish him from the affair?" Verity went on.

Eliza shot her sister a warning glance. "Keep your voice down, will you? And try not to make a fuss about his being present. Jocelin doesn't know we wanted to keep him away. She thinks he just changed his mind about attending."

"Well, he did, didn't he? Last I heard, he was decidedly not coming."

"That's my fault." Quickly, she explained about the officers.

To her surprise, Verity was in Nathaniel's camp. "Surely you don't think that poor girl should be running back off to the Peninsula, do you? It's madness!"

"Everyone keeps calling her a 'girl,'" Eliza snapped. "She's not. You, of all people, should understand that."

"Why? Because I'm only three years older than she? Or because she's a widow, and I can't even keep a suitor?"

"Neither, for pity's sake. Because you've been fighting to be taken seriously by those snide French chefs de cuisine who think you too young and too female to know how to put a meal together. That's all I meant."

Just as Eliza had known they would, her words deflated Verity's anger. "Oh. Well, I suppose Jocelin *is* technically a woman, not a girl. She did have a baby, though I don't know how she stopped blushing long enough to conceive one. But I still say we should match her with someone better than Charlie Crowder."

"*Lieutenant* Charlie Crowder now," Eliza reminded her.

"How he got to be a lieutenant, I'll never know."

"The usual way—by purchasing a commission," said a cheerful male voice behind Verity. "Although Father did use his influence, too."

Verity nearly jumped a foot. "Charlie! You're here!" Casting Eliza a speaking look, Verity turned to face him. "How delightful you were able to come."

Isolde's younger brother, Charlie Crowder, was an old friend of Verity's and Diana's. Clearly, his shaggy red mane had been clipped recently. Tall and burly, he was somewhat less brilliant than his famous father and enjoyed nothing so much as a good ale and a fine day of shooting. But he was also a decent sort, which Eliza appreciated even if Verity didn't quite do so.

"We had heard you might get held up on your way south with your new regiment," Verity added.

"Managed to make it on time, fortunately. But we do only have a month or so in town. We lads are in a frightful hurry to join the war, as you might imagine. Eager to kill as many Boney-ites as we can."

"Boney-ites?" Eliza choked out.

"You know," Charlie said. "Followers of Boney. That's Napoleon Bonaparte. We Hussars call him Boney."

"Yes," Verity said dryly. "We know who he is. *Everyone* calls him Boney."

That caught Charlie off guard. "Are you sure? I thought it was just us lads." He looked around. "Have you seen Isolde? Thought I might give my sis a buss on the cheek. Haven't written her in a while." He winked at Verity. "Too busy with all that training up north, you know."

Verity turned to gaze down the hill. "Oh, look, here she comes now. But sadly, I must go. I have to . . . um . . . put the handles on the chicken baskets."

Charlie blinked. "We have chickens now? Father never mentioned it."

With a roll of her eyes, Verity hurried off, leaving Charlie to Eliza. "I think Verity is referring to a kind of food, actually," Eliza said kindly. "They're little pie crust baskets filled with a chicken mixture. You have to add the pie crust handles at the last minute."

"Sounds jolly good," Charlie said. "I must have some later. Your sister really knows how to cook a fine meal." He bent his head toward Eliza and lowered his voice. "You don't think she's looking for a husband, do you?"

"I doubt it," Eliza said honestly.

Just then, Isolde looked up. "Charlie! You're here!" She ran up the hill to hug him. "I was hoping you'd make it."

Jocelin and Nathaniel climbed slowly up behind her. Taking Jocelin by the hand, Isolde led her forward. "Mrs. March, I'd like to introduce to you my brother, Lieutenant Charles Crowder."

Charlie seemed too intent on staring at Jocelin to speak. He'd always had a fondness for pretty women, and Jocelin was looking especially beautiful. "G-Good evening, ma'am,"

Charlie said when he found his tongue. Hastily, he removed his Busby hat. "It's a pleasure to meet you."

"The pleasure is mine, Lieutenant." Jocelin blinked up at him, as if awed by his size. "I'm very happy to meet a Hussar. Which regiment are you in?"

"How did you—"

"Your uniform. And your mustache. Only the Hussars have mustaches." She ventured a smile. "My late husband was in the army. But . . . but not the cavalry. Just the infantry."

"Infantry is important," Charlie said.

Eliza expected Nathaniel to say something like, "Damned right it is," but before he could, a man came up behind Eliza to say, "It takes many sorts of regiments to make an army, Lieutenant. All of them are important."

She turned to find Major Quinn standing there with Diana and Geoffrey, whom Eliza had dispatched to fetch him. "Major! I'm so pleased you found us. Everyone, this is Major Adam Quinn, our cousin."

"Distant cousin," he added.

"Right." She formally introduced him to the other two ladies and then to Nathaniel and Charlie.

"Honored to meet you, Major," Charlie said with a salute. "I'm in the Eighteenth Hussars."

"I know," Major Quinn said. "I can tell from your uniform."

"I was just saying the same thing," Jocelin said, with a shy smile for Charlie. "Your Hessian boots also show you to be in a Hussar regiment, Lieutenant Crowder. Your lace is silver, but many regiments have that."

Charlie began patting his Hussar jacket. "I have lace on here?"

"Oh, I quite forgot. Lace is what they used to call them."

She raised her hand as if to touch his jacket. "If you'll permit me . . ."

"Of course," he said, his cheeks reddening.

Eliza watched, flabbergasted by Jocelin's uncharacteristic boldness, as Jocelin brushed the ornamentation on Charlie's jacket with great delicacy. "It's these braid things. All the braid used to be called lace. I don't know if they still call it that."

"They do," the major said as he took a second, closer look at Jocelin.

"But how did you know I was in the Eighteenth?" Charlie asked.

Jocelin shrugged. "Your silver buttons say 'eighteen' on them."

Eliza made the mistake of looking over at Nathaniel at that moment. When he rolled his eyes heavenward, she had to fight a laugh.

"Of course they do," Charlie said glumly. "I wasn't thinking."

"It takes a while to get used to the different uniforms," Jocelin said. "I'm sure you forgot all about your buttons, since you use them for practical reasons."

"That *is* a fine uniform you're wearing, Charlie," Diana said, obviously wanting to put him at ease.

Charlie really was a very nice man, aside from his eagerness to kill "Boney-ites."

All his glumness vanished as Charlie puffed out his chest. "It is, ain't it? I prefer a blue uniform to a red one any day on account of my hair. And I like this bag thing here. Very fancy."

"It's called a sabretache," Jocelin offered.

"Even better," Charlie said, winking at Jocelin. "It *sounds* fancy, too."

"Because it is." The major stepped behind Eliza and

looked over her shoulder at Jocelin. "What regiment am *I* from, Mrs. March?"

She eyed him askance. "Obviously one of the infantry regiments, judging from your red coat. The Fifty-Seventh, I believe."

He stepped out from behind Eliza. "How could you possibly have guessed that?"

"I saw *your* buttons, too."

"Despite my standing behind my cousin?"

"*Distant* cousin," Geoffrey muttered. He must have heard that the major had briefly been interested in Diana years ago.

But at present, the major was intent upon watching Jocelin, who laughed. "I saw them when you first walked up, Major. I notice such things automatically."

"Very clever of you," Major Quinn said. "I'll admit you have a wealth of military knowledge for a young woman, even the widow of an army officer."

"My father was also in the army—Major General James Anson," Jocelin said.

"So Mrs. Pierce told me," Major Quinn said. "I never knew General Anson personally, but I knew of him. He was a fine soldier and spent a great deal of time on the Peninsula. Did you see him much?"

"All the time. After Mama died, when I was six, I had no other family but my papa, so I was raised in the regiment."

The major blinked. "Astonishing. How was it?"

"H-How was it?"

"Being raised in the regiment. I can't imagine that was easy for a young woman."

"Oh no, it was wonderful!" It was as if a lamp flared to life in Jocelin's face. "All the places I got to visit . . . all the people I got to meet . . . When I was first brought to Papa, his detachment of the regiment had just gone to Minorca.

What a beautiful island it was. And colorful, too! The ladies wore such pretty costumes that I was always in awe when Papa took me with him to meet with the Spanish."

"That's why I joined!" Charlie said excitedly. "I mean, aside from wanting to serve my country and all. I want to see the world, and how better than in the army?"

"I know what you mean," Jocelin gushed. "I still haven't seen enough of it."

And Eliza hadn't heard Jocelin say so many words in so short a span of time since they'd first met. Nor had the young woman ever shown such enthusiasm for anything. Even her new clothes hadn't made her so chatty.

Meanwhile, the major looked annoyed she was even talking to Charlie. "I spent some time in Spain myself, Mrs. March, and you're right about the ladies. Beautiful gowns. Very bright."

That gained him Jocelin's attention. "When I was a girl, I'd put a flower behind my ear like some of the Spanish ladies. I desperately wanted to own one of their gowns. But the officer's wife in the regiment who looked after me was adamant I didn't dare wear such a dress. She called those ladies heathens because they were Catholics." Her smile turned rueful. "I wished nothing more than to be a heathen."

Charlie laughed at that, although the major didn't seem as amused.

Eliza could only think how hard it must have been for the poor girl to have spent most of her life caught between one world and another. No wonder she didn't know what to do in English society. She'd been part of too many other societies to figure out what this one required.

But she clearly knew what army society expected. She already had both officers' attention.

"What regiment was your husband in?" the major asked.

When Jocelin blinked, obviously taken by surprise, Nathaniel stepped forward. "He was in the Sixty-Sixth."

Major Quinn frowned at Nathaniel. "You knew him, then."

"Only from meeting him before the Battle of Talavera," Nathaniel said.

The major started. "Wait a minute. When Mrs. Pierce said your name, I confess I didn't make the connection, but are you perchance Captain Nathaniel Stanton of the Twenty-Eighth Regiment of Foot?"

"I was. Before my father died and I came into the title. I sold my commission at that point."

Major Quinn thrust out his hand. "You are a legend, sir. I must commend you."

Nathaniel shook his hand, looking a bit embarrassed.

"Why is he a legend?" Geoffrey asked the major, to Eliza's relief.

Eliza ought to know why, but she'd had no idea of Nathaniel's being "a legend" except as it related to his rakish exploits in the stews of London years ago.

"After the Battle of Talavera," Major Quinn explained, "a brush fire erupted on the field of battle. The battle was over, so it didn't affect the combatants, but the wounded of both sides still lay on the field . . ."

He sucked in a heavy breath. "Captain Stanton saw what was happening and began dragging nearby soldiers to safety. Others joined him. And when the fires reached where he was, the captain ran to the brook, wet a horse blanket, then wrapped himself in it to brave the fires and pull more soldiers free."

"I had no idea." Eliza stared at Nathaniel, who was avoiding her gaze. "He never speaks of the war."

"That day was . . . awful," the major said. "None of us speak of it. Although it's worth noting that among those he saved were—as you probably know, Mrs. March —General Anson and his aide-de-camp."

Eliza caught her breath, her stomach sinking. Had Samuel actually died of a fire, and not of his wounds?

With her heart in her throat, she looked at Nathaniel, who now regarded her with such compassion it hurt. She jerked her gaze away, not knowing where to look.

Then Diana tucked her hand in Eliza's elbow, making everything more bearable, as usual.

"I heard that the ADC died a few hours later," the major went on, oblivious to the underlying tensions, "but General Anson lingered for a week, I believe, before succumbing to his injuries. And others that the captain and his fellows saved went on to recover fully."

Jocelin shot Eliza a furtive glance. "Major, I think you should know that the ADC was your cousin's husband."

Now it was the major's turn to look embarrassed. "Good God, I had no idea! And here I was babbling . . . I am so very sorry, cousin. I don't suppose they told you how he died."

"No," she choked out. "Lord Foxstead was my husband's closest friend, so he was the one to tell me of Samuel's death. He didn't . . . give many details."

"Now I have done so and made it worse," the major said. "Do forgive me."

"There's nothing to forgive. You didn't know." And now she wished she didn't, either. The thought of Samuel wounded *and* on fire . . . He might not have been the best of husbands, but no one deserved such a horrible death.

She mustn't think of it, or her grief would return anew. With another squeeze of her hand, Diana walked off with Geoffrey to follow Jocelin and Charlie, who were wandering down the path. Someone had to chaperone, after all.

Meanwhile, the major must have seen Eliza's feelings in

her face, for he stepped up close to murmur, "Let me make it up to you. Come with me to have some wine and victuals."

Forcing a smile, she said, "I'm afraid I can't, sir. I should tend to the orchestra that will be playing while people enjoy their refreshments." She lowered her voice. "But perhaps Miss Crowder would join you?"

He looked over at Isolde, who was speaking quietly to Nathaniel, and said, "An excellent idea. Or I could ask Mrs. March . . ." He glanced around. "Wait, where is she?"

"I'm afraid Lieutenant Crowder jumped in to snag Jocelin while you were talking to me. They just left."

"Ah. Then Miss Crowder it is." He took Eliza's hand in both of his and pressed it. "I will make amends at some future date."

"I look forward to it."

And she would manage to be busy. She wasn't sure how she felt about the major or his revelations, but she certainly had no interest in him as a prospective husband. At least he was showing interest in Jocelin. An older, settled man in the army might be good for the young woman. Or for Isolde, come to think of it.

She watched as the man spoke to her friend, and the two of them left.

As she stood staring after them, Nathaniel walked up to her, looking concerned. "I thought you had to hurry off to take care of the orchestra."

"Actually, no. I set that all up as soon as we arrived. Most of it was prearranged anyway."

"So you lied to your cousin?" he asked with raised eyebrow.

"No, indeed. I purposely said I *should* tend to the orchestra, not that I would."

"Ah. That was the nicest bit of prevarication I've ever seen. But just so we don't run into the man you were avoiding, let's walk in the opposite direction." He offered her his arm. "Besides, I wouldn't want you accusing me of trying to ruin Jocelin's big introduction into society. So I must stay away from her."

She ignored that gibe, but tucked her hand in the bend of his arm.

As they walked down the winding path that eventually led to the stables and carriage house, he asked, "Was it what he said about Samuel's death that made you refuse to go with him?"

"Not really." She gazed up at Nathaniel and swallowed hard. "D-Did he suffer much?"

"Not at all. I know the major said he died a few hours later, but I could tell he was dead when I pulled him from the field. The flames hadn't even reached him yet."

"You're not just saying that to keep from further upsetting me, are you?"

"No. I assure you, Samuel died of a blade through the heart. Probably instantly."

Relief coursed through her. If a soldier had to die, an instant death was the best he could hope for. "Why didn't you tell me you tried to save him?"

"Because then I'd have to tell you what I tried to save him from, and I didn't want you to start imagining all those people in such misery. I'm sorry I didn't stop the major before he blabbed everything."

"I'm sure he took you by surprise."

"He did. I had no idea I was 'a legend.' I never wanted to be. Not for that. And I wasn't the only one, anyway. Plenty of other soldiers helped me." Looking grim, he patted her hand. "Can we talk about something else?"

"Yes, please." Deliberately she thrust the image of Samuel's death from her mind. "So, what do you think of our May Day celebration?"

"Thus far, I think it quite . . . fine." He smiled down at her. "You certainly found a good use for my flowers."

When he dropped his gaze to her bosom, where she'd tucked several blooms into her bodice, she felt heat rise in her cheeks. "It's not as if I could have carried them around in a vase."

"I'm just glad I didn't give you roses."

She stifled a laugh. "So am I. Although I'm not so stupid as to tuck roses in my bodice. I would have put *them* in my turban."

He lifted his gaze to her turban. "Ah, yes. I see that the rest of my flowers are there. They make you look like a Queen of the May."

"Thank you, kind sir," she said, stopping on the path to give a little curtsy. "But I believe I will leave the maypole to the young people."

"You are not that old, dearling."

When he stared at her warmly, she got the feeling he might kiss her, and that wouldn't do, not out here on the path where they could encounter anyone.

She walked on, leaving him to follow. "So, what did you think of the two officers?"

He came up beside her, took her hand and tucked it firmly in the crook of his arm again. "Charlie Crowder is too dimwitted for Jocelin."

Eliza sighed. "Jocelin may have a certain native intelligence, but she's not exactly brilliant herself. And perhaps she would *like* a man she could lord it over a bit. He didn't seem to mind when she instructed him on military uniforms. Although honestly, I think he's more intelligent than he lets on sometimes. At least I would hope he is, since an officer must lead, and one needs brains for that. Also, judging from his sister and father, cleverness runs in the family."

"So I gathered from talking with Miss Crowder," Nathaniel said.

"Do not go toying with my friend's emotions," Eliza warned him. "She deserves better than your use of her to annoy me."

"Is that what I was doing?" he quipped. "How do you know I don't see the potential of her as a wife?"

"Because you've said time and again that you don't want to marry."

"Am not ready to marry, madam. It's not the same thing."

"True." But the thought of him marrying Isolde truly irked her, and she felt disloyal to her friend for thinking that. So she changed the subject. "What did you think of the major for Jocelin?"

"Aside from his indiscretions at speaking of her father's death in front of her, Major Quinn is too old for her."

Eliza raised an eyebrow. "You don't even know his age."

"I can guess," Nathaniel said grimly. "Even a young major would have to be at least my age. Judging from the threads of gray in his hair, he's older than I. And that's far too old for Jocelin."

"Perhaps she just likes older gentlemen." Eliza couldn't resist teasing him. "She certainly seemed to like *you* well enough."

"Watch it, minx, or I'll think you're jealous of Jocelin."

"Why would I be? You've made it clear you have no interest in her."

That sobered him at once. "And I think . . . I hope I've disabused her of the notion that we could have any kind of romantic relationship."

"She hasn't said much of you recently, so you probably have." She patted his hand. "How old was Jocelin's late husband? I'd assumed he was young, given that he was only a lieutenant, but she hardly talks about him. Was *he* older? Or was theirs just not a love match?"

He stiffened. "Let's just call it one of those cases where he appeared to be quite a catch until he didn't anymore, and she was trapped."

"Hmm. Sounds like my marriage to Samuel. I wonder if all women feel that way after they marry?"

"Diana doesn't seem to have that impression of her husband," he pointed out. "There are plenty of happy marriages if you look for them. And plenty of unhappy ones. Why do you think I've always been skittish about the institution? You start out with the deck stacked against you. Or so it seems."

"It does indeed seem that way." They had stopped in front of the carriage house, but she paid it no mind. "My parents' marriage taught me most of what I know of bad marriages. Samuel taught me the rest." She tossed her head back. "But I already got married once. You haven't had a 'trial' marriage to learn from."

"I don't need a trial marriage." He gazed at her intently. "Unless you call an affair a trial marriage. I'm willing to engage in one of those, given that you told me two weeks ago you could use a lover."

She'd rather hoped he'd forgotten that. Especially after he'd ignored her that whole time. She just didn't know if she was ready to start anything with him. Especially when he was always so secretive about his life. "I was joking."

"We both know you were not." After glancing around to make sure they were alone, he pulled her to him and kissed her.

And it was glorious. Sweet and sensual, with the taste of port mingling with lemon on his breath.

She drew back to whisper, "You were drinking negus earlier, weren't you?"

"I was. And now I intend to drink *you*." He bent close to whisper in her ear, "If you'll let me."

She really shouldn't, especially when his very touch sent her pulse pounding. But at the moment, she wanted him to drive thoughts of Samuel's death from her mind. So she stretched up to kiss him on the lips.

And he took that for the answer it was. With need flaring in his eyes, he released her only to pull her around to a side door of the building.

"Where are we going?" she asked, though she didn't resist.

"Inside the carriage house. All the grooms will be busy placing the guests' equipages out by the road, and none of the Crowders will be calling for one of their own carriages." He flashed her a knowing look. "It's perfect for a secretive encounter."

She glanced around, but no one was walking in this part of the property. "If you're sure . . ."

"Are you worried about being needed for the party? Or about losing your reputation as a respectable widow?"

"A little of both."

He laughed. "I tell you what—let's leave it to chance. We'll see if the door is unlocked. If it isn't, we can walk back to join the others. But if it is . . ." He took her mouth in a long, lingering, and intoxicating kiss.

"All right then," she whispered. "We'll leave it to chance. But *I* get to try the door handle."

He swept his hand toward it. "Ladies first, I always say."

She squeezed the handle and pushed. The door opened easily. She hadn't expected that. But then, the Crowders weren't used to having a large property and all that it entailed.

He reached around her to push the door open the rest of the way, and she tugged him inside before they were caught.

The minute they entered, he pressed her against the door to close it, then leaned against it with one hand while gently extricating his flowers from her bodice with the other.

"Worried that our . . . intimacies might ruin your flowers?" she teased him.

"Absolutely. Because if you leave here with crushed flowers—or worse yet, no flowers—in your bodice, *every-one* will notice."

She blinked. "I hadn't thought of that." How astonishing that *he* had. Samuel would never have. Then again, Samuel would never have had a secret encounter with her in a carriage house. They hadn't consummated their wedding until after they'd married.

He laid the flowers on a table by the door. "Don't forget them or we'll have to make up a story that involves stones and you tripping and goats."

"Why goats?"

"They eat everything, trust me. I saw many a goat on the Peninsula. Ate many a goat, too."

With a chuckle, she looped her arms about his waist. "Sounds as if you've already got the story ready."

"Except that I haven't seen any goats on the property, have you?"

"Not yet. But you never know."

She started to kiss him, and he put a finger to her lips. "I'm not taking you against a door. I'm a gentleman, damn it."

"Except for how you curse," she said lightly.

Taking her hand, he led her to the carriages. "I figured you wouldn't mind."

"How could I? Geoffrey curses regularly, and not even Diana has been able to cure him of it."

"Love only takes you so far," he quipped.

Well, that was something they could both agree on.

When he pulled her past the first carriage to the second, she asked, "What was wrong with the first one?"

"Too easy to see from the side door and the front doors, if someone should open any of them."

"My, my. You certainly know how to think ahead for your seductions."

"I did used to be a bit of a rake." He grinned as he opened the carriage door and put down the step. After tossing his hat inside onto the far end of the bench seat, he murmured, "Up you go." He put his hand out to help her in, but as she grabbed it and bent her head to enter, he stayed her and lifted her skirt just enough to make her legs visible.

Something about that sent a shiver of pleasure from her feet to her mons. And somehow, he knew, because he ran his hand with a silken stroke up one stocking-clad calf, turning her warm and wet in an instant.

"God help me," he said hoarsely. "I never guessed you had such shapely legs under your gown. I can't wait to have them opening for me."

No man had ever said anything so erotic to her, and it thrilled her beyond measure. That could mean only one thing.

She was in deep, deep trouble.

# Chapter 11

Nathaniel's arousal was so intense, he thought he'd collapse before he could release his erect cock from his tight trousers. Why had he thought *those* were a good idea? Meanwhile, the woman he wanted sat next to him, patiently waiting for him to undress.

"Do you need help?" she asked in that smooth, unruffled voice of hers.

If he did only one thing today, he wanted to make her ruffled. Very, very ruffled.

"I've got it," he said hoarsely as the buttons finally came free, and he could wriggle his trousers down past his hips. "But the next time we do this, it'll be in a bed."

She gave a musical laugh. "I think the carriage is rather cozy. And it's certainly more private than I expected." She shifted on the seat so she could undo his drawers, and his cock practically leapt out at her.

"A cozy bed, then," he said. When she drew off one of her gloves and began stroking him, he grabbed her hand. "You do that, and it'll be over before it's begun. Besides, I want to see you and touch you first."

"My, my, aren't we the bossy fellow?" She cast him a coy smile. "What do you wish to see?"

"You know what—those perfect breasts of yours."

"Then you'll have to unbutton me."

She turned her back to him. He drew off his own gloves and tucked them in his coat pocket, only to undo her buttons in a fever of need. Just the sight of her thin shift beneath her gown stoked that fever even higher.

"Do you really think my breasts are perfect?" she whispered.

Did he imagine it or was there a hint of self-consciousness in her voice? "They're magnificent, minx. As I'm sure you're aware."

Her shoulders relaxed. "Samuel always said they were vulgar."

Damn that arse. Nathaniel would drive Sam from her thoughts if it killed him. He chose his words carefully. "I'm beginning to think Sam was quite possibly out of his mind while he was married to you."

With a laugh, she turned to face him. "I think you might be right." She shrugged her gown off her shoulders, then pulled down the cups of her corset and worked loose the buttons of her shift. "Look your fill," she whispered as she unveiled both breasts.

He allowed himself to feast his eyes on them, but the sight of their lovely fullness only frustrated him at the moment. He dragged her skirts up enough to part her legs, then looked down. "I was surprised to see you wearing drawers. I thought those were considered wicked."

She colored a little. "They are. But I like having something soft and pretty between my legs."

They were lacy and beribboned, not at all what he would have expected of her. Still, as with when she'd climbed into the carriage, he could see through the slit in them just enough of her satiny thighs going up to her shadowy curls to rouse him to painful heights.

"Then I suppose I'd best warn you that you're about to

have something hard and not so pretty between your legs."
Before she could even answer, he shifted her over to strad-
dle his thighs.

"Oh!" she said in surprise. "So that's how it's to be, is it?"

"You said you've seen me ride. Now I want to see *you*
ride."

"I think riding might be . . . interesting." Judging from
her ragged breaths, the ruffling had begun.

"But first . . ." He parted his legs enough to widen hers
farther, so he could slip his hand between them to caress
her. As he felt the sweet, slick heat of her, he leaned forward
to whisper, "I intend to make you come, dearling. More
than once, if I can manage it. Which I may not be able to do
since I want you so very badly."

Then he kissed her, feeling a moment's satisfaction when
she encircled his neck with her bare arms. His cock surged
instantly, straining toward her as if of its own accord.

He knew he must control his desire, manage his needs so
he could give her pleasure, too. But all he wanted was to be
inside her, joined to her. His craving pounded in his temples, beat in his blood, ached in his cock.

Fortunately, he didn't seem to be alone. She was rubbing
against his hand, obviously aware of exactly what she
wanted and needed and craved.

Her low moan made him chuckle. "Like that, do you?"
He liked ruffling her. A lot. "Let me make it even better."
He found her firm little pearl and fondled it until he had her
squirming and wriggling on top of him.

"Hold on, dearling," he murmured. "Rise up on your
knees. I need to be inside you, or I swear I'll perish."

"P-Perish?" She gave a choked laugh, and nothing else.
That was how he knew she was fairly far gone. Otherwise,
she would have gone on to tease him about it.

She was teasing him in a different way now, with her

bouncing breasts and her slick pearl. But she did as he'd directed, rising up to come down on him, engulfing him in her fierce heat.

"Ahhh," he said. "That is . . . so . . . *so* . . ."

"Good?"

"Good . . . is a . . . gross understatement."

"I-I see what you mean."

She wriggled atop him, and he really did lose his mind. "If you're finding your seat, minx, do it quickly, because I can't take much more."

Then she caught on to what he wanted and moved up and down. *Finally.* He filled his hands with her breasts, reveling in her soft gasps. He could see her above and feel her above and below, and he'd never seen or felt anything finer.

He wanted to tear off her turban, but mustn't. Others would notice if she showed up with her hair undone. Instead, he plumped up her nipples for his mouth, then sucked them hard as he pushed up into her, unthinkingly guiding her motions.

To his surprise, she let him.

"That's it, my sweet lady—ride me. Ride me hard." She quickened her motions, and he groaned, "Ah, yes. Like that."

God help him, she was driving him mad with all her delicious female flesh . . . wiggling and . . . jiggling . . .

The drumbeat of his release sounded louder in his ears. Mustn't come without her. He'd promised.

He worked her tight pearl again, fighting back his own climax. Until her eyes shot open, and she breathed a startled "Oh, *Nathaniel*!"

That sent him over the edge into oblivion.

As he spilled his seed inside her, her inner muscles convulsed around him, draining him dry. Damn, but she was glorious as she threw her head back, his Mermaid of the May—all pink cheeks, blond curls, and bountiful breasts.

She collapsed on top of him, and he held her close. For a while, he was insensible of anything but her body atop his, her sweet breath wafting over him . . . her arms draped across his shoulders. He wished he could have taken her hair down . . . seen her naked from head to toe . . . made love to her more leisurely and not like some frenzied beast.

Instead, he let himself glide on the ocean of pleasure he shared with her. It was . . . unlike anything he'd known before.

How could that be?

No, he didn't want to think about that. Not right now. But one day soon he would lay her out beneath him and pleasure her until she screamed herself hoarse.

"Are you all right?" he murmured in her ear.

"All right . . . is a gross understatement of what I feel." She pulled back to stare at him, a smile trembling on her lips. "May I ask you something?"

"Whatever you like."

"Is it always like this for you?"

"Like this?" he echoed warily.

"Wonderful." She dropped her gaze from his.

"Ah. Not generally."

She released a long breath. "So it wasn't just me . . . feeling that."

"No. As you said—*wonderful*." Then realizing he was revealing too much, he added, "Although I try to have a bit more control than that. And I generally prefer to do this in a bed."

She gave a rueful smile, her gaze drifting down to his neck. "I can't believe you didn't even remove your cravat, waistcoat, and coat."

"I can't believe you didn't even remove your turban."

Startled, she felt for it, then laughed. "I didn't, did I? But I should have. I've probably crushed it in my . . . enthusiasm. Then again, if I'd removed it, my entire coiffure would have been ruined."

"You can remove it next time," he said.

"What makes you think there will be a next time, sir?" she asked coyly.

He caught her under the chin, smoothing his thumb over her reddened lips. "What makes you think there won't?" Then before she could answer, he kissed her with deliberate skill, determined to ensure there would be.

If she wanted an affair, he would give her one. Because that's what he wanted, too.

After a moment, she pulled back to lock her gaze with his, assessing and measuring. He caught his breath and prayed that her scrutiny didn't unearth what she did to him, how she made him want more than just to bed her. Because if she ever guessed, he'd never escape her thrall.

Then she dropped her eyes to her open clothes and started buttoning her chemise. "We should get back."

He swallowed his sigh of relief. "Probably."

In silence, they pulled apart to straighten clothing and fasten buttons and generally make themselves presentable. They had to climb out of the carriage to do some of it, but Eliza paused to take one last look inside.

He thought it was so she could remember it. Then she reached out to straighten the seat cushion.

"No one will notice anything wrong," he said, amused. "And even if they do, they won't know it was us who . . . mussed things."

Her head whipped around. "Good Lord, I hope not! That would be mortifying!"

"Not for me. I have a reputation, you know." He smirked at her. "They'd just chalk it up to that."

"Yes," she said dryly. "Men are always exempt from being shamed."

"They shouldn't be," he said in a hard voice, thinking of Jocelin and Jimmy.

"I agree." She faced him with a nervous expression. "How do I look?"

"Beautiful as always."

"Nathaniel!" she protested. "I meant, is my clothing and my turban all straight? Do I look as if I've just . . ."

"Been well pleasured? Sadly, no. I probably look like a rakehell as usual, though, so they might guess."

"I swear, if you don't tell me—"

"You look fine, I promise. Except for one thing." He went over to the table by the door. "You're forgetting these."

She brightened. "Oh, yes, my flowers!"

"They look a bit forlorn now. Perhaps we should go pick some replacements from Crowder's gardens."

"Perhaps not." She hurried out the door. "How about this? I'll wear them until we encounter someone, then make a show of having to discard them because they're wilted."

"Good God, Eliza," he said as he strode after her, "you're such a wily woman."

"When I have to be." She walked briskly back the way they'd come. "But I'm not the one who just happened to choose a route that led us to the carriage house so we could . . . enjoy ourselves. Unless you've been here before?"

"No, indeed. When we arrived, however, I did ask a groom if there was a carriage house on the property." He winked at her. "Because I'm fond of carriage house architecture, you see. Or so I told him."

"Nathaniel! What if someone realizes that two people were in there . . . doing *that*? They could trace it right to *us*!"

"I can't believe you were married and still allude to swiving as 'doing *that*.'"

She halted on the path to glare at him. "You're avoiding answering my question."

"Because it's ludicrous. How would anyone know we were in there 'doing *that*'?"

"What if one of us left something behind? Like a glove, for example?"

He started and looked down at his hands, "Damn."

"You left your *gloves*?" She poked him. "Go back and get them, for pity's sake! You can't just—"

"I didn't leave them anywhere." He reached into his coat pocket and pulled them out. "Merely forgot to put them on."

She scowled at him. "You did that on purpose just to torment me."

"No, I didn't." When she cocked her head, he laughed. "All right, I did. You're just so much fun to tease."

"You remember that 'next time' we were discussing earlier?"

That turned him instantly wary. "What about it?"

"'Next time' I will contrive to be busy." She marched off ahead of him.

"Eliza!" He hurried up to her. "You know I would never do anything to tarnish your reputation."

"Do I know that?" she asked tartly. "Are you sure?"

"Of course I'm sure. I don't want to see you publicly humiliated. I care too much about you for that."

Surprise crossed her face. Then she let out a long breath. "I know. It's just that sometimes you can be so . . . so frustrating."

They walked a little farther in silence, with her looking deep in thought.

He wanted to break whatever melancholy mood she was

in. "Thank you for indulging my . . . desire for an intimate encounter. When I thought you were going to hurry off to work, I was disappointed."

"I do have to do a few things."

"But you seem to have dressed for attending rather than for working. I thought you and your sisters usually did the latter."

"I didn't exactly have a choice. I had to introduce Jocelin to Charlie and the major."

"Diana could have done it."

"True, but . . . well . . ." She colored a bit. "I . . . er . . . promised my sisters that if I couldn't dissuade you from coming, I would make sure you stayed away from Jocelin. So I had to . . . you know . . . draw you away from her."

He gaped at her, then burst into laughter. "You certainly did a good job of that."

"I knew you would take it that way," she said with a roll of her eyes.

"How could I not? But feel free to use that sly tactic whenever you please. I won't even put up a fight."

"Do you ever resist a woman?" she snapped.

That quelled his amusement. "I do. To be honest, I've been celibate since I returned from the war. Until today, that is."

It was her turn to be shocked. "You're . . . you're lying."

"Actually, I'm not. I can see why you wouldn't believe me, but it's true. Some of the things I saw in the war . . ." He thrust those painful images to the back of his mind. "Suffice it to say, it changed how I view casual encounters with women."

"So ours wasn't just some casual encounter?"

He shrugged. "You said you wanted an affair. So do I. I only hope this is the beginning of one."

"It could be," she said with a coquettish air. "Since we both like to ride and all."

A laugh escaped him. "Good God, Eliza, I do believe you just made a bawdy joke." He stared at her. "Tell me something. When did you see me ride?"

"You're joking, too, right?" she asked, looking up at him.

"Pretend that I'm not, and tell me."

She thrust out her chin. "If you'll recall, you and I and Samuel used to ride in Rotten Row all the time when he was courting me. The two of you would flank me and take turns vexing me."

"Ah, I'd forgotten about that. As I said, you are always great fun to tease." He winked. "And vex."

She snorted. "You were both children."

"Good point."

"I only wish I'd seen it then." She sighed. "But I was young and under Samuel's spell."

"When, exactly, did you stop being under Sam's spell?"

"When did you?"

Nathaniel scowled. "I was never under anyone's spell, but certainly not Sam's."

"Then he must have been under yours. Or so he gave me to believe every time the two of you got into trouble."

"Did he?" Nathaniel said. It didn't surprise him, but it did disappoint him. All this time he'd thought Sam was owning up to the things he did, when instead he'd been laying it all at Nathaniel's feet. It was hardly fair. And it wasn't even true most of the time.

"At least you two had a real friendship," Eliza said. "Samuel only married *me* for my fortune."

"That's not true," Nathaniel said, then cursed himself for it. He certainly wasn't going to get Sam out of her head by making his friend sound *better*.

She halted to face him. "He told me he did. Then he blamed *me* for not convincing Papa to give him my dowry." Her eyes were haunted. "I tried, you know. But Papa was angry I'd ignored his warnings not to let Samuel court me, so he cut me off after Samuel and I eloped. And that was that. So you see—there's no need for you to lie for my late husband anymore. I know how he felt about me." Her voice turned bitter. "He reminded me of it often enough."

"I'm not lying. Samuel was just rather . . . petty. He could be a downright petulant arse sometimes. If he didn't get what he wanted, he blamed everyone around him for it, and generally said some nasty things in the process. But he *should* have blamed himself—for eloping instead of finding a way to ingratiate himself with your father."

"I doubt that would have worked. It certainly hasn't ever done so for my sisters or my mother or me."

"My point is, no matter what he said in his attempts to blame you, he was insanely jealous of any man who came near you, including me. That's not the behavior of a chap who married a woman for her fortune." When she didn't answer, Nathaniel added, "You were caught between two bull-headed fools, and you were the prize. In the end, they both lost. Which means that essentially, you won. Although I can see how it probably doesn't feel like a triumph sometimes."

"No." She stared thoughtfully across the pretty pond they were passing. "But I never before thought of it that way. Thank you."

"You're welcome. He didn't deserve you." Nathaniel knew that for a fact, but he didn't dare tell her how.

"No, he didn't. It took Elegant Occasions to convince me of that, but now I am fully persuaded." She stared him down. "And I'm not likely to forget it anytime soon." She said it as if to warn him.

"Do you think I *want* you to forget it? I don't. I liked the old Eliza, but I like the new one better, the one who speaks her mind, who doesn't let anyone push her around. If Sam had returned from the war, I daresay you would have run him a merry dance."

"I like to think so," she said, then flashed him a tentative smile.

"And I hope you're running your father a merry dance, too."

"To be honest, Papa tries to get my attention from time to time . . . but I've mostly been ignoring him. After he pursued the divorce proceedings so vigorously with Mama, laying waste to our lives, I couldn't find it in my heart to forgive him. I'd had enough of his behavior."

"I can understand that. And you have every right to—" Something caught the corner of Nathaniel's eye. "Um, is that your sister hurrying up the path toward us?"

Eliza followed his gaze and groaned. "I'm afraid it is. And that likely means our private interlude is over."

# Chapter 12

"I've been looking for you *everywhere,*" Verity said to Eliza as she came within hearing range. "Where the devil have you two been?"

"Viewing the grounds," Nathaniel said, as if he were used to lying to cover up bad behavior. Which he probably was. "I've never visited here, so I asked Eliza to show me about."

Verity rolled her eyes and fell into step with them. "A likely story. Judging from Eliza's wilted flowers, you've been doing something entirely different. Well, you may not realize this, sir, but my sister has other duties. So pray do not keep her from them."

"I would never—" he began.

"What's wrong?" Eliza asked sharply, knowing that Verity would never be so rude under normal circumstances.

"You remember that blasted singer you didn't want to hire, whom I insisted upon us hiring?"

Eliza knew exactly where this was leading. "Your opera singer friend?"

"Yes." She sighed. "I confess I was wrong about her. She was supposed to arrive around the time you did, but she didn't. Just now, I received a message from her saying she couldn't come. She gave no excuse and no apology."

Panic rose in Verity's voice. "As you are well aware, she's scheduled to sing 'Venite inginocchiatevi' in an hour. Do you know it?"

"I've heard it but never sung it. Fortunately, I know and have sung 'How Pleasant the Banks' many a time, which is perfectly apt for May Day. And the orchestra I hired has played it for me, too. I also . . . er . . . made sure they had their music with them for that and a few other songs in my repertoire. I can give a veritable concert if I must."

Verity winced. "You knew she wouldn't show up, didn't you?"

"Believe me, I would much have preferred she came. But some singers have a reputation for unreliability, so it's best to be prepared."

"I was hoping to help her improve her reputation," Verity said. "But I see she comes by it honestly."

"Perhaps next time you should leave the music decisions to Eliza," Nathaniel put in.

Eliza shot him a quelling look. The man didn't even know he was playing with fire.

"And perhaps next time, sir, you should keep your opinions to yourself," Verity snapped. "After all, you did hire us to make the decisions concerning the parties that your ward attends. Why, you're not even supposed to be here!"

"Verity, stop that!" Eliza said. "He's just trying to . . . to . . ."

"Point out my mistakes? Thank you, but I already have you and Diana for that. Besides, what he's actually trying to do is get you into his bed, and you're helping."

Nathaniel began to cough, obviously attempting not to laugh. "Perhaps I should just—"

"Stay!" Verity turned to point her finger at him. "Do not accompany us any farther. We need Eliza to focus on singing, and she turns all . . . sappy and distracted when you're around."

Nathaniel blinked, clearly not used to being told what to do by the likes of Verity. "May I ask one question before I'm summarily dismissed?"

Verity let out a frustrated breath. "What is it?"

"When and where will Eliza be singing? Because I don't want to miss that."

Eliza choked down a laugh. For once, Nathaniel's refusal to take things seriously was rather amusing.

Verity clearly didn't see it that way. Shooting him a dirty look, she grabbed Eliza's arm and began marching down the path, dragging Eliza as she went.

"I sing in an hour, by the big tent!" Eliza called over her shoulder. "Now, stop following us, so Verity will stop yanking my arm out of its socket!"

He must have halted because she could hear nothing more from behind them.

Verity released her. "Sorry," she mumbled. "I always forget you have short legs."

"Believe me, I'm well aware that you forget," Eliza said. "You and Diana with your long strides. You leave me in the dust." Eliza frowned at Verity. "And I don't get 'sappy' when I'm around Lord Foxstead. I certainly don't get 'distracted.' That's ludicrous."

"Yes, you do."

"What does that even mean, 'sappy and distracted'?"

Verity folded her hands together over her breasts. "Ohh, Lord Foxstead, do you really think I sing like an angel? Shall I sing for you now instead of helping my sisters? Shall I sit in your lap whilst I do so?"

Eliza struggled not to laugh. It would only encourage her mouthy sister. "I have never used the word 'whilst' in my life. Nor have I ever sat in Nathaniel's . . . in Lord

Foxstead's . . ." But she had, less than an hour ago. "You're just being ridiculous. And I don't sound like that, all syrupy and silly."

"Oh, look, Diana's coming," Verity said. "Let's see what *she* says about you getting all sappy and distracted."

"You found her!" Diana exclaimed as she neared them. "Thank heavens."

"Wait!" Eliza said. "Where's Jocelin? Is no one chaperoning her?"

"Lady Crowder is with her, as is Geoffrey. Jocelin's holding court with the soldiers—apparently there are more than two here—regaling them with tales of life in the army as a girl and then a woman."

"And they're *listening*?" Eliza said. "I would never have expected Jocelin to regale anyone with stories."

"Apparently, all it took was finding some army people to bring her out of her shell. It seems nearly Charlie's entire company of Hussars is here." Diana had turned to walk on Eliza's other side. She'd slowed her strides a bit lately, now that she practically had to waddle everywhere. "So don't worry about Jocelin. It's the orchestra leader you need to worry about. Last I saw him, he looked a wreck. He's not a terribly hardy character, is he?"

"You know these musical sorts," Eliza said. "Very dramatic. I'll soothe him. It will be fine." She cast Verity a pointed glance. "I'll sit in his lap, Verity. What do you think?"

As Verity's eyes shot daggers at her, Diana drawled, "That's a bit extreme. Plus, he's Papa's age, and much pudgier. Although I suppose that means his lap would be soft. Why are we talking about laps, anyway?"

Eliza sniffed. "Verity thinks I get 'all sappy and distracted' around Lord Foxstead."

"Verity is jealous. Because anyone can see he's fond of you, and she wishes she had someone herself."

"I do not!" Verity crossed her arms over her chest in a most unladylike fashion. "And I'm not jealous. If she's fool enough to fall for a rakehell, I don't give a farthing. I don't accuse *you* of being sappy around Geoffrey, do I? Even though you are." She looked over at Diana. "When I found Eliza, she was alone with Lord Foxstead and looking a bit disheveled."

Diana burst into laughter. "I would be surprised if she wasn't. First of all, Eliza isn't some naïve thing like Jocelin. Second, she can handle herself and any man perfectly well."

"Yes, that's what I'm afraid of," Verity said. "She's been 'handling' him, if you know what I mean."

Diana shot her a stern look. "Third, it's none of our concern. Leave her be. Widows of a certain age can . . . well . . . indulge in such activities as long as they're discreet and no one sees it going on." When Verity opened her mouth as if to answer, Diana added, "*You* seeing it doesn't count."

"Happy to hear I've reached the advanced age to do as I please," Eliza said wryly.

"You know what I mean," Diana said. "You *are* being discreet, aren't you?"

"I'm trying. It's a bit difficult around you two. And I don't think Verity is jealous. I think she's afraid she'll be left alone to run Elegant Occasions."

"Nonsense," Diana said. "She has Rosy. And I still have my hand in. I'm sure you will, too, if you should happen to marry Lord Foxstead."

"I'm not marrying Lord Foxstead." Eliza was fairly certain of that. "So there's nothing for you to worry about, Verity."

Verity increased her pace. "This is absurd. I'm not jealous, and I'm not worried about anything, unless it's Eliza getting hurt. Now, if you two will excuse me, I am going to run ahead of you dawdlers and reassure the orchestra leader that help is on the way."

Without being impeded by short legs or a pregnant belly, Verity quickly left them behind.

"She generally enjoys talking about how she is feeling more than anyone I know," Diana told Eliza.

"Unlike Lord Foxstead, who'd rather chew off his tongue than speak of his feelings." She looked at her sister. "Did you realize he was a 'legend'?"

"I didn't. Geoffrey was shocked. Just now, when I left him, he was questioning the soldiers about it, who were assuring him it was true. Geoffrey has always assumed the man was only a 'legend' in terms of his bedchamber exploits."

"I confess I thought the same thing until today." Eliza kept to herself Nathaniel's assertion that he'd been celibate since his return. She wanted to believe him, but after Samuel . . .

Samuel had affected her thinking in far too many ways, unfortunately. She found it hard to trust men. Nor did it help that from time to time they'd dealt with clients whose fathers, husbands, or brothers thought them easy prey. Fortunately, all it took was a sharp reminder of who the Harper sisters' father was to make sure the men left them alone.

Men assumed that their father would leap in to defend them. She and her sisters were lucky that most people didn't know about their contentious relationship with their father. Because Eliza had witnessed, through their charities, how easy it was for a man of wealth, rank, and connections to prey on servants, spinsters, and tradeswomen.

It wasn't right. That was one reason she was determined that no one take advantage of Jocelin.

"So," Eliza said, "how do you like being married?" Between Elegant Occasions and planning Rosy's wedding, she and Diana had scarcely had a moment to talk about anything since Diana's wedding several months ago.

"I like it, but it has taken some getting used to. Did Samuel snore?"

That set them off on a conversation about married life that took them until they reached the area where the musicians were tuning their instruments. Then the orchestra leader rushed over to discuss matters with Eliza. They worked out which songs she'd be singing, and he returned to his musicians to ease their minds.

They could do with a bit of practicing, but they wouldn't get that when guests were already wandering down to see what was going on. Besides, the orchestra was about to start playing the music for the maypole. Young people were gathering for a chance at dancing round it.

Meanwhile, Verity was directing footmen on how to lay out the first course—white soup. Until she spotted her sisters.

At once, Verity hurried over to pull her and Diana out of hearing distance of the crowd. "Have either of you seen the Jack in the Green I hired? He seems to have disappeared."

Eliza surveyed the area. "Given that his costume is a bush, I'm not sure he has disappeared so much as . . . blended in. There are several bushes back there. He could be any of them, couldn't he?"

Verity gazed heavenward. "It's not as if he's sitting in a corner. He's supposed to be dancing about like a . . . like a Jack in the Green."

"Isn't that him over there?" Diana said helpfully, pointing to a bush-like creature moving through the crowd.

"That's not the man I hired," Verity whispered.

"How can you possibly tell?" Eliza asked. "He's encased in greenery, for pity's sake, and his face is heavily smudged with soot. I mean, the chap *is* a chimney sweep, but still . . . his face is *really* dirty."

"That's my point. The face of the sweep I hired and met with when he arrived today was like that of any other sweep—a trifle darkened by soot, not 'heavily smudged.' And I think it's possible that this one is my Phantom Fellow in the guise of a Jack in the Green. After all, I only hired the one Jack. And it definitely wasn't—" She jerked her head toward the fellow walking about. "Him."

"Perhaps the Crowders hired another," Diana said. "Perhaps you should check with them before you leap to conclusions."

"Why would the Phantom Fellow disguise himself as a Jack in the Green anyway?" Eliza asked. "That makes no sense. And why does he let you see him but not the rest of us?"

"Why does he show up at so many of our events?" Verity snapped. "If I had an answer to that, I wouldn't be fretting over him!"

"Well, then go talk to that . . . Jack creature," Diana said, with a flick of her hand in that direction. "He's trapped in that costume. Just grab him by the branches and demand to know why he's here. Or pull him up by the roots."

Diana looked at Eliza, and they both burst into laughter.

"Very amusing," Verity said coldly. "You're not taking this seriously, but I know that's not my Jack in the Green. That one is wearing boots, not raggedy shoes. Also, mine wore a box bush sort of cone costume. That is very definitely a *yew* bush sort of cone costume."

"So he brought a friend," Diana said. "I don't understand your concern."

"She's lost her mind is what it is," Eliza said. "A box bush versus a yew bush? Are you really that keen an observer of bushes, Verity?"

"I know my bushes."

As Verity started off toward the supposedly faux Jack in

the Green, a sudden guffaw nearby made her and Diana glance over to see Geoffrey and Nathaniel trying futilely to hold in laughter. The sisters hadn't even noticed the two men approach.

Geoffrey elbowed Nathaniel. "Verity's a keen 'observer of bushes,' did you hear that? I had no idea she had such a proclivity."

"She does know her bushes, after all," Nathaniel said with a wink.

Eliza rolled her eyes.

"What on earth are they laughing about?" Diana asked Eliza.

"Clearly, you do not spend enough time with the Fallen Females. 'Bush' is slang for a woman's . . . er . . . nether hair, and thus also for a woman's . . . you know."

"Good Lord," Diana said, color creeping up her neck.

"'Nether hair,'" Geoffrey said, which sent the two men into fits of laughter.

"Ignore them," Eliza snapped. "They're clearly both fresh out of the schoolroom. Or they've been drinking. Or both."

"On my honor, we haven't been drinking." Geoffrey grinned. "Much. Just enough to know that Verity hiring bushes for one of Elegant Occasions' fancy affairs is . . . is . . ."

"The height of irony?" Nathaniel said.

They both laughed.

"Stop this nonsense!" Diana marched over to her husband. "Please, Geoffrey, before Verity hears you! You're being incredibly vulgar, and you know it."

"You like me vulgar," he said with a waggle of his eyebrows.

"Not if it might embarrass my little sister," she said.

When that sobered him a bit, Diana and Eliza both looked down the way to see Verity being stopped by a servant. She used a flurry of hand gestures as if giving him instruction and then glanced around. In a fury, she marched back to them.

"While I was talking to that kitchen servant, my quarry disappeared," she said. "Again. He must have seen me heading his way. I looked around and couldn't see him at all. You'd think it would be easy to spot a walking bush, but—"

Geoffrey and Nathaniel erupted into laughter again.

Verity nodded at them. "What are they going on about?"

"Who knows?" Diana sent them a dirty look. "They're men."

"I have to find him," Verity said. "Both of them. The fake Jack in the Green might have decided to do something to the one I hired and take the poor fellow's place."

The music had begun for the maypole, and Eliza could see people dancing about it. People were already sitting at the tables, having been informed by the Crowders' butler that dinner was being served. Eliza had been told she would perform after the Morris dancers, and they were next, so she couldn't leave.

"I don't think you should go alone," Eliza said.

"I agree." Diana walked over to Geoffrey. "Would you and Nathaniel mind accompanying my sister while she searches for the two Jacks in the Green?"

Geoffrey stood there slack-jawed, like a small boy caught stealing pies. "But . . . but aren't they serving dinner?"

Nathaniel frowned. "I was hoping to hear Eliza . . ." He halted when he caught sight of Eliza's scowl. "Of course. Happy to help. Come on, Geoffrey."

"What the devil, Diana?" Verity said. "I do not need a

male escort, and I certainly do not need Lord Foxstead—or your husband, for that matter—to act as a protector when I go hunting for two Jacks in the Green."

"Hush, Verity," Eliza said. "If the one you didn't hire is an impostor, he could be dangerous."

Geoffrey cocked his head. "Couldn't be any more dangerous than those soldiers I was just hearing tell war stories. None of them even know how bridges are built—only how they're blown up. That lot are the most incompetent, foolish fellows ever. I can't believe the army even gives them rifles." He looked over at Nathaniel. "Sorry, old chap. Didn't mean to disparage your friends there."

"Oh, no, I'm right there with you. The last things I ever wish to hear again are war stories."

Verity was beside herself. "We are wasting time with this foolishness. The impostor is on the premises and has probably discarded his costume by now, so I'll never find him. I'm going this very minute, with or without these two."

"What is this about?" Geoffrey broke in.

"Verity thinks the Phantom Fellow has sneaked onto the grounds dressed as a second Jack in the Green," Diana explained.

"The Phantom Fell— We're back to that again?" Geoffrey shook his head. "This is about her imaginary friend?"

"Not a friend, to be sure." Verity planted her hands on her hips. "And definitely not imaginary. You saw him yourself at your sister's come out ball."

"If you say so."

"You did!" Verity said, a hint of betrayal in her voice.

Nathaniel met Eliza's gaze. "Geoffrey doesn't have to go. I can just go look for the two bu— The two Jacks myself. Do you want me to?"

That he would ask her, as if he were a knight riding off to defend his lady, touched her deeply. "If you don't mind,"

Eliza said. "But take Verity before she has an apoplexy. I'd go, too, but I need to sing shortly."

Diana nudged her husband, who sighed. "I can handle it, Foxstead. You stay and listen to Eliza sing. Come along, Verity. We'll do a quick sweep of the grounds. I'm sure we can find both Jacks."

"Thank you, my love!" Diana called after him as he and Verity headed up the hill.

"Wait, where is Jocelin?" Eliza asked.

"She's at one of the tables with Lady Crowder and Charlie," Nathaniel said. "Do you think I should go chaperone?"

"No!" Diana and Eliza cried in unison.

Then Diana said, "I shall go make sure she is properly chaperoned, Lord Foxstead. You stay here and talk to Eliza until it's time for her to perform."

Nathaniel approached Eliza warily. "Are you even going to *want* me there? I know Geoffrey and I were annoying you and Diana with that whole 'bush' thing."

"May I make a small confession?" she whispered.

"Of course."

"When she said she knew her bushes . . . I confess my mind went right where yours and Geoffrey's did."

"It did not." He crossed his arms over his chest. "I don't believe it."

She sighed. "I spend more time with the Fallen Females at Filmore Farm than the other ladies, so I hear . . . things they don't."

"Do tell," he said, eyes gleaming.

"Stop that," she warned. "Although I do wonder sometimes . . . If Samuel hadn't actually taken me to Gretna Green—if he'd been some sort of scoundrel just hoping to get under my skirts and abandon me—might I have ended up like the Filmore Farm ladies? They are my age or younger, and some never had a chance to choose. It's not right."

"No, it's not." He paused, looking as if he wanted to tell her something. Then his face cleared, and she wondered if she'd imagined it. "But you're doing all you can to help the Fallen Females."

"And that's another thing. I loathe that term, 'fallen.' No one calls the men who seduced them 'fallen,' even though they're just as culpable in the ruination of the women. It's utterly unfair."

"I hate to tell you this, dearling, but the world is unfair and the scales of justice uneven," he said in a hard voice. "That's why you have to put your thumb on them to *make* them balance out."

"I try." She smiled faintly. "Meanwhile, you're going about saving soldiers from death by fire. What I do seems inconsequential by comparison."

"It isn't, I promise." He stepped closer, looking as if he was about to say something else.

Then a voice called out behind her, "Mrs. Pierce? We're nearly ready for you."

She looked over to see that the Morris dancers were already performing on the stage as people were eating the first course. "Forgive me, Nathaniel. I have to go sing in just a moment or two."

"Of course." He took her hand and pressed it ever so briefly, yet she felt the sweet touch of it to her toes. "I'm looking forward to it."

"Quick—do I look all right?"

"You look lovely as usual." He leaned close. "Although your turban is a bit crooked, and you should probably remove those wilted flowers."

"Oh, dear, yes." She surreptitiously tugged them out of her

bodice and tossed them on the ground. Then she straightened her turban. "Better?"

"Looks fine to me."

With a smile, she left him and headed for the area where the orchestra was seated. On the way there, she was accosted by Charlie Crowder, of all people, who still had managed to keep Jocelin by his side.

"Mrs. Pierce, I have a request," he said. "The lads and I would really like it if you'd sing 'O'er the Hills and Far Away.' Since we're about to leave for Spain and all."

"I miss hearing it," Jocelin added. "The men used to sing it all the time in the camps."

Eliza glanced from his hopeful expression to Jocelin's. "If the orchestra knows it well enough to play it, I'll do my best to fit it in."

And that would be no small feat. She'd already chosen to sing "The Blue Bells of Scotland," Rabbie Burns's "How Pleasant the Banks," and "The Suffolk Miracle," that last one because her sisters would enjoy the significance if no one else did. But she could drop it in favor of "O'er the Hills and Far Away." With so many soldiers in the audience, it did make sense to sing something else military.

Having decided on that, she made sure the orchestra could play it and had the music. Then she sat at the front table watching the Morris dancers. A servant asked if she wanted dinner, but she refused it. She could never eat before she sang.

Before long, Lady Crowder made her way to the stage to introduce her, explaining that their opera singer had taken ill. Eliza and her sisters had agreed to that little white lie. No point in insulting their hosts and guests by implying that the opera singer couldn't be bothered to attend. To her surprise, the announcement that Eliza would be singing instead was met with enthusiastic applause. Then she reminded herself that a good number of her friends were here, so of course they would support her.

As she rose and headed for the stage, she silently rehearsed her speech about the songs she'd chosen. But when she turned to face the crowd of guests ranged along the tables and eating and drinking, she saw one person who changed her plan entirely. Now she would *have* to sing "The Suffolk Miracle," if only to provoke the man sitting at the back table, glowering at her.

The scandalous Earl of Holtbury.

Her father.

# Chapter 13

Nathaniel had chosen to sit at the back table, in case he was needed by Verity or Geoffrey or both in their quest for this Phantom Fellow chap. No one had yet explained to him who that was, but he wasn't concerned. He would learn the truth eventually.

Besides, he was about to hear Eliza perform. That was all he cared about at present. He wanted to make sure his captivation with her singing had been genuine the first time. He watched in utter fascination as Eliza spun a tale about why she'd chosen these particular songs. She seemed at home in this setting, the way Jocelin seemed at home around soldiers. So at least Eliza wouldn't need him for anything.

It bothered him a bit. He *wanted* her to need him. For everything—attention, acceptance, advice, affection, and any other bloody *a* word he couldn't think of. He was a glutton when it came to Eliza—he couldn't seem to get enough.

A servant placed a plate in front of him—apparently the second course of their meal—but he could only pick at the salmagundi. Oddly enough, he was nervous on her behalf, which made no sense.

Near him, someone cleared his throat, and Nathaniel

happened to look the man's way. He'd been so entirely
focused on Eliza that he hadn't realized who'd taken a seat
beside him: Eliza's damned father.

Nathaniel hadn't seen the man in years, so he was surprised to find how much the gaunt fellow had aged. If
Nathaniel remembered correctly, Holtbury was only in
his midsixties, but his snowy hair and face mapped with
debaucheries made him seem older.

For a brief moment, Nathaniel felt pity for the former
Lady Holtbury, twenty years the man's junior. Sam had
described it as an arranged marriage, and clearly Eliza's
mother had received the poor end of the arrangement.

The orchestra had just begun playing the accompaniment
to her first song when Holtbury leaned over to say, "I know
what you're about with my Eliza." The man's sharp blue
eyes betrayed his keen intellect.

Nathaniel forced himself to remain calm. "Oh?"

"You are hoping to ruin her so she will be forced to
marry you."

Nathaniel shifted in his chair to give her father his coldest,
most aristocratic glance. "Why on earth would I wish to
gain her hand by deceit? Why would I even *need* to do so
when I can court her—and win her—perfectly well? It's
not as if I need her fortune. Oh, wait, she no longer has a
fortune, does she? Her blasted father kept her dowry, meant
to take care of her in her widowhood."

When Holtbury looked astonished that anyone would
challenge him, Nathaniel added, "Now, if you'll excuse me,
sir, I would like to hear your daughter sing. In case you
were unaware, she has the voice to rival a nightingale."

She absolutely did. Around him, people stopped eating
Verity's admittedly delicious food to listen as every note of
Eliza's first song trilled beautifully in the dusk hours. That
gained Eliza ample smiles and nods, although no one was

so rude as to applaud, which would be considered improper until the end of the entire performance.

When she sang her second song, a pastoral, cheerfully lyrical piece with a happy tune, people were nodding their heads in time to the music. No one was eating *or* talking, a sure sign they were listening.

Then she began to sing a song he knew, called "The Suffolk Miracle." The ballad told of a young maiden whose father disapproved of her true love and sent her away to live with relatives in a distant town. Weeks later, her love came to fetch her back to her father. During the trip on horseback, he complained of a sore head, so she tied her holland handkerchief around it as a bandage.

When the young woman entered her home, she asked her father why he'd relented in his disapproval and sent her true love to fetch her. Horrified, the father admitted that her love had actually died a few days before. And when she had the man's grave dug up, she found her handkerchief tied around his head.

The way Eliza sang the ballad chilled Nathaniel's blood, especially since she kept her gaze on Holtbury during the first verse about the unfeeling father who disapproved of her daughter's choice. Though Nathaniel knew she wasn't singing about her sorrow at losing Samuel, it almost felt as if she'd heard what Nathaniel had said to Holtbury and was adding her own coda.

Holtbury clearly recognized it, for he turned stiff in every part, muttering under his breath about foolish daughters and their unacceptable suitors. A quick glance at Diana showed her smiling to herself.

"I don't have to sit here and take such ridiculous nonsense," her father mumbled, and half rose as if to leave.

Nathaniel grabbed him by the arm and said in a low voice, "The least you can do, old man, after beggaring Eliza and forcing your other two daughters to endure scandal, is to sit here and take your medicine. God knows you deserve it."

Holtbury tried to free himself, then resorted to snarling, "Release me, Foxstead, or I will send my bloodhounds to unearth your secrets. There were rumors about your parents back in my day that you might not want resurrected, and I'm sure if my men did a bit of digging . . ."

As rage rose within him, Nathaniel could barely resist throttling the man. Instead, he leaned in to growl, "Let them dig. I, too, can dig, which you'll discover if you spew lies about my parents to *anyone*. Because I'll be digging your grave in a place no one will ever find you."

Only then did he let go of Holtbury's arm, hoping he'd left bruises. The damned arse was the worst of his kind—bullying and belittling the very women he should be treasuring.

Meanwhile, up on the stage, Eliza's face had turned as stony and cold as a field in winter. Had she seen their interaction? If she had, she still managed to imbue her song with such pathos and feeling that when she finished, a hushed silence came from her audience. There was no need for their applause. Their faces showed she held them in the palm of her hand.

After that, she brightened to end her performance with a rousing rendition of "O'er the Hills and Far Away." It had every soldier in the crowd singing along, of course, which she encouraged with her smiles and hand gestures.

God, she was a work of art. What's more, she seemed utterly unaware of it. Nathaniel surveyed the crowd and saw more than one handsome, *young* fellow eyeing her with interest. He didn't like that at all. But he conceded she was the kind of woman many men would kill for. Would die for.

Would marry.

Damn it. How had he come to this pass? He hadn't

expected to care so much. Or want her so much. Once she learned the truths he'd been holding close, she would have a hard time forgiving him. And he wouldn't blame her.

Eventually, he would have to tell her. But not yet. He couldn't risk her finding out the truth until Jocelin was settled with *some* good fellow—preferably not the witless Lieutenant Crowder nor the aging Major Quinn. Then Nathaniel would make himself so indispensable to Eliza that she would no longer care about what he'd hidden from her.

After the soldiers leapt to their feet in thunderous applause, it took several minutes—and quite a few of her bows—until the applause died down. When she left the stage, people instantly surrounded her, clearly eager to tell her what they thought of her performance. By the time she was done with them, most of the rest of the crowd had finished eating and were headed for the house where there was to be dancing in the ballroom.

She skirted the tables, walking toward the house.

Clearly, she was trying to avoid her father, and Nathaniel would have kept the man there, too, if the sly devil hadn't already slipped away while Nathaniel was still watching her leave the stage to chat with admirers.

Nathaniel jumped up and looked around for her arse of a father just in time to see Holtbury head toward her as if to cut her off. Nathaniel hastened that direction . . . in case bloodletting was involved.

Just as he came up beside Holtbury, her father accosted her. "Still hoping to become an opera singer, I see," he said in a snide voice.

She'd wanted to be an opera singer?

"Fancy meeting you here, Papa," she said coolly. She gazed around the grounds. "And where is Sarah? Did she attend? Or did you make her stay home like a good little wife instead of allowing her the freedom to move about society?"

"Watch your tongue, girl. You are a fine one to talk, entertaining a crowd of raucous soldiers like a singer on the stage."

"I'm hardly a girl anymore," she said with a mirthless laugh. "And how appropriate of you to bring up aspirations I long ago laid aside. You haven't seen me in . . . oh . . . five months? Six? Yet you don't ask how I am. You start right out with insults."

"Don't mistake me for one of your gushing admirers, girl. You're the one avoiding *me*."

"True. A pity I didn't move faster, or I would also have avoided you this time. Sadly, I didn't inherit your long legs."

"Is that why you're spending time with this damned rogue?" he asked, jerking his head toward Nathaniel. "Because of his long . . . legs?"

When she colored, Nathaniel said, "See here—"

"Whom I choose to befriend is no longer your concern, Papa." Eliza planted her hands on her hips. "You gave up that right when you disowned me years ago. Now if you'll excuse me, I have to go see about Verity."

"I did not disown you, girl," Holtbury snapped.

"You might as well have," she said. "You didn't try to make arrangements for a settlement for me after Samuel and I married. You didn't give him my dowry. So, for all intents and purposes, you *did* disown me. If not for Grandmama bequeathing her house to me, Samuel and I might have ended up living in St. Giles. As it was, we could scarcely afford to live in Grandmama's house."

"Because you married a gambler and a scoundrel."

"I did indeed. And, as usual, when any woman in your care goes against your wishes, you punish her by stripping her of any funds she might be entitled to."

"So *that's* why you went into trade. To shame me for my supposed disownment of you."

"I went into trade to save myself from poverty and my sisters from becoming governesses . . . or, worse, your virtual servants, always at your beck and call." She thrust her face up to his. "I went into trade because I wanted to be free of *you*. And now I am. I only wish I'd thought to become an opera singer. *That* would have taken me entirely out of your sphere."

"Yes," he snapped. "Then you would have become *this* fellow's mistress, I suppose."

To Nathaniel's surprise, she said lightly, "Perhaps. You never know. Lord Foxstead? Are you ready to go inside?"

"Absolutely."

They started to leave, but this time her father blocked their path. "Do not walk away from me, girl. I *made* you. You will listen to what I have to say." He tried to wave Nathaniel off, as if dispensing with a servant. "No need for you to stay, sir. This is between me and my daughter."

"The two of us are leaving," Nathaniel said, "and there is naught you can do to stop us."

"You think I can't thrash you and whisk my daughter away? I'm not so old as all that. You caught me by surprise last time. You won't get a chance like that again."

"Perhaps not," Nathaniel said. "But you seem not to have noticed the crowd of young soldiers standing to your left and watching to see how the wind blows over here. I daresay *they* can hold you here fairly well with just a word from Eliza. What's more, they seem rather eager to come to the rescue of a woman who just entertained them so well."

Startled, Holtbury looked over to where Major Quinn, Lieutenant Crowder, and a number of Crowder's compatriots were moving slowly toward them.

Holtbury backed away. But before retreating, he said to her, "Ask his lordship about his parents before you agree to any . . . 'friendship' with him. Ask him about the rumors. Because if he won't tell you, I will."

"I have no doubt." Her expression remained resolute. "Fortunately, Papa, I don't care what slime you think you have dug up about Lord Foxstead." She turned to Nathaniel with a saucy smile. "Come, sir, let us go inside. Now that my work is done, I should like to dance."

"That sounds like an excellent notion, my dear." Giving her father a wide berth, they continued toward the house.

"Are you all right?" he asked as they moved out of earshot.

She didn't answer, and judging from her tight grip on his arm, she was still reacting to her father's words.

"I can take you home if you wish," he said.

"And let him think he upset me? Not on your life." She drew in a deep breath, then pasted a smile on her lips. "Besides, aren't we going to dance?"

"Do you really want to?"

She seemed to consider that a moment. "Eventually, yes, but first—"

"You want me to tell you what your father meant when he spoke of rumors about my parents." And Nathaniel would, too, now that her father had raised the ugly specter of it.

"Actually," she said, "I was going to mention I hadn't eaten since early this morning, but since you insist . . ."

He gave a rueful chuckle. "Perhaps we could do both." But he damned well planned to fudge some of the facts. Given the uncertainty of their friendship, it was probably unwise for him to reveal the full truth about his parents. "I barely touched Verity's delicious dinner. Could we sneak into the Crowders' kitchen and snag whatever was left?"

"Or some cold collation. I don't need much." Her tone

of forced gaiety didn't fool him. Clearly, she was still upset about her father.

"I need more than a cold collation, I'm afraid," he said, lightening his tone. "I kept a certain female vastly entertained earlier, and now I'm starving."

That caught her attention, for she cocked her head. "'Vastly entertained'? Are you sure?"

"I think I can tell when a woman is enjoying herself."

"No doubt," she said dryly. "You did have years of experience at it, didn't you?"

"You're never going to let me forget that, are you?"

"Can you blame me?"

"No, I suppose not."

She halted. "Where the devil are you going?"

"I have no idea. I've never been to the Crowder home before, and I certainly have never been in their kitchens."

"Oh, right. Of course." She tugged him back to a different path. "This way."

Within minutes, they were inside a busy place unlike anything he'd ever seen. He'd been forbidden from entering Amberly's kitchens as a boy, and thus it had never occurred to him to enter them—or the kitchen at Foxstead Place—as a man. But now he wondered why he hadn't.

Rich scents tempted his senses—meats roasting, savory pies baking, aromatic spices dancing in the air. The number and variety of people fascinated him. Cooks made sauces and mixed things in bowls, other kitchen staff arranged delicate slices of ham and cheese in fanciful whorls on plates, and a kitchen maid turned a spit of beef while somehow also beating eggs.

Now he knew why it was called beating. It literally sounded like the rhythmic beating of a drum, although how he could hear it over the other sounds assailing his ears was anyone's guess. The place resounded with the clanking of pots, clacking of crockery, and the cries of staff needing items from other staff. Between them all, a robust, dusky-skinned fellow with close-cropped salt-and-pepper hair ordered people about.

The man caught sight of Eliza the moment she and Nathaniel entered. "Madame Pierce!" he cried in a French accent, hurrying over to kiss her on each cheek. "It is very good to see you, but this time is not the best—"

"I know, Monsieur Beaufort, but my companion and I missed dinner, so we were hoping to eat something, anything you have left. I promise we'll make up our own plates and won't disturb anyone."

"Non, non, Madame!" he protested. "You will not have *les restes*—how do you put it in English—'leavings.' I shall not allow it." He called a fellow over and told him in French to make up a plate of the food being prepared for the ball supper.

Then the Frenchman gestured to a door. "*Le salon* for the cook of the Crowders is just there. She is *très occupée*, so she will not mind your use of it. I shall see that food and drink is brought *tout de suite*."

"*Merci beaucoup,* monsieur," she said. "We are most grateful." When he bowed and started to walk away, she said, "One more thing—have you seen Verity?"

"I have not seen *le mademoiselle* since she left to ensure *le dîner* was served properly."

"*Merci encore,*" Eliza said, though tiny creases formed between her brows.

They went through the indicated door to find a perfect little room arranged for eating and socializing. Only then did he ask, "Are you worried about Verity? Because she should be safe with Geoffrey."

"Unless she tries to go off on her own."

Nathaniel held out a chair for her at the small table. "Would she do that?"

"Probably not." Eliza took a seat. "She *likes* Geoffrey. It's you she's unsure of."

"Are you certain?" he asked as he sat down. "And here I thought her continual insulting remarks were signs of affection."

"Don't count on it," she said, though she smiled.

The smile relieved him. Verity might be worrying her, but Eliza was worrying *him*. That's what one did with a lover, wasn't it? Worry about them? Want to take care of them? Although it was odd he'd never done it before.

He shook off that thought.

She smoothed her skirts. "It just bothers me that some fellow may actually be coming to our events for Lord knows what reason. Until now, I thought Verity might be imagining it."

"She might well be. Let's see what she and Geoffrey find out. Even if some man is lurking at your parties, perhaps he does so at other people's fancy balls as well. Perhaps he just enjoys sneaking into places."

"Perhaps."

She was wearing that frown again, so he changed the subject. "I take it that Monsieur Beaufort isn't the Crowders' cook."

"No, although they'd steal him in an instant if they could. And before you ask, he's not exactly my personal cook, either. I could never afford a French chef of his caliber. He's head cook, or chef de cuisine as the French call it, for Elegant Occasions. We use him only for large affairs like this."

"That must be expensive."

She raised an eyebrow. "You aren't being billed for him. The Crowders are."

"That's not what I meant. Do you keep him on staff, or does he generally work somewhere else?"

"He used to cook for The Society of Eccentrics, but he was getting older and couldn't keep up with the demands of the club. So with us, he keeps his hand in but isn't run off his feet. His food is excellent, as you will see. He and Verity work closely to develop bills of fare and choose the recipes. But she isn't really a cook, so she needs him, and he isn't interested in kitchen management or planning meals anymore, so he needs her."

She was babbling, which meant she was nervous. Perhaps he should find yet another subject to relax her.

He smiled. "So, you wished to be a professional singer, did you?"

She blinked, then settled back into her chair. "Ages ago. Before I was even married. At eighteen, I told Mama I didn't want a début. I wanted to sing opera."

"She must have been horrified. You certainly have the talent for it, but no family in polite society would have wanted their child in that world, especially a man like your father. What did she tell you?"

"To talk to my father." She gave a dry chuckle. "At that point, I think she didn't have time to deal with her daft daughter, since she was already engaged in an affair with Tobias Ord."

Everything Nathaniel had heard about the former Lady Holtbury indicated she was an indifferent parent. If she hadn't been, perhaps Eliza might never have married Sam. Then Nathaniel might never have met Eliza.

The thought did something unsettling to his insides. "I did see that Ord had been made Viscount Rumridge, and they had finally married."

"Yes. She's Lady Rumridge now. Although I don't think she enjoys being stuck up in Cumberland. Unlike Jocelin, she had absolutely no interest in following her new husband, a Major General like Jocelin's father, to the Peninsula."

"I can't say I blame her."

"So instead, Mama is holding court up north. Not that there's much 'court' to hold in Cumberland. I think she's bored, to be honest."

"You've seen her since the divorce?" he said in surprise. He would have thought the Elegant Occasions sisters wouldn't wish to hurt their business by associating with their outcast of a mother.

"She invited us all to attend her wedding, so we did. It was rather nice to go to one we didn't have to plan."

He laughed. "I can see how that would be the case."

At that moment Monsieur Beaufort's man entered, carrying a tray with two plates of food, utensils, napkins, and a bottle of wine with glasses. Within moments, he'd set everything out, rattled off in French what the dishes were, and left before they could even thank him.

Eliza examined the items on their plates. "Oh, good! He gave us a couple of the chicken baskets. They're new in Verity's repertoire, and I've been eager to try them." She bit into one. "Mmm, heavenly. I always seem to be gone when she tries them on Diana or Rosy or, most often, Geoffrey. He's practically Verity's official taster these days. That man can eat."

"He has to." Nathaniel poured the wine. "A stalwart build like his requires sustenance."

"And what does a build like yours require?" she asked gaily, clearly perking up now that she was being fed.

"Exercise," he said, fixing her with a purposely rakish look. "Lots and lots of exercise."

She colored faintly. "Of the . . . er . . . carriage kind, you mean. I daresay Geoffrey gets plenty of that, too."

"I daresay he does."

"Ooh, try these," she said, holding out some red things. "They're prawlongs, one of Verity's most delicious sweets, made with imported pistachio nuts."

"Forgive me, but I prefer to put my sweets last."

"Suit yourself. They're my favorites, so they may be gone before you get to them."

"I'm sure if they're on the supper menu, I'll have a chance to try them." He eyed her closely. "Do you not eat in any order?"

"Not usually. Sometimes. It depends on my mood. And what I'm most craving at the time."

He bit into a piece of roast duck breast with slices of truffle and delicate spices laid under the skin. Then he closed his eyes in something near to ecstasy. "That is truly spectacular." He cut another piece. "Perhaps I've been courting the wrong sister."

"She didn't cook them, remember? And is that what you're doing? Courting me?"

Damn. He probably shouldn't have mentioned courtship. "If courting includes seduction, then yes."

"That's not courting, and you know it. But feel free to court Verity whenever you like. It won't get you anywhere." Her eyes gleamed as she ate a bite of red beetroot salad. "Verity has sworn off marriage."

"What about you?" he asked, despite knowing he was treading dangerous territory. "Have you done the same?"

"I've sworn off men," she quipped.

"Funny, I didn't get that impression when we were in the carriage house earlier. You seemed to be enjoying your encounter with a male companion."

"Very well. Then I've sworn off rakehells." When he started to protest, she added, "And soldiers. Let's just say you caught me at a weak moment."

Then she laughed, and he didn't know if she was teasing

him again, or cloaking her discomfort in humor, which she had a tendency to do. As did he.

She devoured another prawlong, this one white. "So," she said, "are you ever going to tell me about the rumors concerning your parents?"

Just like that, the time had come to explain her father's remarks. If he could.

# Chapter 14

Nathaniel looked taken aback. Had he not expected her to pursue it?

Perhaps she shouldn't. Whatever tales had been told about his parents were really none of her concern, and hearing them would only create more intimacy between them. Which she wasn't sure she wanted.

Besides, she could hear the music from the ballroom even in here. They could leave right now and join the dancing. But she was loath to leave their cozy little dining room.

Finally, he glanced away. "I've merely been waiting for you to ask."

"I'm only asking so I can tell my father he's wrong about . . . whatever he thinks." That was mostly the reason, actually. Papa always embellished people's faults, including those of his wife and daughters, and it was always up to them to set him straight. "Keep in mind that I know how Papa exaggerates, so I'll believe whatever you say."

He shot her a sharp look. "That would be a first." When she made a face at him, he sighed. "Fine. But there's not much to tell."

"Anything you say will be more than I know."

"Very well." He sipped his wine. "Two years after Tess was born, my parents conceived me, although they didn't yet know it, of course. Then Father had a tragic riding accident that resulted in his . . . er . . . how do I put this . . . his genitories . . . being crushed."

She gazed at him, baffled by the unfamiliar term. When she worked it out in her head, she rolled her eyes. "Do you mean his *testicles*?"

"I was trying to be delicate," he grumbled.

"Then you're not very good at it. Honestly, for a man who uses his 'genitories' regularly, I should think you'd choose a blunter term."

"Oh, I generally choose a full score of 'blunter terms,'" he drawled. "They're just unfit for a lady's ears."

"I've heard them all, I assure you, since the Fallen Females have no compunction with throwing them about."

"Right." He crossed his arms over his chest. "Do you want to hear the rest of the story or not?"

"Of course. Pray continue. However, since no one is in here but us, there's no need for delicacy."

"Trust me, from now on I will be vulgar to the point of obscenity, if you wish."

"I didn't say I wished it—just that I knew the words already." She blotted her mouth with her napkin. "But do go on."

"As I said, Father's *balls* were crushed."

She ignored his use of a very vulgar term. "And he survived it? I mean, given that he only died a few years ago, I know he must have survived it, but—"

"He lived on, yes." He dragged in a harsh breath. "Unfortunately, the local barber surgeon, who was little more than a quack, said my father would need to have his ballocks removed."

"*Removed*? Good Lord, your poor father! That sounds awful!"

"It would have been had he agreed to it. To be honest,

I try not even to think about the particulars. Fortunately, both were skeptical about his enduring such torment. My mother convinced my father to travel to Italy to see a doctor my mother had heard of from her own family there."

"Your mother lived in Italy?"

"Did I never tell you that?"

"No, and no one else did, either, not even Samuel." She paused a moment. "Then again, he might have feared it would make you more appealing to me, given my infatuation with Italian opera."

He smiled. "And has it?"

"It depends," she said lightly. "Was your mother living there temporarily with her British family? Or was she born there?"

"Born there. When she turned twenty-five and was considered a confirmed spinster among the Italian aristocracy, she visited an English friend in Gloucestershire with whom she'd attended finishing school. Then she ended up marrying the local lord of the manor. I gather Father was past thirty at the time."

"Like you," she teased.

"Not as far past thirty as my father was. Not that it changed a thing between them." A sudden warmth crossed his features, making her wonder if, unlike her own parents, his had been in love. "Anyway, while they were in Italy, and Father was enduring a series of painful operations intended to save his ballocks, Mother discovered she was enceinte. They actually remained in Italy for nearly two years, during the whole of Father's recovery and Mother's lying-in period."

"So you, too, were born in Italy."

"Yes. Which is why I can't sit in the House of Lords. I'm an Italian by birth, so I inherited the Foxstead title and estates but not the right to sit in Parliament."

"I never knew that."

He lifted an eyebrow. "There's a great deal you don't know about me."

And more she still wished to know. "I'm beginning to see how very intriguing you are. But we did put the carriage before the horse. So to speak."

With gleaming eyes, he murmured, "Something I don't regret for one moment. I hope you don't, either."

A little thrill coursed down her spine. "Not regret so much as . . . wonder how wise it was." *And when we'll do it again.*

She shouldn't. She dared not. But she would. She knew that as surely as she knew her own name.

"You will tell me if you find yourself with child, won't you?" he asked in a most earnest tone.

That took her aback. "Why? So you can marry me to save my reputation?"

"If I have to."

She swallowed her disappointment. "And therein lies the problem. 'If I *have to*.' Do not do me any favors, Nathaniel."

He stiffened. "That's not what I meant, and you know it."

"And *you're* avoiding the subject." With her hunger somewhat sated, she sipped some wine. "Finish telling me what happened to your father in Italy."

He muttered a curse under his breath. "Very well. The physician there managed to help Father keep his nutmegs, but—"

"Nutmegs? Now that one I have never heard. But I've heard 'baubles' and 'cods.'"

His eyes narrowed on her. "Stones. Tallywags. Thingumbobs."

She sniffed. "Now you're just making terms up."

"No, indeed. I have a whole quiver full if you wish to hear it."

"I *want* to hear what happened in Italy that spawned rumors. Unless the tale of your birth was merely to warn me you can't serve in Parliament, which would disappoint me exceedingly."

"No need to be sarcastic," he said mildly. "My parents' arrival home with a child was what spawned the rumors. I was rather small for my age—"

"So was Diana, apparently," she said softly. "And look at her now."

He blinked, as if stunned she would take his parents' side and not the average person's.

"I told you," she added, "I know how my father works. He unearthed every rumor ever spoken about Mama for the divorce proceedings. Granted, I'm sure some of them were true, but . . . I seriously doubt even my feckless mother ever slept with the Regent. She prefers her lovers a tad younger."

His lips curved in a reluctant smile. "To be honest, people in our small village seemed to have nothing better to talk about than our family." His tone hardened. "And the barber surgeon had, out of spite, told villagers that Father's injuries had made it impossible for him to sire children, and Mother had not been enceinte when they left for Italy. No one thought to question how he would know such a thing."

Just like that, she understood. "So they claimed that your father hadn't really sired you. That some Italian fellow had impregnated your mother."

She must have been right on the mark, given the bitter glint in his eyes. "Something like that," he said. "It's not as if it mattered. The law says I inherit the title regardless, unless my father claimed I wasn't his and a physician proved he couldn't have done it. But my father claimed me, of course."

"Still, it must have been hard for you to hear such slurs as a child." She reached over to cover his hand. "I'm sorry.

I know how painful vicious gossip can be. And my mother actually *was* unfaithful to my father."

He gave a shuddery breath, then slid his hand from beneath hers as if he was uncomfortable with her sympathy. "True. But it wasn't as if I played with the village children or anything." He met her gaze with a certain defiance. "And no one dared throw those rumors up at me at Eton. I outranked most of them."

She knew bravado when she heard it. "Is that when you became friends with Samuel?" Because that would explain so very much.

"How did you know?"

She laughed humorlessly. "Just a wild guess." Samuel had always been the sort to gravitate toward people higher ranking than he, people who were also vulnerable. If she'd realized that before they'd married, she might not have eloped with him. He'd wanted her for only one thing, after all.

Although Nathaniel had said that wasn't entirely true.

Then something else occurred to her. "Is that why you were so wild in your youth in London? Trying to forget the rumors?"

For some reason, that seemed to throw him off balance. "Do not paint me a saint, Eliza, just because I've told you a bit about me," he said, with a sardonic lift of his eyebrow. "I have faults, like any man. Or woman."

The rebuff stung, though she knew he was probably only speaking the truth. "Is this the place where I tell you mine, so you can mock me for caring about yours? Because—"

"Eliza," he said in a remorseful tone.

"I think perhaps it's time we go." She rose and swept crumbs from her skirt. "Otherwise, we'll miss the dancing. Besides, I'm a bit worried about Verity, and I should like to find out what has happened to her and Geoffrey."

"Eliza!" he said sharply.

She halted but refused to look at him. "I will not let you spoil this day by being . . . you. If you wish to dance, we should go. If you don't, then you may stay here and ponder your . . . secret sins, whatever they are. But I intend to kick up my heels for a while."

He sighed heavily. "Fine. Let's go." He followed her as she hurried to open the door to their private little dining room.

She had to escape the mounting intimacy of their discussion. She couldn't stand watching him put up barriers every time they grew closer. It shouldn't bother her so, especially if all she wanted was an affair, but it did.

So she should focus on finding Verity, and let the Earl of Foxstead fade out of her life as he apparently was eager to do now that they'd had their physical needs met.

As soon as they were back in the bustle of the crowded kitchen, she tried to hail the closest footman. "Sir, if you could please go see if my sister is anywhere around the food tables—"

The man didn't even pause to look at her. "I am in the service of another," the servant said and continued stalking away.

"That was damned rude," Nathaniel murmured under his breath.

"It certainly was." Then, just as the servant disappeared through a nearby door into the ballroom, Eliza spotted a dusting of soot on his white collar, and a chill ran through her. "Nathaniel, get him! That's the . . . the Phantom Fellow!"

"What?"

"The Jack in the Green man!" She hastened for the door. "He's . . . he's not wearing the bush costume anymore. That was him, I'd swear! That's why he kept his back to me—because I saw him once at a ball. He thought I would recognize him!"

Nathaniel raced ahead of her to the ballroom door, but when it swung open, he was swamped by a phalanx of footmen coming through with trays. By the time he fought his way through, with Eliza on his heels, they were in the ballroom with dancing couples swirling past them.

Eliza scanned the room. "I-I'm too short to spot anything but dancers."

"And I didn't see the fellow well enough to distinguish him from anyone else. Still, unless he found a partner within seconds, we should be able to find him. He'll be dressed like the servants." He peered over the heads of other guests. "It's odd. I don't notice anyone who isn't paired up or wearing appropriate clothes."

"The footmen!" Eliza threw her head back in frustration. "After he saw us, he knew we might get suspicious, so he grabbed a tray and came right back through here. We were so focused on dodging the other footmen that—"

"He walked right past us." Nathaniel looked at her. "He's as clever as Verity gives him credit for being."

Verity came running up to them. "Where have you two been? We found the Phantom Fellow."

"You did?" Eliza let out a long breath. She hadn't lost him after all. "Thank heaven. Where is he?"

"Well, we didn't actually *find* him," Verity said. "Geoffrey and I found the empty Jack in the Green costume stuffed behind a garden wall." She tipped up her chin. "And I was right—it *was* a yew bush. I told you, I know my bushes."

This time there was nary a laugh from Nathaniel.

"So he was definitely here," Eliza mused aloud.

Nathaniel looked from her to Verity. "Exactly what does he want with you three?"

"I wish I knew," Verity said. "Today makes eleven times I've seen him at one of our events over the past year and a half. None of us knows why he attends. Obviously, we don't invite him. And I seem to have been the only one to notice him all those times. No one else does."

"Until tonight," Eliza said, rather pleased with herself. "Not counting the time I encountered him before, though I think he wore a disguise then, too. His blond hair was odd, as if it were a wig. Just now when I saw him, his hair was a strange shade of black. Come to think of it, that could have been the soot."

Verity stared hard at her. "You actually saw him? When? How? Can we follow him? How recent was it?"

"He's long gone, I'm afraid." Nathaniel related what he and Eliza had seen and figured out.

After that, they had to endure Verity trying to eke out some detail from them that would reveal everything. Which, of course, their paltry encounter did not.

Verity huffed out a breath. "Very well. I will question the kitchen staff all the same. He may have interacted with them."

"Perhaps," Eliza said, "but I sincerely doubt it."

When Nathaniel wandered away to look out over the floor, Verity drew Eliza aside. "And where were *you* all this time, pray tell?"

"Talking to Lord Foxstead."

"Alone?" Verity asked.

"What concern is it of yours?" Eliza stared her down. "Stop trying to mother me, Verity. I didn't let our own mother do it after I married, and I'm certainly not going to let you."

Verity sighed. "I just worry about you."

"As I do you. But I'm in good hands." When Verity looked alarmed, she added, "My own." She smiled. "I'm fine. I swear I will never again let myself be taken in by a man like Samuel."

"To be fair, I don't think Lord Foxstead is as much like Samuel as I initially feared."

"He isn't." She pushed her sister. "Now go ask your questions of the staff and leave me be."

With a nod, Verity disappeared through the nearby kitchen doors.

For a moment, Eliza watched Nathaniel, who wore a pensive look as he observed the dancers. What was she to do about him? Should she let him pursue her. Should she pursue him? Did all of these encounters of theirs mean anything to him, or was he just killing time until he could get Jocelin married off?

If she knew the answer to that, it would help her enormously. But he wasn't saying, and she wasn't sure how to compel him to do so.

With a sigh, she turned to look toward where the chaperones were all sitting as they waited for their charges. When she spotted Diana among them, Eliza joined her. "How is Jocelin?"

"See for yourself," Diana said, inclining her head toward the dance floor.

This time Eliza saw Jocelin dancing a jig with Charlie, her face positively radiant.

Eliza chuckled. "Please tell me she hasn't danced with him the *entire* time."

"This is their second set, and, as you know, even that is significant."

Eliza shook her head. "I told her repeatedly she's not supposed to dance with the same fellow for more than two sets and it's ill-advised to dance for more than one."

"To be fair, she also danced a set with Major Quinn and

at least three other gentlemen, two of them officers. They've kept her busy."

"Does she seem to be enjoying her dances?"

Diana cocked her head as if considering. "She certainly does the steps in a lively fashion. She seems to have laughed the most with Charlie, although Major Quinn captured her attention several times while they were standing here waiting for their own dance to begin."

"Good," Eliza said. "I want her to enjoy this. I gather she mostly spends all her time with Jimmy, and that simply will not do."

"We shall merely have to hope that after this the gentlemen invite her out for rides, walks, visits to museums, and the like." Diana laid her hand on her belly. "But you shall have to be the one to chaperone her. This fellow kicks like a mule, and it quite takes me aback when he does."

"Wait, I thought you swore you were bearing a long line of heirs to Elegant Occasions," Eliza said with a teasing grin.

"I thought I was." Diana sniffed. "But no lady would ever kick like this, I'm certain. It's ill-mannered."

Eliza laughed heartily. "A tomboy is exactly the sort of daughter you need. Geoffrey would certainly enjoy teaching her all about buildings and canals—"

"And skew bridges. Did I tell you I finally found out what those are?"

"No, but I already know. *I* looked it up in a dictionary."

"Of course you did. Probably just so you could lord it over the rest of us with knowing what it is."

Eliza suppressed a smile. "You are a tad cranky these days."

"Only because your mule-kicking nephew is keeping me up at night."

They fell silent when the music stopped, and people

either drifted from the floor or joined new partners for the next dance.

"I see that Major Quinn was not to be outdone by Charlie," Eliza said. "It looks as if he'll be dancing a second set with Jocelin himself. And Charlie appears rather forlorn."

"He's not the only one," Diana said, and nodded toward Nathaniel, who was deep in conversation with Geoffrey while casting disapproving glances at Jocelin's partners.

"He's very protective of her," Eliza said. "It baffles me."

"He *is* her guardian. And he strikes me as the sort of fellow who takes such responsibilities seriously."

"I hope that's all it is."

Diana patted her hand. "He doesn't look at her as if it's anything more than that. And why do you care? You said you had no intention of marrying again."

"I don't. I just . . . wouldn't want to see Jocelin taken advantage of."

Her sister eyed her askance. "Yes, this is all about concern for Jocelin, and not in the least jealousy over Lord Foxstead."

Eliza frowned at her. "I don't have to sit here with you, you know."

Diana laughed. "Who is the cranky one now? And you don't even have an excuse. Well, except for jealousy."

They were silent a few moments. Then Eliza forced the scowl from her brow. "He's afraid a soldier will carry Jocelin and Jimmy back to the war."

"It's a legitimate fear." Diana's voice turned fierce. "I would die before I let my son—or daughter—go off to the Peninsula. The accounts of those battles in the papers have been awful."

"I know. But I think Jocelin really wants to return. To the army, anyway. And at least she'll know what she's in for."

"With a child in tow? I should hope she does. Although

she didn't have him abroad, did she? So she might not have realized how much harder army life is when one has a child."

Nathaniel turned abruptly and headed toward Eliza, his features set in a grim expression, which he only briefly smoothed away as he approached her and held out his hand. "May I have this dance, madam?"

Eliza rose. "I would be honored, sir." Though she was a bit wary of his mood just now.

As soon as they joined the dancers, waiting in two long lines for the jig to begin, Nathaniel glanced around, apparently to make sure the other dancers were paying them no mind and having their own conversations. Then he said, "My ward seems only to be dancing with soldiers."

"She accepted dances with a couple of other gentlemen, too," Eliza said defensively. "Or so I'm told. But yes, it's mostly been soldiers. I suppose you blame me for that."

He released a long breath. "No. Geoffrey told me she's been approached by a number of gentlemen, both for dances and conversation, but she gravitates to the soldiers."

"I confess I didn't know how many were planning to attend. I wasn't even sure Charlie would be here, and I certainly didn't know he'd bring so many of his fellow officers."

Nathaniel shook his head. "I don't understand her. To me, the endless marches punctuated by days of fierce fighting weren't things I enjoyed, especially after I'd been given a company of green recruits to command."

"Yes, but you were in battle. She was not."

"True. She had a gig to travel in with her duenna, and officers who paid attention to her at every turn."

"Sounds like the ideal life for a young woman who probably already worshipped her father."

"But not so ideal a life for Jimmy."

Eliza grimaced. "I confess I didn't think she'd be quite so eager to go off to war. I now fear she might take him with her. Until tonight, I honestly didn't believe she would." She looked away. "Has she seemed to be a good mother otherwise?"

"Mostly. Although once she realized she could possibly marry . . . again, for love, she took to all the début trappings like a duck to water."

His slight pause after "marry" made her wonder if she was missing something. Then again, she was probably reading too much into it.

"But she was still shy around everyone," he went on. "So I didn't worry too much about it. Today, however . . ."

"Yes, the soldiers have really brought her out of her shell. You must admit she does seem more comfortable with them."

"You were right about her wanting to find a soldier husband above all else. Once she marries, though, it won't be the same. If she marries Lieutenant Crowder, he won't have the standing to provide her with a gig and a donkey or whatever mount is available."

"Ah, but he'll have the funds for it," she said absently. The thought of Jocelin actually considering carrying Jimmy off to war still disturbed her. "Charlie is his father's only heir, so I daresay he has a fine allowance."

The dance began, but they were close to the bottom of the very long lines of the reel, so they had a few minutes before it was their turn to move. She added, hoping to relieve both his and her worries, "Besides, they're still a long way from marriage, wouldn't you say?"

"I certainly hope so."

"They just met today, Nathaniel. She's having a lovely time, but who knows what will happen once they're not seeing things through the bright gleam of May Day?"

It was their turn to move. He took her hands, and she felt the impact even through her gloves. At least she wouldn't have to worry that he'd return to the war again, speaking of people who were "still a long way from marriage."

Yet the intensity with which he fixed his gaze on her mouth was so all-encompassing that it sent a delicious shiver through her. She remembered how his lips had felt against hers, by turns hard and then soft. And when he'd taken her breast in his own mouth, she'd thought she'd gone to heaven.

Lord help her.

"You're blushing," he said in an undertone.

"I'm not. This ballroom is hot, that's all."

"I know when a woman's blushing, dearling," he whispered, low enough to be heard only by her.

They did the figures in silence, unable to do more than stare at each other. She swallowed, and his eyes followed the motion of her throat. She wished he'd kissed her throat earlier. She wanted to feel that.

She wanted something more than just a quick tumble in a carriage. But she doubted that he did. And she dared not trust her own judgment. The last time a man had made her heart race, she'd ended up in a disastrous marriage.

*I was a blushing virgin then—every handsome fellow made my heart race.*

Even that didn't encourage her to allow this to go too deep for her comfort. Quick tumbles must be enough. Period.

To distract her from her wildly vacillating feelings, she forced a bright smile to her face. "You dance better than I remembered, Lord Foxstead."

"You dance as well as I remembered. That's probably why Sam was so careful to keep us apart once you married."

She frowned. "Was he?"

"Haven't you ever wondered why I didn't go to your home to lounge about and drink port with Sam?"

"I . . . I assumed most men went to their clubs with their friends."

"Most did both. But Sam never invited me to join him at your home."

"I did tell him to invite you for dinner sometime, but whenever I did, he seemed rather reluctant to do so. He never gave me a reason."

"I told you, he was jealous of any man in your circle, worried some other fellow would cuckold him."

When he'd said that earlier, she hadn't quite believed him, but she'd had a few hours to consider how often Samuel had refused invitations to dances, how he had maneuvered situations so that he had some pressing reason *she* could not go. Jealousy made as much sense as anything else.

"I don't know why he was that way," she said. "I would *never* have been unfaithful to him."

"I wouldn't have expected you to, either, especially given how your parents wrecked you and your sisters' lives with all their catting around."

Catting around. She stifled a snort. As if Nathaniel hadn't been famous for "catting around" himself. Had it been Nathaniel's reputation that had sparked Samuel's concern? Or had Samuel just been so possessive that he looked on any fellow as a prospective rival?

They were motionless in the dance lines again. All around them others were chatting to their partners, making it feel as if the two of them were all alone, even though they really weren't. "Tell me something," she murmured. "When and if you marry, would you be faithful to your wife? Or are you one of those fellows who believe that monogamy cannot be sustained throughout a marriage?"

"I want what my parents had," he said bluntly. "But without the . . . er . . ."

"Removal of the family jewels?"

"Exactly."

There was so much more she wished to ask, wished to say to him, but now was not the time or place. Already she was afraid people might be listening, and not for the world would she revive the gossip about his parents. Gossip about parents was the bane of her own existence, after all.

So they danced and she let herself enjoy just being with him. It was better than she'd anticipated. And worse, too. Because eventually they would have no excuses for such intimacies. Jocelin would marry *someone* and probably soon, too. There was no doubt of that. Then Eliza would be a widow without a partner again.

For the first time since her disastrous marriage, she couldn't stand the thought.

# Chapter 15

After that day at the Crowders, Nathaniel had been forced to return to Gloucestershire for two damned weeks, away from Eliza. But he'd had no choice. There had been an accident at Amberly involving the new horse-drawn tramway built to transport building stone from the quarry on his land.

No one had died, thank God, but the track had to be relaid in a new direction that might prevent future accidents. He'd taken care of setting all of it up as quickly as possible, but then his estate manager had wanted some time after his long absence, and there had been other investments he needed to check on. It had been a constant barrage of duties and responsibilities.

Meanwhile, his sister had overseen Jocelin's new social calendar in London as well as chaperoning her with her suitors. He'd received a full report from Tess last night . . . or what he hoped was a full report, given Jocelin's many interruptions. He was anticipating a clearer one from Eliza.

Assuming she'd be willing to see him. Disappearing for two weeks without a word had probably not endeared him to her. He should have sent her a note, a letter, anything to tell her he hadn't forgotten about her. He *had* tasked Tess with explaining the situation, but that wasn't the same.

He just . . . hadn't known what to say. Which he supposed was no excuse.

At least Norris wouldn't give him any trouble. Being a former soldier himself, the butler had heard of Nathaniel's exploits on the Peninsula and was usually ready to go along with whatever Nathaniel asked.

Then again, perhaps not. Today, as Nathaniel entered Eliza's house at proper visiting hours, the man gave him quite the cool reception.

"Will Lady Usborne and Mrs. March be joining you as well, my lord?" Norris asked in a frosty tone.

Damn. "Perhaps later. At present, they're shopping on Bond Street." Trying to pretend he hadn't just disappeared for two weeks, Nathaniel handed his gloves and hat to Norris as a matter of course, then glanced around. "Where is your mistress?"

"In the garden feeding the swallows." Norris held himself as stiffly as a sentry. "They gather in London this time of year, although they are a tad late this season."

Nathaniel suppressed a chuckle. "Are you a bird lover like Mrs. Pierce?"

"I like swallows, my lord. They have predictable comings and goings."

Ah, that was a direct jab. "Unlike earls, I suppose," he said dryly.

"I wouldn't know, sir."

Nathaniel flashed the man a thin smile. "How is she?"

"You will have to ask her yourself . . . my lord."

"I will." He looked at the stairs. "Are her sisters here, too?"

"Not at present."

The man's officious behavior was starting to annoy

Nathaniel. "Well then, since I know the way to the garden, there's no need for you to bother showing me back there."

When Nathaniel started to walk that direction, Norris blocked his path. "I would be remiss in my duties if I did not announce you, sir."

Nathaniel was tempted to say in no uncertain terms that his association with Eliza was none of the man's concern. But Norris was merely protecting his mistress. And Nathaniel understood, since he had the same inclination.

"I need to see your mistress alone for a few minutes," Nathaniel said earnestly. "What will it take?"

With an arch of one supercilious eyebrow, Norris said, "Your promise to be a gentleman, sir."

"I am always a gentleman," he said steadily. Although he had no intention of engaging in the sort of "gentlemanly" behavior Norris expected. Indeed, Nathaniel doubted that Eliza would want him to.

The servant looked him in the eye as if to assess his sincerity. Then, with a curt nod, Norris stepped aside.

Stifling an irritable oath, Nathaniel strode past him and down the hall to the door leading to the garden. A quick search of the area didn't at first turn up Eliza. Then he spotted a garden shed at the back, with the door open.

Eliza stood with her back to him, filling a bucket with spadefuls of seeds. He paused a moment to take in the sight of her, and their conversations the night of the Crowder affair flooded his mind. How she'd sympathized with his situation regarding his parents. How her heart had gone out to him over his experiences in battle.

Part of him had expected to banish her from his mind through distance, but apparently absence really did make the heart grow fonder. Although it wasn't his heart growing fonder. It was his lustful desires. That was all. Seeing her just made him want her more.

Her body. Yes.

*Liar.*

He ignored that small voice. Moving up behind her, he covered her eyes with his hands.

"I missed you." The words just popped out, in spite of his determination to proceed with caution.

"Major Quinn?" she said lightly. "Why, how could you have missed me? I just saw you yesterday when you came to call."

A surge of jealousy so fierce it cut him gave an edge to his voice. "Quinn! Has that arse been courting you? How dare he?"

She twisted out of his hands to face him, her eyes as cold as a winter forest. "Do we know each other, sir?" She touched a finger to her chin. "You do remind me of someone I once knew. But he disappeared without a word, so I assumed he was dead."

Ah. She was angry. That, he'd expected. "I deserve that."

"Yes. You do."

He steadied himself against the sinking in his stomach. He could talk her around. Surely, he could. "Did Tess not tell you why I was gone?"

"She did. And I understood completely. Then I heard nothing from you, not even a note saying when you might return." She crossed her arms over her lovely bosom. "As the days passed without a word, I realized you had run away after you shared your life and your feelings. After we had been intimate. That you'd clearly regretted telling me so much. Perhaps even regretted making love to me."

"I didn't regret a bit of it," he said hoarsely.

"No? It certainly felt as if you did. To be honest, I didn't expect you to come back to my house even after you'd returned to London. You'd given me no reason to believe you would. I'd prepared myself for the very abrupt end of our affair."

That last was said in a trembling voice that showed she wasn't angry. She was hurt. He'd hurt her, and that hadn't been his intention.

He'd made a huge misstep. And if he considered her words carefully, he had to admit she was partly right. "I . . . it wasn't . . ." He ran his fingers through his hair. "Perhaps there's some truth to what you're saying. I did . . . sort of run away. But it's also true that I thought of you the whole time I was overseeing the repairs to the tracks and dealing with my estate manager and talking to tenants."

He placed his hands on her rigid arms. "I craved your presence while I was in Gloucestershire. I imagined how you'd enjoy Amberly's gardens, where you'd want to put a birdhouse . . . how much pleasure you'd gain from the new pianoforte I'd had installed for my mother."

She'd softened a fraction under his hands. "And I was supposed to guess these feelings of yours? To infer them from your silence?"

"Of course not." His throat felt tight. "I should have written. I thought about it several times. But I didn't know what to say."

Her gaze lifted to his. "You could have said all the things you just told me."

"And you would have expected a proposal of marriage upon my return." God, he hadn't meant to say *that*.

She dragged in a long breath. "I wouldn't have expected it *or* wanted it. We both agreed this would be only an affair."

That should have reassured him that their thoughts were on the same plane, and he was safe. Instead, it agitated him. "What if I want more?"

Her throat moved convulsively. "We don't always get what we want."

"And what do *you* want?" He bent to kiss her forehead, and her eyes slid closed. "This?" He slipped his hands about her waist. "Or this?" He could smell her perfume, feel the softness of her muslin gown, taste the fine salt on her brow. But it wasn't enough.

"Every night while I was gone," he whispered, "I imagined you in my bed. You have bewitched me with your voice and scent and lovely laugh. I hear your singing in my dreams." He bent toward her mouth. "I remember how soft your lips were when I—"

She pulled back, with a furtive glance toward the bend in the building that barely hid the entrance to the garden. "You promised me that the next time we made love it would be in a bed."

He drew back a fraction. "I did. And I wouldn't want to make love in a garden shed, anyway. But I hardly think we can sneak upstairs without being noticed." Something occurred to him. He nodded toward the windows and small balconies above them. "Which of those connects to your room?"

"Why? I assure you I am not able to scale walls in this gown."

"No, but I can scale them tonight. In the dark. At whatever time you wish."

Her laugh held enough warmth to encourage him. "You're quite daft, you know that?"

"Do you doubt I can do it? I scaled cliffs as a soldier. Scaling the side of your house would be nothing."

"The watch might see you. Then what would they think?"

He leaned in. "You let me manage all that. Just tell me which window belongs to your bedchamber."

"Fortunately for you, the window directly above this shed.

It looks out over the garden, which is why I chose it after Samuel died." She flashed him a half smile. "I *am* the mistress here, after all. And I'd rather be able to hear and see my birds when I awaken." Her smile abruptly vanished. "You're assuming, however, that I'm willing to let you in my bedroom window. I haven't forgiven you yet, you know."

"But you will," he said and brushed his lips across hers.

She didn't pull back right away, thank God. "Perhaps. You won't know until you try."

"So this is a test, is it? You mean to leave me hanging about on the shed roof while you make up your mind?"

"I suppose you'll find out at midnight," she said saucily. "But whatever happens, don't wake Verity. She would probably march down and call the watch herself to come catch you."

He chuckled. "That does sound like something she'd do."

With scarcely any warning, they heard voices coming from the garden door. "Nathaniel? Mrs. Pierce?"

Bloody hell. His sister. He stepped away from Eliza. "Back here!" he called out. "Mrs. Pierce is filling a bucket with seeds for the birds."

Hastily, Eliza picked up her bucket as if to reinforce his claim.

It was just in time, too, for Jocelin came tripping about the corner seconds later, with Jimmy holding her hand. "Oh, there you are! Jimmy wanted to say good afternoon to you before we headed home from shopping."

"I'm heading home myself," Nathaniel said. "He can say good afternoon to me there."

"Not you, silly," Jocelin said lightly. "Eliza. Especially since we have no fixed engagements this evening."

From what Tess had told him, whenever Eliza *had* come to Foxstead Place, Jimmy had insisted on spending time with her. Nathaniel didn't know if that was good or not.

If the lad became too attached, it might cause trouble down the line.

Then again, Nathaniel hated to deny the boy anything.

Now, as his sister joined them, Jimmy broke free to run over to Eliza and seize her about the legs. "Missis Pears!" He peeked inside her bucket. "Jimmy like seeds, too."

Eliza laughed. "You wouldn't like these, my boy. They're only for birds." Setting down the bucket, she hefted him up in her arms so naturally that Nathaniel wondered how often she'd done it while he was gone. "You like seeds in cakes. They're not the same kind of seeds. Come with me. We'll see if any seed cakes are left from breakfast."

They all followed her and Jimmy inside. Once they were settled in the dining room with seed cakes and cups of tea, Jocelin said, "Guess who we saw on Bond Street today, Eliza? Your beau, Major Quinn!"

The major again? Nathaniel bit back an oath.

"He's not my beau, I assure you," Eliza said, though she wouldn't meet Nathaniel's gaze. "He didn't say he was, did he?"

Jocelin smiled knowingly. "He asked if you were going to be in for callers tomorrow morning because he wished to pay you a visit. I told him you would be. He was acting strange, though. Very stilted with me. He's probably just nervous about this particular call. You may not think him your beau, but clearly, he thinks otherwise."

"Nonsense. He's my cousin, that's all." Eliza stirred sugar into her tea. "If he's anyone's beau, he's yours."

"Jocelin prefers Charlie to the major," Tess told Nathaniel. "Although I'm trying to convince her that the major is a better choice."

"He's too old," Nathaniel grumbled. "And Charlie is too stu—"

Eliza kicked him under the table.

"Too . . . green a recruit."

"I like Charlie," Jocelin said. "He makes me laugh. Major Quinn just makes me sad."

"He *is* a rather serious fellow," Eliza said.

Jimmy began to bounce on her lap. "Jimmy have tea, Missis Pears?"

"Milk goes better with seed cakes, love." Eliza looked at Nathaniel. "Don't you agree?"

"Yes. Much better." Nathaniel frowned. She was trying to distract him from the discussion of suitors. "Perhaps I will call on you in the morning as well. I can see what the man's intentions are."

"And why on earth should I need your opinion on the subject?" Eliza asked lightly, though her eyes looked grave.

"It never hurts for another man to give his opinion of a suitor."

"Major Quinn isn't my suitor." She rose abruptly. "Now, who would like to help me feed my birds?"

Eliza paced her bedchamber near midnight. Would Nathaniel decide not to come? Should she let him in even if he did?

She didn't quite have the courage to keep the window locked against him, but it still angered her that he thought he could waltz into her home after not so much as a word for two weeks and expect her to accept him with open arms.

All the same . . .

It had been so good to see him. To hear his voice, to have his mouth against hers, even if only briefly. Before the group had left, and him with them, he'd managed to whisper, "I'll see you at midnight," and her need had tugged at her breasts and belly as if his hands were already touching her.

She was more than ready for him. She'd taken a bath and put on her favorite perfume. Then she'd had the good sense to insert a sponge soaked in olive oil up inside her, because the Fallen Females had suggested that to another woman as a way to prevent children.

The downstairs case clock chimed midnight. When the last chime finished echoing, she determined one thing. If he could not be bothered to arrive on time—or early even—then she wouldn't spend half the night awaiting him. She'd waited two weeks to hear from him already, and if he couldn't make up his mind to have an affair, she saw no reason to continue hoping for it.

It felt as if she'd spent half her life waiting—for marriage, for children who hadn't come, for her husband to return from the war, for her mourning to end, and on and on. She was young, true, but not by society's standards. So she'd just as soon grow old doing what she loved and mothering her nieces and nephews than wait and long for things that didn't happen and that she wasn't even sure she wanted.

With that decided, she glided over to the window to reach for the latch. Then a face appeared in the glass. Meeting her gaze, Nathaniel tapped on the pane. She hesitated, but couldn't bear to deny him. With her heart in her throat, she opened the window, and he tossed his boots in before climbing inside in stocking feet.

"Still couldn't decide whether to let me in?" he asked in a rough voice.

He raked his heated gaze down her night rail, which she knew left little to the imagination since she hadn't worn her usual wrapper over it.

She wished she had when his eyes fixed on her breasts. Her nipples tightened, and with nothing to shield them from his all-consuming gaze, she prayed he couldn't tell. "When you were late, I did consider not doing so."

"Turns out it's harder to scale your walls than I expected," he muttered. "Why do you think I had to take off my boots?" He slid his riding coat off his shoulders, letting it fall where it would, then pulled off his riding gloves and dropped them.

"You are very casual with your clothing, sir. Your stockings are ruined."

"It was the only way to get up onto the roof." Eyes gleaming, he lifted his hand to thumb her nipple, slowly, smoothly. "But it's a good thing you didn't lock me out. Once I had seen you in such undress, I might have broken the glass to get to you."

Desire pooled in her belly. "Like a . . . thief in the night?" she asked shakily.

"More like a stallion scenting a mare."

She frowned. "At least you didn't say . . . 'a mare in heat.'"

"Are you in heat, Mrs. Pierce?" he asked hoarsely. "Because I am deeply in lust, having waited two long weeks for this."

Catching her at the waist, he drew her to him for a deep, hungry kiss that roused her own hunger. She unbuttoned his waistcoat and shoved it off, then tugged his shirt out of his buckskin breeches. With a groan, he pulled back, only to walk her backwards to the foot of her bed.

"I suppose you were sure of me," she whispered as he halted just shy of the bed.

"Not by any measure." Slipping his hands down over her hips, he began to drag her night rail slowly up her sides. "You, dearling, I see as a wild bird, to be wooed into my hand. I have never been so unsure of any woman in my life."

"Good," she said, trying to sound less needy and eager than she felt. "Because I certainly am not sure of you."

"You may be sure of this." He caught his breath as her night rail cleared her hips, exposing her mons to him. "I have wanted you far longer than even you realize."

She barely had time to consider what he meant before he lifted her onto the edge of the bed, without letting her night rail fall below her hips. It felt odd to be sitting on her coverlet naked, and when he dragged her night rail off her entirely, she wondered if he ever meant to remove the rest of *his* clothes.

Almost as soon as she thought it, he stood back to admire her, as if he'd been posing her for his gaze. Then, still pinning her with his dark eyes, he removed his cravat and shirt, revealing a chest sculpted with muscles and overlaid with a dusting of black curls.

There were also scars and burns, places where the puckered skin showed he'd been wounded more than once. It was a soldier's chest, not a dissipated rakehell's. He hadn't lied when he'd said the war had changed him.

When he unbuttoned his breeches and slid them off, leaving him wearing only his drawers and stockings, she couldn't help admiring the fine form he made. And apparently he read her admiration in his eyes, for he murmured, "Even our first joining didn't slake my hunger or my thirst for you. And now I intend to slake both."

She'd thought he'd meant it poetically . . . until he knelt at her feet and more provocative images leapt into her head. She'd once seen an erotic print of a man with his head between a woman's legs. At the time, she hadn't been able to imagine what the man was doing. Samuel had certainly never done anything like that to her, and even the Fallen Females didn't talk about such a practice.

But Nathaniel looked as if he was about to do exactly

what she'd seen, especially when he spread her legs and held them apart with his strong hands while he kissed the inside of her thighs.

It was maddening . . . and thrilling and so very carnal that she was sure she blushed. Perhaps even down *there*.

Then he moved higher, spread her curls apart with his fingers, and placed his warm mouth on her . . . her . . . altar of Venus, as the Fallen Females sometimes called it.

What on earth? He was *licking* her there. "Wh-what are you doing?"

He paused to shoot her an odd look. "Did Samuel never—"

Wordlessly, she shook her head.

"Ah. Well, how else am I to slake my hunger and thirst? I want to taste you . . . suck you . . . make love to you with my mouth before I make love to you with my cock." A smile crept over his face. "If you don't mind."

"No. I-I mean, yes. I mean, please do." She was babbling. Who could blame her? He was caressing her with his mouth in a . . . most intriguing way . . .

Good Lord.

He drew back, and she caught his head. "Don't . . . stop. *Please*."

"I won't. Not until you come, dearling." He fumbled with his clothing. "Just . . . undoing a few . . . buttons."

"*Come*?" she repeated. She'd heard Samuel use the word before. "Like . . . what happened . . . in the carriage?"

"Exactly."

She hadn't told him yet that she'd never "come" before. Except with him. And she'd certainly *liked* it the first time. Could he make it happen twice?

He returned to what he'd been doing, and her body was in raptures. How did he know . . . how could he sense . . . what she felt . . . what she wanted to feel . . .

Her eyes slid shut. She let him have his way with her, and it was glorious. The more he laved her with his tongue, the more aroused she became, her thighs quivering as he sucked at the part he'd fingered in the carriage.

Good *Lord*, how had she never known this was possible? Every part of her skin felt sensitive, even the brushes of his curls against her thighs increased her need, her want, and yes, her hunger.

Within minutes, she felt as if she could fly, as if her body strained up toward the sun.

Oh . . . *oh yes . . . OH YES!*

Even as she thought it, she took flight, barely able to keep from screaming his name aloud, though his name reverberated inside her. "Nathaniel . . ." she whispered. "Oh, *Lord*!"

Now she was quaking inside, her body trembling and shivering under the exquisite pleasure of it.

His motions slowed, and he only nuzzled her where before he was sucking and rubbing and thrusting with his tongue. How could her arousal—and her coming—have been even better than before? She was still shaking, still basking in the release of it, when she heard him say, "My turn, sweet lady," in a throttled voice that made her eyes shoot open.

She was so drunk on her enjoyment, she nearly asked, "Your turn for what?"

But before she could, he wiped his mouth on her night rail and stood to yank off his drawers. She barely glimpsed his long, thick "cock," as he called it, fully aroused from its nest of dark curls. Then he was half lifting, half pushing her farther back onto the bed and onto her back, so he could kneel between her legs and plunge himself inside her.

"Forgive me . . ." he choked out. "Seeing you come . . . I just can't . . . wait to be inside you . . ."

"And I can't . . . wait to see *you* come," she whispered as she clutched his muscular arms.

The words seemed to stoke his need higher, because with a groan he began to thrust hard and deep into her, so fast that the bed shook. And to her surprise, she felt echoes of that same rising pleasure as before—not quite as intense but strong enough that she began moaning.

Hastily he covered her mouth with his hand even as he plunged in one last time and spilled himself inside her.

And as he collapsed atop her, his warm body heating hers, she realized she could never give this up. Not the intimacy, not the lovemaking . . . not the sweetness of knowing he wanted her so badly that he would scale a wall for her. If she were honest, she'd admit she wanted him as her husband.

Now if only she knew what to do about that.

# Chapter 16

A short while later, Nathaniel leaned his head back against one of her frilly pillows and gave a contented sigh. He should say something worthy of her. Like, *When can we do this again?*

No, not that. It sounded too desperate, too out of control.

What about, *Marry me, dearling?*

Not that, either. He wasn't quite ready for marriage, was he? Not while so many things in his life were unsettled.

He could say, *I love you.*

Definitely not that! Talk about sounding out of control—that was the rakehell's one rule—never say *I love you.* But he wasn't a rakehell anymore.

So why did he feel the panic of a rakehell who has sunk in too deep? Why did the way she curled up next to him, all soft and naked and lovely, make strange feelings bubble to the surface?

The most important one being that he didn't deserve her. He didn't. He wasn't even the person she thought he was, for God's sake. He still wasn't the person *he'd* once thought he was.

"I'd better go," he murmured.

When he rolled over to leave the bed, she caught his arm. "You can stay a while longer if you wish."

"I can't, or I'll never be here in time for Major Quinn's 'important visit' in the morning." Having not meant to make it sound so snide, he stood and began gathering up his clothes.

She sat up in bed with a bemused look. "Are you jealous of *the major*?"

"Should I be?" he asked with an edge to his voice he couldn't quite hide.

"No, indeed. I have no interest in him, even if he wanted to marry me, which he doesn't."

He pulled on his drawers with jerky motions. "How can you be so sure?"

"Because he's barely spoken to me since you've been gone." Frowning, she watched as he buttoned up his drawers. "You said Samuel was jealous of me. Well, you were right. I always took it to mean he didn't trust me somehow, which made no sense. But it was worse even than that. He was possessive, even obsessive. Sometimes it frightened me, but . . . then he'd turn charming again, and I'd assume it was all in my head."

Nathaniel paused in the middle of what he was doing, as it dawned on him why she was saying all this. Because *he'd* been jealous today and just now. She wanted to know exactly how much he was like her late husband.

"I'm not Sam," he said softly and bent to kiss her lips. "And I trust you implicitly." His voice hardened. "It's just the major I don't trust. I haven't from the moment he blithely told you how your husband died, without a care for your feelings."

She stroked his face. "That's very sweet."

When her words gave him a surge of satisfaction, he scowled. Pups like Charlie were sweet, not men of his consequence. *They* were supposed to be strong and brave. "If you say so," he said gruffly.

"Anyway, I'm sure this meeting has nothing whatsoever to do with me. He's been trying to court Jocelin, that's all. But she only has eyes for Charlie, I'm afraid. The major probably just wants to find out if he has any chance with her."

"Fine. I will be there to tell him he doesn't." *And to tell him he has no chance whatsoever with you.*

God. Perhaps he *was* like Sam when it came to her. Obsessed. Possessive.

No, indeed. Even once he married her, he would not—

Wait, *once* he married her? How had that thought slipped past him? He still had to be careful, had to remember what was at stake.

Forcing himself to be calm, he pulled his breeches on and fastened them, setting his stocking foot on the bed to button up the leg.

"You missed one," she said, startling him.

"One what?"

"Button." She scooted over, still naked, to rebutton that leg of his breeches and then button the other, too. "There," she said, dusting off her hands. "Perfect."

Her domestic skills amused him. "I like having you play my valet."

He couldn't imagine any of his former mistresses buttoning up his breeches. They had usually been asleep when he'd left them.

He bent to fondle both her breasts. "And I love what you wear while you're doing it, too."

She swatted him with a frilly pillow, and he chuckled. Then he donned his shirt and waistcoat. "Do you wish to fasten these as well?"

"I think you're perfectly capable of doing those on your own." Her eyes brightened. "But I'll be happy to critique your efforts, if you wish."

"Very funny."

He'd finished dressing and had just picked up his boots when a knock came at the door, startling them both.

"Are you all right, Eliza?" Verity asked through the door.

With a roll of her eyes, Eliza nodded to the window. It took every ounce of his control not to laugh aloud. As he threw his boots out, then climbed through and eased the window down, he saw Eliza hastening to don her night rail and her wrapper.

When she was respectably covered, she extinguished every candle but the one by her bed. Then she walked to the door with it in hand, pausing only to blow him a kiss before she opened the door a crack and said, in a drowsy voice, "What do you need, Verity?"

Throwing his boots onto the grass below, he shimmied down. He was able to tug them on before anyone sounded an alarm. By the time he'd walked out past the mews to the street, he looked as normal as any buck of the first head returning from—or going toward—his club, late at night.

Just for good measure, he weaved a bit and hummed, as if he were foxed. But he didn't relax until he reached the next street over, where he'd tied up his horse outside a friend's town house. He wasn't taking any chances with Eliza's reputation. She would find that unforgivable, as well she should.

Fortunately, he arrived home to find everyone abed, with only a sleepy footman waiting to let him in. He had a hard time falling asleep himself, however. Despite being bone-tired after two days of travel, followed by the past two days in London, he had to consider what he might do tomorrow if Major Quinn really was visiting Eliza to offer her marriage.

She said she wasn't interested, and Nathaniel believed her. Still, she'd be a fool to turn the man down, especially if Quinn was considering retiring soon. And selfish as it might be, Nathaniel didn't want to give up his chance of marrying her.

It *was* selfish, wasn't it? He wanted to wait until his affairs were more settled, but waiting wasn't fair to her. Men could wait for decades to marry, but women, if they wanted children, couldn't wait forever. He wasn't exactly sure how *long* they could wait, but he knew it was less time than men.

He didn't even know if she wanted children. He had never asked. He'd merely taken her at her word when she'd said she didn't want to remarry. He'd assumed that if *he* wanted to marry *her*, she'd readily consent.

What if she didn't? What if she really didn't want marriage *or* children? Why hadn't he considered that possibility? And why hadn't he at least taken steps not to get her with child tonight?

Damn, he really *was* a selfish arse.

Thoughts like these, along with different schemes for dealing with Quinn if the man offered for her, swam through his head as he lay in and out of sleep. By the time he rose, just after dawn, he knew he would get no sleep until after the visit from Quinn to her. So he might as well prepare himself for it and go over to Grosvenor Square. He'd rather already be with her when Quinn arrived than show up later and not be admitted because Quinn had asked to see her alone.

A few hours later, at the earliest possible time for paying calls, he found himself facing down Norris again. Except that he was prepared this time.

"Lady Eliza is expecting me," he told the butler. Which was the truth. Mostly.

To his surprise, Norris nodded. "So is Lady Verity. Come with me, sir."

At the entrance to the drawing room, he saw Verity with

a young woman who looked like a lady's maid. "Just stall her a few more minutes," Verity said to the servant.

The maid nodded and hurried off toward the stairs as Nathaniel reached the drawing room. Verity caught sight of him and told Norris, "Thank you, Norris. That will be all for now." Then grabbing Nathaniel's arm, she pulled him into the room and pulled the door enough to keep them respectable, but not so much that they wouldn't spot someone coming.

"You can't let Eliza marry Quinn," Verity said in a low voice.

His heart stopped. "Is she . . . considering it?"

She rolled her eyes. "Who knows? My sister keeps her own counsel sometimes. But if he's coming here to offer for her today . . ."

"Don't worry," Nathaniel said firmly. "I'll do whatever it takes to prevent it."

"Offer for her yourself?" Verity asked.

That caught him by surprise. Then he narrowed his gaze on her. "I thought you disliked me."

"*She* likes you. That's all that matters."

Good to know. "Why are you against Quinn anyway?" Nathaniel asked.

"He rubs me the wrong way," she said with a shrug. "And lately he's been asking so many questions about Eliza, as well as Samuel and you on the Peninsula—"

His stomach dropped. "What kind of questions?"

The door swung open to reveal Eliza dressed in a beautiful pink gown. Her bodice of a darker pink draped in silver cords seemed to accentuate her bosom rather than mask it.

He swallowed hard. How was he supposed to ward off Quinn with Eliza looking like that? The man would trip over his feet to see it.

"What's going on?" Eliza demanded, then turned to him.

"Aren't you here rather early, Lord Foxstead . . . for someone who isn't a relation?"

"I didn't want to take the chance that your actual relation, Major Quinn, would try to get you alone before I could be present," he drawled.

"Distant relation." Eliza fixed Verity with a questioning look. "And what's *your* excuse for being closeted in here with Lord Foxstead?"

"Um . . . I was . . . just making him feel comfortable as a visitor. Would you like tea, sir? Toast?" When Eliza snorted, Verity headed for the door. "I'll see that some is brought in. I have to consult with the kitchen about tonight's ball anyway."

"I'm sure you do," Eliza said dismissively.

As soon as Verity was gone, Nathaniel asked, "Is she referring to the ball Jocelin is attending this evening?"

"Yes. It's an affair at Lady Sinclair's. I suppose you're attending, too?"

"This is the first I'm hearing of it, but I'm happy to accompany her and Tess." He lifted one brow. "That's assuming I've been sufficiently absent in the past two weeks to convince everyone of my lack of interest in marrying my own ward."

She smiled, but her eyes darted nervously toward the open door. "I believe that has been reinforced well enough."

"For you, too?" he asked in a low voice as he approached her.

"For me, too. Now stay back," she warned him. "The last thing I need is to be caught in your arms when Major Quinn arrives." When he scowled, she said, "Not because I care what he sees, mind you, but because I don't know if I can trust him to keep quiet about it."

He breathed a little easier. "I'm not sure I can either."

He drank in her fetching gown. "You look ravishing this morning."

"I can't imagine why, given how little sleep I got last night."

"Did Verity quiz you too much after I left?"

She chuckled. "She knows better. She did say she'd heard voices, and I told her I was talking in my sleep and would like to get back to it." At his smile, she added, "I'm very adept at pretending to be sleepy."

"I'll keep that in mind for the future." With a glance at the door, he whispered, "I wish I could kiss you right now."

"I wish you could, too, but I don't know how far I can strain society's idea of respectability, even as a widow."

"A young widow."

"Not so young a widow as all that."

God, it was as if she'd read his mind. "I did want to ask you . . . Well, this is probably not the time for such questions, but—"

"Major Adam Quinn!" Norris announced from the door.

Damn Quinn to hell. He was always interrupting. Still, Nathaniel rather enjoyed watching the major's face drop as he saw who was there with Eliza.

"I beg your pardon, Mrs. Pierce," Major Quinn said stiffly. "I did not realize you already had a caller."

Normally, Nathaniel would follow the prescribed behavior for such cases and would politely leave her to her new visitor. But he wasn't about to do that this morning and not with Quinn, for damned sure.

Eliza held out her hand so Quinn could press it. "It's not a problem in the least. Why don't we all take a seat, Major?" She turned to Norris. "Verity seems to have become lost on her way to fetch tea and toast. Would you please see to that?"

"Of course, madam," Norris said and left, but not before

Nathaniel caught the servant smirking to himself. Apparently, Nathaniel wasn't the only person not that admiring of the major.

"Good to see you again, Major," Nathaniel lied.

"I'm rather surprised to see you, Lord Foxstead. I'd been given to understand you were at your estate."

"I just returned. Indeed, Mrs. Pierce and I were catching up on all that has happened during my absence."

Eliza sat down in an armchair, leaving Nathaniel and Quinn to share opposite ends of the settee. But no sooner had the major sat down, than he jumped back up. "If I could be so bold as to ask for a moment alone with you, cousin . . ."

She motioned for him to sit down. "Please, there's no need, *cousin*. Anything you could say to me can be said in front of Lord Foxstead. He's an old family friend."

*And her lover. For God's sake, Quinn, recognize a hint when it hits you in the face. She doesn't want to be alone with you.*

Still, Quinn refused to be seated. "Very well. He would learn of it eventually, anyway. And I should hope the two of us can behave like gentlemen. I suppose it's even possible he's unaware of the situation."

The situation? Now the man had piqued Nathaniel's curiosity. What possible situation could Quinn mean?

"If, however, he is not," Quinn went on, "then he is abusing your trust mightily, cousin. And I simply thought you should know of it."

Nathaniel tensed, ready to call the man out right there, although he wasn't yet sure what he'd call him out for.

Reading Nathaniel's mood as well as she usually did, Eliza shot him a wary glance. "I can't imagine what you mean."

"The young lady that you have been championing these past few weeks is not who you think. She is not a widow of any kind." Scowling at Nathaniel, Quinn added, "She is certainly not the earl's ward. And given that she has a small child, I can only guess she's his mistress."

Eliza's face cleared. Obviously, she thought Quinn was laboring under the same misapprehension she herself had been a few weeks ago, and that they could all clear this up in a matter of moments.

But Nathaniel wasn't so hopeful. Quinn had once made some assumptions that Charlie had called him out on in front of Nathaniel. The man hadn't become a major by making the same mistake twice.

Feeling as if he were watching a carriage wreck from close at hand, Nathaniel couldn't even think of how to stop it. His stomach roiled, and he had to fight to keep his composure.

"These are grave accusations, sir," Eliza said in her usual calming voice. "I assume you have some proof?"

"I do," Quinn said.

Nathaniel stifled a groan.

The major continued without looking at Nathaniel. "I have a friend who was a member of one of General Anson's regiments until recently being wounded. When I visited him in the hospital a few days ago, I mentioned having met Lord Foxstead and Mrs. Jocelin Anson March. He informed me that there was no such person as a Mrs. March. That the so-called Mrs. March might very well be Jocelin Anson, for the general did have such a daughter, but that she'd never been married, and he knew of no Lieutenant March who might have married her."

Unsurprisingly, that brought Eliza up short.

"So I did some investigating at the War Office—discreetly, of course, for your sake—and discovered that at least in the matter of Lieutenant March, he was correct. No such man exists. As far as I'm concerned, that proves my friend to be speaking the truth."

Bloody, bloody hell! Nathaniel cursed the day he'd ever met Major Quinn. He could only pray that Eliza wouldn't figure out who Jocelin's seducer was, because if she did, she'd turn all her anger on Nathaniel, even though he hadn't had a damned thing to do with any of it. Somehow, he had to salvage this. But how?

Quinn went on. "Now you can understand why I thought this situation should be brought to your attention. I would hate for word to get around and thus ruin you and my other cousins and your admirable endeavor to help young ladies advance in society. I'm sure you can see my concern."

Nathaniel jumped to his feet, unable to endure another moment. "If 'word' is 'to get around,' sir, it would only be because you—or your so-called friend—spread it."

Now apparently certain of the rightness of his position, Major Quinn sat down to gaze coolly up at Nathaniel. "My 'so-called friend' was once in *your* regiment. I believe you know Captain Wainwright?"

Of course he knew Wainwright. The man was a good officer but an incurable gossip. Damn, damn, *damn.*

"To be fair, *he* defended you," Quinn continued. "Said you would never take advantage of your general's daughter. But she left the war as an unmarried young lady and arrived in London a few weeks ago as a mother and a widow of a fabricated soldier. I can see no other way to consider the matter."

"Because you assume no one else could have got her with child," Nathaniel snapped. "Well, sir, unbeknownst to you or any of your 'friends,' there were others capable of doing so. One of them, a married man under Anson's command, who deceived us all about his character, seduced her and left her with child, then up and got himself killed in battle."

He couldn't look at Eliza, didn't *dare* look at Eliza for

fear she'd guess who the "married man" was. "Since her father had asked me on his deathbed to be Jocelin's guardian, and I had readily agreed, I held to my word and brought her to England with me. It was only on our way to the Portugal coast—accompanied by her duenna, I assure you—that she told me of her condition."

Raking his hand through his hair, Nathaniel stopped right in front of Quinn, who'd suddenly begun to look a trifle uncomfortable. Good. He deserved it. "Hell, it was only on our way to the coast that *she* discovered her condition. And being the rank innocent that she was, despite her treatment by that . . . that scoundrel, she turned to me for help."

Nathaniel glared down at Quinn. "So yes, I invented a husband for her. I didn't see the harm in it. It was either that or trample on the memory of her late father, a man I admired above all others. *She* was always uncomfortable with the ruse. But I saw no point in sentencing little James to a life of ignominy or her to a life of degradation when a small lie would save her reputation and his future. My mistake was in letting her ever be introduced to *you*!"

Eliza rose to place a hand on his arm. "Come, Lord Foxstead, do resume your seat. As the major has already said, you are both gentlemen and can surely discuss this as gentlemen."

But her hand shook on his arm, and he wondered what she was thinking. He would give anything to know . . . except tell her the truth, because he knew how much it would wound her. "I shall do as you wish, madam, but only because you will it. Not because I have anything more to say to this petty fellow."

Angry beyond measure, Nathaniel dropped onto the settee. Then sat up again abruptly. "Actually, I do have a few things more to say. If you need confirmation of what

I've told you, Major Quinn, feel free to speak to Captain Harris Pembroke's wife aboard the merchant ship *Eclipse*. I hired her to serve as chaperone to Jocelin while we returned home on the *Eclipse*. But you'll have to hunt the ship down, since I've no idea where they went from here. They could be in India by now, for all I know. Besides, I only told Mrs. Pembroke that Jocelin was a widowed friend of my family."

"Another lie, I suppose," Major Quinn said.

Nathaniel refused to answer. It was either tell the truth and open up a different can of worms, or lie, and he was tired of lying . . . at least to Eliza.

Major Quinn stared hard at him. "Perhaps I *should* have discussed this matter with you, Lord Foxstead, before bringing it to the attention of my cousin. But surely you can understand my outrage."

"Frankly, cousin," Eliza cut in, "I'm not sure *I* do. Yes, he lied. Yes, Mrs. Mar— . . . Miss Anson maintained the lie." Her voice softened. "But you have met both Miss Anson and her little boy. Surely you would not want to see either ruined simply because a married man took advantage of her."

Nathaniel could feel her gaze on him, but he couldn't look at her. She would read the truth in his eyes. He still hoped to salvage this, at least for her.

Major Quinn stiffened. "I will admit that Wainwright said, to his knowledge, Miss Anson's behavior had always been above reproach. But when a woman is seeking marriage—"

"I quite agree." Eliza rose to her feet. "Forgive me for having ever introduced her to you. Like the earl, I regret that. And like the earl, I don't think you would be an appropriate husband for a young woman in her situation."

Quinn jumped to his feet and looked about as confused

as Nathaniel felt, though he, too, stood, praying she was not planning to dismiss them both.

She went on coldly. "Young women have enough difficulty finding their way in the world without also having to be punished an entire lifetime for one mistake. I've seen what happens to women who lose their reputations, who *don't* lie, and as a result sink into degradation, along with the poor children they often end up bearing. So I can't entirely blame his lordship. I wouldn't for the world wish to watch a sweet girl like Jocelin and a dear boy like Jimmy suffer for the actions of a scoundrel."

"But cousin—" he began.

"Enough," she said, her voice quivering. "I need to speak to his lordship alone now. So I think you should leave. If you should wish to discuss this further, do return tomorrow, and I will attempt to suggest other possible brides for you—women who might suit your fastidious requirements for a wife. In the meantime, however, I do hope you will keep this knowledge about Jocelin and Jimmy to yourself, at least until I can uncover the full facts of it. Do you think you can?"

Nathaniel held his breath.

"For you, I can," Major Quinn said in a stilted voice. Then he bowed. "And thus, I take my leave of you."

Then she strode to the door and called out, "Norris?"

The butler was there swiftly enough that Nathaniel feared he'd been listening at the door. At the same time, the man had struck him as having a certain fondness for Jocelin and Jimmy. That might work in their favor.

"Yes, madam?" Norris asked.

"The major is leaving. Tell the kitchen they need not bother with the tea and toast. Lord Foxstead will be departing shortly as well."

"Very good," Norris said and ushered the man out.

Eliza kept her back to Nathaniel and remained silent so long that he wasn't sure what to make of her response. Then she faced him with an expression of sheer, unadulterated rage, and he knew he was in deeper trouble with her than he had ever been.

"So when exactly were you planning to tell me that Jimmy's father is—was—my late husband?"

Bloody, bloody hell.

# Chapter 17

Anger, betrayal, outrage all swirled through her body, turning Eliza nauseous. "He was, wasn't he?" she choked out.

The minute Major Quinn had begun his revelations, several things had flashed through Eliza's head at once. Nathaniel and Jocelin both had been secretive about Jocelin's "husband" for no apparent reason. And Samuel *had* been aide-de-camp to Jocelin's father.

Even that moment on May Day when Nathaniel had said of Jocelin, *once she realized she could possibly marry . . . again* had taken on new meaning. Because what Nathaniel had meant was *once she realized she could possibly marry*. As opposed to thinking she could only be a mother known for having a child out of wedlock.

Then there was the way Jocelin had taken so very long to warm to her. Oh, Lord. Because Jocelin had been Samuel's *mistress*.

"Did Samuel father Jimmy or not?" she asked again. "Could you please answer me?"

"Please, Eliza, sit down," Nathaniel said, his face the color of ash, which told her all she needed to know. "Let me get Norris to fetch you some tea."

When he reached for her, she recoiled. Her very blood screamed anger. "How could you . . . *lie* about such a thing to me, knowing who she was to my husband? How could you even think it acceptable that my sisters and I be the ones to . . . to . . ."

An awful thought crossed her mind. "What horrible things did Samuel tell you about me? Did you bring Jocelin here to . . . to shame me because of something he said or did . . . or even something *I* did?"

"God, no! Of course not." He swallowed hard. "I wasn't thinking. At the beginning, I had some foolish notion that if you and your sisters presented her in society, any gossip that might leak out—like that of your cousin just now—would be discounted. Because what woman would help her late husband's . . . that is . . ."

"Mistress?"

"Mistress! She was never that to him." He paused, a sudden frown creasing his brow. "At least, I don't think so. If it had ever risen to that level, surely her father would have noticed and strung Sam up by his ballocks. Then *I* would have strung him up by his ballocks."

She gaped at him. "Are you saying you didn't even *know* who she was to him while you were on the Peninsula?"

"Not until long after Sam died. Not until she found herself with child." When her face apparently showed her disbelief, he placed his hand over his heart. "I swear it! I didn't know until then."

She crossed her arms over her chest. "So you're claiming you had *no idea* of their . . . association even though you were all under her father's command."

He reached for her again, and she glared at him so hard that he dropped his hands to his sides. "Regimental life isn't how you imagine. One regiment alone has over four hundred soldiers, and the ADC spends his time going between various companies and regiments on behalf of his general. I only saw Sam when he was bringing messages to my company. And though Anson saw him every day, the general had his hands full commanding men and strategizing future attacks. Meanwhile, Jocelin spent most of her time behind the lines with her duenna, whom Sam—"

"Charmed into not noticing what was going on." Her eyes prickled with unshed tears. She understood that aspect of her late husband's character only too well. "And I'm sure he charmed Jocelin, too, the same way he charmed every woman he met. Still, how could the two l-lovers have managed to share a tent or . . . or whatever they did share, without anyone noticing?"

"I don't know. I wish I did. Jocelin didn't give me details. She said it was only once, but she seemed so mortified by the experience that even if it had been more, she wouldn't have admitted it to me. As it was, it took me a week just to get that much out of her once she revealed she was pregnant. She wouldn't even tell me the name of her seducer at first, just that he was dead."

How horrible it must have been for a shy girl like Jocelin, who could only seem to talk to soldiers, to be in such a position. Although Eliza supposed Jocelin *could* have tempted Samuel into her bed, Eliza had trouble seeing it.

"And you're sure she was telling the truth about Samuel having been the one to seduce her."

"Eliza." He cast her a pitying look that somehow made everything worse. "Why would she lie about it?"

She tried to come up with a reason, but he was right. One man's name would have been as good as another to Jocelin at that point. The damage had been done. And she couldn't possibly have anticipated she'd later end up encountering Eliza in England.

"By then she was four months along," Nathaniel went on. "I knew I had only one way to protect her—invent a dead husband for her. So I did." He lowered his voice. "I'm sorry, dearling. I didn't mean for you to find out this way."

"You didn't mean for me to find out at all, did you?" she said through the thickness in her throat.

He dragged in a heavy breath. "Not so soon, no. I'd hoped to wait until she married. Until she and Jimmy were settled. I never dreamed—"

"That someone would question your story? Would seek out the truth?" She shook her head. "I can't believe you didn't tell me from the very beginning. Do you realize how much you've risked by not at least warning me of what was going on? If this gets out, it could destroy Elegant Occasions! We built it from nothing. It means everything to us. But how can it continue if people think we're hiding something whenever we put clients forward in society?"

"I know," he said, remorse filling his gaze. "Honestly, I was only thinking about how to ensure a decent future for Jocelin and Jimmy, one that did not involve them hiding in shame on my estate."

"And if you had explained all that—"

"Would you have taken her on if I had?"

That brought her up short. "I don't know. And now we'll never know, will we?" She paced the rug. "But even if you'd chosen not to tell me everything, you could have told me the same thing you told Major Quinn—that a married man had seduced her."

"And you would have wanted more details about his background and the circumstances, and after a few days of seeing how she was around you, you would have figured it out." Nathaniel crossed his arms over his chest. "Then we would have been precisely where we are now. I couldn't . . . I didn't want to take that chance."

"It's not as if I have any illusions by now about Samuel's character, you know." Her stomach churned. "Samuel hadn't ever been a saint. I just . . . never imagined him to be quite so much a sinner. Clearly, I'm inept at distinguishing good from bad when it comes to men."

He blanched. "You're including me in that number, I suppose."

"About the only thing I'm certain of with you is you want me in your bed. Beyond that . . ." She dropped onto the settee. "Well . . . I assume you and Samuel used to spend countless hours in the stews with women of ill repute. I'm aware you had more than one mistress—he told me that much."

"Yes, he told you so much about me," Nathaniel said, then scrubbed his lips with one hand as if to wipe off the bitterness that his words left on his mouth. "Half of it was lies, as you well know. I did have mistresses before we left for the war, but Sam and I never went to brothels together. I wouldn't have been that disrespectful of you, and he knew it. I'm unaware if he went to them on his own, but if he did, he never spoke about it. It was the one area in which he seemed to control his urges."

"I can see how well he controlled his urges. All I have to do is look at Jimmy now to be reminded—" A sob escaped her. "That poor mite. He thinks his father was a man who doesn't even exist. You'll have to wait to tell him the truth until he's grown. It's too big of a risk otherwise." She sat up straight. "But you have to tell Charlie Crowder the truth if he offers for Jocelin. He can't marry her without knowing!"

"Why?" Nathaniel exclaimed. "For God's sake, don't punish Jocelin because of what I did!"

"I'm not. But if he marries her and then learns about it the same way my cousin did, Charlie might take it out on her."

Nathaniel looked alarmed. "Is he that sort of man?"

"I don't think so, but I only know him from encountering

him at Isolde's house. Which I rarely have, since she was closer to Verity and Diana than to me. And as I said, my ability to tell good men from bad is clearly suspect, anyway."

She knit her hands together over her waist. "Still, if he did grow high-and-mighty once he learned the facts, that would be horrible for her and Jimmy. Her husband would always think himself superior, or worse, suspect her of low morals and watch her every move for evidence of it. She'd be locked in an awful marriage for life. Can you imagine?"

"You mean, as you were," he said softly.

"Don't you dare speak of my marriage!" she cried, her voice trembling in spite of her attempts to control it. "All this time, you've obviously known more about it than I, but you didn't have the consideration to warn me that Samuel—"

"Had been unfaithful to you? Had profaned your marriage bed? Did you really want me to tell you the truth after he was gone, and it no longer mattered?"

"It mattered to *me*! All this time I thought that whatever his faults, he loved me. But even that is a lie."

It shifted how she saw Samuel. How she saw herself. What if she wasn't capable of capturing a man's affections fully? How could she even trust anything she thought she knew? None of it seemed true.

He sat down beside her and grabbed her hands. "He did love you in his own way. As far as I know, Jocelin was the only woman with whom he strayed. Plenty of men get lonely on campaign, and they do things they might never do at home."

"Would you?" she asked. "Get lonely while away and do things you might never do at home?"

"We're not talking about me," he said uneasily.

"Just answer the question."

"I don't think so, no."

She slid her hands from his. "Then again, what else would you say? It's not as if you're going to admit to something like that. What man would?"

"So now you're calling me a liar?" he said, then caught himself and sighed. "Right. I suppose that's how you see me now. As an opportunist determined to have things his own way even if it means lying and cheating his way to get them."

He rose, his eyes searching her face. "Fine. Then let me continue to act as an opportunist and ask you—what do you intend to do about Jocelin?"

"What do you mean?"

He ran a hand over his chin. "Now that you know the truth, what will you do? Will you . . . refuse to continue with her as a client?"

Once again, Jocelin was the only one he cared about. "It's too late for that now. She's in the midst of a début. If we halt any activities we already have planned for her, it will reflect badly on us. And people might speculate on what reason we had for stopping our association with her. If you give them enough rope, they *will* hang her. I wouldn't do that to her or any woman, even knowing who she was to Samuel. I certainly wouldn't do it to Jimmy. I'm not as vindictive a sort of woman as you apparently assume."

"I didn't mean . . . I don't think you a vindictive sort of woman at all. You're a good person. I just . . . wanted to know your plans, so I could plan."

Anger clogged her throat. "For Jocelin, you mean. Why does her future matter so much to you? Did you owe her father something? Did he . . . he save your life in battle, or what?"

He blinked, clearly taken off guard by that question. "He

asked me to be her guardian, and I take such responsibilities seriously."

"But *why you*?" She rose to face him. "What is so blasted important about Jocelin that you would risk destroying me and my sisters for her?"

"I didn't mean to risk . . ." He paused, then tried again. "I swear I never meant to harm you or your sisters or Elegant Occasions. Clearly, I was being selfish and not thinking through the consequences."

"Clearly," she repeated sarcastically.

When he said no more, obviously not planning to answer the question at all, she realized he'd made his choice. He'd chosen his ward over her. He would do whatever he must to protect Jocelin.

Normally, she would find that admirable, but under the circumstances she simply couldn't.

She swallowed her hurt. "I will have to tell my sisters of what has transpired. And when Major Quinn returns tomorrow, I will ask him to keep things quiet for my sake and the sake of Diana and Verity. We are also his cousins, after all. But if I can't convince him . . . you will have to find another strategy for protecting Jocelin from his gossip."

"Of course." He looked as if he might reach for her hand again, but if he did, she knew she would fall apart in front of him.

So she swiftly turned away. "I'll send you a message letting you know the results of that conversation."

"Eliza, please . . ."

"I don't know who you are anymore, Nathaniel. Perhaps I never did, since you spent these past weeks around me living a lie."

"Not all the time," he said in a low voice fraught with emotion.

"But I can't tell which parts were real. And until I can figure that out . . ." She swallowed, praying she could get through this. Steadying her breath, she went on, "I can only . . . do that if you aren't around. Jocelin may come as usual, and your sister and Jimmy will, of course, always be welcome. I just can't have you here."

"For how long?" he asked hoarsely.

"I don't know."

Then, before he could say anything else to further erode her control, she hurried to the door and called for Norris, who came in record time.

"If you would please see Lord Foxstead out, Norris . . ."

"Of course, madam," he said, although the daggered look he shot Nathaniel showed that Norris could tell how upset she was.

Thank heaven for faithful servants. He'd always been so good to her.

She held her breath, praying that Nathaniel didn't make some flippant remark or heated protest that showed he had no idea of how this was affecting her. Because if he did, she was liable to say things she would later regret.

When he merely followed Norris out, she nearly collapsed with relief. Hastily, she closed the door, then leaned against it until the sound of footsteps diminished.

She slowly started falling apart. Sliding down onto the floor, she began to cry, then weep, then sob, and take great gulps of air in a vain attempt to calm herself. She soaked her handkerchief and couldn't even get up to find another.

So she was a red-eyed, red-nosed mess of a woman by the time her sisters burst through the other entrance into the drawing room.

"Should have . . . have closed that door . . . too," she sobbed. "Go away!"

"Not on your life," Diana said. "Something must be

horribly wrong if *you* are crying. You *never* cry." She waddled toward Eliza.

But Verity got there quicker. "Oh, Eliza, oh, my dear sister." She dropped onto the floor next to her and dragged Eliza into her arms. "Sh, sh, sweetie. We're here. We'll take care of you. Did that awful fellow hurt you somehow?"

"Wh-which awful f-fellow?" Eliza choked out.

"There was more than one?" Diana asked in alarm.

Verity took the damp handkerchief from Eliza and tossed it aside, then pressed a fresh handkerchief into her hand, for which Eliza was grateful. But her tears were beginning to dry up anyway, leaving her numb. She blotted her eyes and blew her nose while trying not to think of all she'd learned. Trying not to think of her fight with Nathaniel.

"Tell us what happened," Diana said, taking a seat on the settee. "Sorry, love, but if I get down on that floor, I'll never get up again." When Verity shot their sister a dirty glance, Diana rolled her eyes. "I'm not inventing that, you know. You try getting up while carrying a boulder in your belly."

"It's fine," Eliza said, placing a hand on Verity's arm.

Eliza pushed herself to a stand as Verity leaped up to help her. Then they headed to the settee to squeeze onto it next to Diana, with Eliza in the middle. Both women enveloped her in their arms, and she nearly burst into tears again. There was something vastly comforting about having them holding her just now.

Until the hugging became a trifle overwhelming. "Enough," she whispered. "I'm all right now. Truly, I am."

"If you're sure," Verity said with one last squeeze before she released Eliza and sat back.

But Diana continued to hold Eliza's hand. That, too, was comforting.

"I'm glad you two ignored me . . . and stayed," Eliza

said. "I would have had to tell you about it eventually, anyway, but thank you."

Then Eliza proceeded to explain, in halting words, why Major Quinn had called on her, what Nathaniel had said in response, and what Eliza herself had guessed after the major had left.

"*Jocelin?*" Diana said, clearly shocked. "*Our* Jocelin?"

"Samuel's Jocelin," Eliza said, then nearly cried again. But this time she was able to maintain control over herself, and that small triumph relieved her. The wild spate of tears had terrified her.

Verity jumped up to pace in front of the settee. "I swear, if your late husband weren't already dead, I'd kill him myself."

"No, you wouldn't. Because you're a good person. He . . . was not."

Next, Eliza related her argument with Nathaniel and how it had ended. "But I should have guessed about Samuel and Jocelin long before this. She wouldn't talk about her supposed husband to me, and she seemed quite slow to warm to me—"

"Which is odd, because everyone likes you," Diana said. "It's me they find a bit difficult."

Diana then looked at Verity, who snapped, "I know what people say of *me*, but I don't care. I'm not overly critical at all. I merely prefer perfection."

"The point is, with all that before me," Eliza went on, "why did I not guess about Samuel and Jocelin's . . . er . . . friendship until today?"

"Because you trusted Lord Foxstead," Verity said. "All of his attentions and deceptions kept you from guessing. He deliberately misled you."

"He's not so bad as all that," Diana said.

"Stop defending him," Verity retorted. "You only like

him because he's Geoffrey's friend." She turned to Eliza. "I will call Lord Foxstead out if you wish." When Eliza looked skeptical, she added, "I mean it. If I thought the earl wasn't too much of a gentleman to duel with me, I would damned well make him do so."

"Nobody is fighting Lord Foxstead, least of all you." Eliza rubbed her temples, which were throbbing now from all her crying. "You don't even know how to shoot. Or fight with swords or whatever men do when they duel."

"True," Verity admitted. "But I would learn. Just for you." Brightening suddenly, she looked at Diana. "Would Geoffrey consider calling Foxstead out for Eliza?"

"No," Diana said, "because I'd kick him out of bed if he did."

When Verity gaped at Diana, Eliza gave a dry chuckle. "You want her to send her husband off to possibly get killed because Nathaniel never told me that my devil of a husband impregnated some seventeen-year-old girl? Are you daft? Diana and Geoffrey are about to have a child, for pity's sake, and Nathaniel is a trained soldier. Do you really want our niece or nephew to grow up without a father?"

"I suppose not," Verity grudgingly admitted.

Diana looked pensive. "I hadn't thought about it until you said it just now, but Jocelin *was* only seventeen when he got her with child, wasn't she?"

Swallowing hard, Eliza nodded. "Nathaniel told me the truth from the beginning about how old she was when Jimmy was sired. He just lied about who did the siring." She sucked in a shaky breath. "That's what makes this so hard. Samuel was twenty-nine when he seduced Jocelin— far too old for a naïve girl her age."

"Are you sure Samuel did the seducing?" Diana asked.

Eliza and Verity eyed her askance.

"What?" Diana said. "Someone had to mention it."

"You were never the recipient of Samuel's considerable charm," Eliza said. "That man could seduce the habit off a nun, trust me. And a girl like Jocelin, enamored of officers and prone to hero worship? She was easy pickings for someone like Samuel."

"Remind me of why you married him again?" Verity asked.

"I fancied myself in love." Eliza sighed. "Perhaps I was. But it didn't take long to figure out that love wasn't what Samuel had in mind when we eloped." She stared down at her hand in Diana's. "Although Nathaniel insists it wasn't money that prompted Samuel. And we've already established that my late husband could get any woman he wanted into his bed, so it couldn't have been my physical attractions."

"I daresay it was both combined," Diana said, squeezing her hand. "He wanted to have the rich *and* sensual wife of his dreams."

"And it turns out I disappointed him in both respects." Eliza sighed. "Thanks to Papa, I was never rich. And thanks to Mama, I was afraid of becoming *too* sensual, so I could never let myself relax in the bedchamber. He probably found a more appreciative companion in Jocelin."

"Don't you dare blame yourself for that," Verity said fiercely. "Samuel was a blackguard, pure and simple, no matter what gentlemanly trappings he might have had. You deserved better, and he knew it."

"And Lord Foxstead knows it, too, I daresay," Diana said. "Why do you think he's been so . . . cautious around you? He didn't want to trample your husband's memory, but he also thought you deserved better."

"I deserved a liar? A man who even now won't tell me the truth about a girl who is only his ward?"

"Did you ask him why he's doing all this for such a girl?" Diana asked.

"I've asked him twice. He avoids the subject or simply points out he's her guardian. He won't say anything beyond that. The only reason I can think is that he's secretly in love with her."

Her sisters burst into laughter.

"What?" Eliza said. "Unrequited love seems to be popular enough in novels and plays."

"Then why even have this 'début' for her?" Diana said. "Especially when, by your own admission, Jocelin was already enamored of him and probably would have married him if he'd only asked."

"If Lord Foxstead is in love with anyone, it's you," Verity retorted. "I don't generally believe men capable of love, yet even I can tell he's feeling *something* for you."

"He's in lust with me, that's all," Eliza said, wishing Verity was right.

Did she *want* Verity to be right? Did she want Nathaniel to be in love with her?

She very much feared she did.

"He may *think* he's in lust with you," Diana said, "but men often refuse to recognize love even when it hits them in the face. I wouldn't give up on him so soon if I were you."

Eliza lifted one brow. "Or you may merely be biased toward your husband's friend. But I'm afraid Samuel has made me cynical."

"I suppose only time will tell," Diana said. "He may yet surprise you."

They fell into a companionable silence.

Finally, Verity asked, "So what will you do about Jocelin? I mean, I know you told Lord Foxstead we would finish out her début—and indeed, I think we should, assuming that Charlie doesn't offer for her before it's even over. But are you going to tell her you've learned the truth?"

"I don't know. What would be the point? To embarrass her? She's clearly already uncomfortable with the ruse. Even Nathaniel said that. To shame her? I'm not going to shame a woman who was only a girl, and a naïve one at that, when my husband took advantage of her. Especially not when she might be on the verge of marrying a decent fellow like Charlie. There's Jimmy to think of, after all."

"I do think you're right, though, about Charlie," Diana said. "We have to tell *him* if he offers for her." She slipped her arm about Eliza's shoulder. "But not today. There's no reason you must go to the ball tonight. Rosy and Winston return from their honeymoon trip today, so I can handle Jocelin's hair with Rosy's help. Besides, Geoffrey will need to spend time with Winston anyway."

"And I can make sure the orchestra is settled in the proper place and the music is all correct," Verity said.

Diana pushed herself to a stand. "So we're going to send you up to your room where you can rest, read, and drink tea and eat cake. Or you can stay down here and practice your harp lute or the pianoforte. You can sing the most melancholy songs you wish, and we won't even complain."

"If it helps," Verity said, "the kitchen is making plenty of prawlongs for the ball tonight. Feel free to have some."

"Oh, yes, prawlongs, the perfect cure for heartbreak," Eliza said as she, too, stood. "While they do sound tempting, I doubt they can wipe the memory of Nathaniel's deceptions from my mind." If anything, they'd remind her of her wonderful private dinner with him at the Crowders.

Tears stung her eyes again, and she dashed them away with a swipe of her hand. Enough of that nonsense.

"You could always cry some more, if you need to," Diana said in a gentle voice.

"Thank you, but I've turned into a watering pot sufficiently to last me a few years at least," Eliza said ruefully. "And with the house party coming up soon, I know you both need my help, so I can't be walking around bursting into tears at every turn."

"Don't worry about the house party," Verity said. "We can handle that, too, if we have to. Although I must say, I'm pleased Diana agreed to do it this month instead of whenever she has the christening. That way we don't have to have Mama and Papa there together."

Diana snorted. "I don't know what I was thinking. The two of them at a house party? I can't imagine." She gave Eliza a quick hug, no small feat with her ungainly shape. "The point is, you do what you like today. Tomorrow will be soon enough, I assure you, to figure out what to do about Jocelin. Who knows? Tonight she might meet yet another officer she fancies, who's willing to fight Charlie for her and won't give a fig about her past."

"I don't think Charlie does give a fig about her past," Verity said. "He just likes that she has the perfect figure and a pretty face."

"And knows what laces and sabretaches are," Eliza added.

All three of them laughed.

It felt so good to laugh with her sisters. She'd been spending so much time with Nathaniel—or worrying over Nathaniel's feelings for her—that she'd forgotten how important Verity and Diana would always be to her.

Now if only they could find a way to heal the bruises on her heart.

# Chapter 18

Nathaniel sat at the desk in his study at Foxstead Place and attempted to answer letters from his estate manager. But he couldn't keep his mind on the work. He just kept hearing the pain in Eliza's voice, the cry of betrayal. He shouldn't have lied to her. How could he have been so foolish?

He simply hadn't expected to end up caring for her quite so much. Only three days later, it already felt as if he'd lost a limb. Worse yet, he had cut off his limb himself, cavalierly, stupidly. He really had no excuse for causing his own pain, let alone hers.

God save him. His missing her during those two weeks at Amberly was nothing compared to missing her because of this. Because he'd lied to her so egregiously that she would never be able to forgive him.

"Lord Foxstead?" came a voice from the door.

He looked up to see Jocelin. Damn. How long had she been standing there? "Yes?"

"Are you well?"

He blinked. "Why do you ask?"

"Your sister wondered. The staff is concerned. But you always snap at them if they ask, so . . . well . . ."

"They sent you. Because they knew I'd never snap at you."

She gave a half-hearted smile. "Something like that. They're worried, that's all. And I'm worried. You don't eat with us, you spend all your time in here with the account books, you don't go out at night, and by all accounts, you don't even go to bed. And you don't go to Grosvenor Square."

He sat back with a muttered curse. "It's complicated, that's all."

"So it's not because of your quarrel with Eliza?"

He frowned. "How do you know about that?"

"All the servants at Grosvenor Square are talking about it."

That made him sit up. "What are they saying?"

She shrugged. "That you quarreled. I told you."

"Did they say what we quarreled about?"

"No one knows. Why, is it important?"

Was she asking because she suspected the truth? He should tell her the source of their argument. But then he'd have to say why the subject had come up in the first place. He'd have to reveal that Quinn knew the truth and now so did Eliza. It would hurt Jocelin deeply, especially if she'd been hoping for an offer of marriage from the major.

That bastard. Nathaniel would never let him marry Jocelin now.

"It doesn't matter," he said.

"If you don't want to tell me—"

"I don't." When her lower lip trembled, he cursed his quick tongue. "It's private. I'm sure you understand."

She nodded, although clearly, she did *not* understand. Fortunately for him, Jocelin wasn't the sort to press him on it, even if she did suspect the reason.

So he kept talking, though God only knew why. "I

tried to see her the day of our . . . disagreement. I attended the ball."

"I know. You and your sister took me."

"Right." God, he sounded like an idiot, stating the obvious. "She wasn't there." Why not? Had he hurt her so badly that she wouldn't even show up to places she would normally go?

Diana and Verity had both been there. Diana had been kind enough to talk to him, but when he'd asked how Eliza was, she'd said, "Give her time." Which was essentially the last thing Eliza had asked of him before she'd had him ushered out by Norris.

So he'd done what Eliza had asked. But he didn't know how much longer he could bear to do so. She had forgiven him so easily for his two weeks of bachelor panic. He doubted she would do so that easily again. And he deserved whatever punishment she gave him. Because he'd brought this on himself.

"The night of the ball, Verity said Eliza wasn't feeling well," Jocelin admitted. "But the next day she left town to go—" A distressed expression crossed Jocelin's face.

He ignored it to pounce on her tidbit of information. "To go where?"

"I can't tell you! I wasn't supposed to say anything at all about her leaving. I-I forgot! They swore me to secrecy." She slumped. "I can't believe I said something."

"You didn't say *anything*," he bit out. "All you said was she left town, damn it!" When she flinched, he forced himself to calm down, to get control over his voice. "Surely you can see that's of no help to me. Can't you at least tell me *where* she went?"

"I swore I wouldn't." Jocelin chewed on her lower lip. "Please don't make me. They're my friends."

And he was no longer theirs. Not anymore. He wanted

to pound the desk, but that would *really* alarm Jocelin, and she was clearly already upset. Besides, if he got what he wanted by bullying Jocelin, then he deserved to lose Eliza.

At least her leaving town would explain why she hadn't come to visit him or send a message for him. Even now, a letter might be in the post. "It's fine, dear girl. She needed time and distance, obviously, and I . . . must give that to her."

Even if it drove him mad, which it did. He was not a patient man.

Now he knew how Eliza must have felt when he was gone for two weeks without a word. Like *shite*. Closing his eyes, he rubbed his temples.

Jocelin let out a relieved breath. "So you understand. Thank goodness."

Understand? Hardly. Less than a week ago, he'd had the woman of his dreams in his arms, and now he'd driven her away.

"Was there anything else you wished to tell me?" he asked, wanting only to get Jocelin out of his study so he could try to figure out how to find Eliza. He ought to put his skills as an army captain to good use. She couldn't have gone to too many places.

"Well, now that you ask . . . I think Charlie is going to offer marriage. And if he does, I mean to accept."

Bloody, bloody hell! Could things get any worse? "And what will you do about Jimmy?"

"I don't know. I can't talk to Charlie about it until he offers." A hopeful look crossed her face. "Has he spoken to you yet? Since you're my guardian?"

"Not yet." And when he did—if he did—Nathaniel would have to decide whether to reveal the truth about Jocelin's past.

*But you have to tell Charlie the truth if he offers for Jocelin. He can't marry her without knowing!*

Eliza had had a point. A very worrisome point. "Doesn't it bother you, Jocelin, that you've only known him a few weeks?"

"Not really. I've known women who got married on even less of an acquaintance. It does happen."

"True. But that doesn't make it wise."

"I don't have time to be wise. If he does offer, it will be soon. The regiment leaves for the coast in two more weeks. Will you accept his suit?"

He sighed. "It depends on how he answers my questions."

She swallowed. "You won't be *too* hard on him, will you?"

He took one look at the yearning in her face and knew he couldn't refuse her anything. How could he, when he knew what it was like to care about someone who might never care about him again? And since Sam, whom she never would have met if not for him, had ripped her innocence from her, it was only fair that Nathaniel help her to happiness even if it meant she squandered that happiness by following the drum with her husband.

Although he would do his damnedest to make sure that Jimmy remained safe. He still had connections within the army. Perhaps he could get a safer posting for Charlie.

"Lord Foxstead?"

Right. She'd asked him a question. "I'll try to be fair. That's all I can promise. And we may be assuming a great deal about Lieutenant Crowder, anyway, so there's no use in borrowing trouble."

That didn't exactly reassure her, but she bobbed her head and rose. "I have to go to Grosvenor Square. I'm helping them prepare for the house party next week. We are still going, aren't we—me, you, and Lady Usborne?"

"Of course. As far as I know, Geoffrey is still my closest friend. That's not likely to change because Eliza and I have quarreled."

A smile tipped up her lips. "I did hope we would attend. Since Charlie is staying in Richmond with his parents, it will be easy for him to visit me."

"Ah, yes, I forgot that the house party is at Geoffrey's hunting lodge by Richmond Park. It's larger than one would expect. You'll like it."

She cast him a sly glance. "And Eliza is sure to be there."

He blinked as the ramifications of that dawned on him. Eliza would be there! And so would he. As Jocelin flounced out the door, it occurred to him that he could court Eliza during the house party. When was it again?

Fumbling through the papers on his desk, he came up with the invitation and held it up to the sun streaming through the window. Yes, in four days. Surely that would give her enough time to have thought through her feelings. And she could hardly accuse him of being too aggressive in pursuing her. They were all invited. It would be as natural as could be.

He folded his hands behind his head and lay back to contemplate that august event. This time he would win her, whatever it took. Because he began to think he couldn't bear to live much longer without Eliza in his life.


Two more days passed, and Nathaniel began to wonder if he could even wait two more. If he could just figure out where Eliza was, he wouldn't need to. But he'd asked at Grosvenor Square about where she was, and for his trouble, he'd been refused entry by Norris. Eliza hadn't shown up at any of the events he'd escorted Jocelin to, and her sisters had declined to tell him where she'd gone.

He'd even waited like a smitten fool outside the house, figuring she had to return home sometime. But no, she had not. So now he had no choice *but* to wait until the house party.

That was why, five days after Eliza had thrown him out, when his butler announced that Geoffrey was there to call on him, his spirits lifted at once.

"Excellent," Nathaniel said. "Show him into the drawing room. I'll be there shortly."

Geoffrey probably knew precisely where Eliza had gone. Damn, Nathaniel should have considered that sooner. He took a moment to make sure he didn't look too much like the bedraggled fellow down on his luck that he felt like. Then he headed to the drawing room.

But when he walked in, he was surprised to find his friend circling the room, his frown deepening the longer he circled.

"Good God, Geoffrey, I didn't take all *that* long." Nathaniel strolled over to where he kept his brandy. "Shall I pour you some, too?" he asked as he poured a glass for himself.

"I don't drink brandy in the morning, for God's sake." Geoffrey wouldn't meet his gaze. "And I . . . won't be here long, anyway. Indeed, if not for our friendship, I would have written this in a letter. But I thought that would be in particularly poor taste."

That brought Nathaniel up short. "*What* would be in 'particularly poor taste,' and since when do you care about such things?"

Drawing himself up straight, Geoffrey said in an offended tone, "I *am* a gentleman, sir."

"I wouldn't go that far, but . . ." When Geoffrey didn't

laugh, Nathaniel realized the man had something serious on his mind. "So, tell me what you wished to write in a letter." Nathaniel sipped some brandy, wondering if he should call for tea or coffee for Geoffrey.

"I'm afraid I have to . . . um . . . rescind my invitation to our house party at Grenwood Lodge."

Nathaniel stared at him, his heart freezing. "What do you mean?"

"Diana and Verity feel that your presence there, in such close quarters with Eliza, would make her uncomfortable."

"Oh, they do, do they?" He knocked back the rest of his brandy and set down the glass with a bang. "And does she agree with them?"

"They didn't say. I haven't spoken to her myself."

His temper rose as he walked up to his so-called friend. "Let me get this straight. Despite not knowing how Eliza even feels about all this, you are putting the wishes of your wife and her sister above that of your friend, who has known you longer than you've known the three of them!"

Geoffrey scowled. "Don't make this harder than it needs to be." He tugged at his cravat. "I should think you'd be glad to get out of attending a house party. You know how deuced boring they are."

"I know that I haven't seen Eliza in five days, and I was counting on—" He glared at Geoffrey. "If you want me not to attend, you'll have to get her to tell me herself."

"Diana?"

"No, for God's sake. *Eliza.* If she doesn't want me there, I won't come. But until she says so . . ."

"Nathaniel," Geoffrey said softly. "Surely you wouldn't ask that of her. Her heart is breaking. You lied to her, kept crucial information from her. They are trying to spare her from more pain."

Nathaniel swallowed bile. "So you know everything then, I suppose, including the truth about Jocelin."

Geoffrey sighed. "Yes. And about Jimmy's real father. I never met Mr. Pierce myself, but—"

"He was wrong for Eliza in every way." Disappointment weighting his steps, he walked back to where he'd left his brandy glass. After pouring himself more, he took a few slow sips. "Only after I learned that he'd seduced Jocelin did I realize he was also more of a scoundrel than I'd thought." He hesitated a moment. "You . . . you won't tell anyone about Jocelin, will you?"

"Of course not! I *am* capable of being discreet."

"I had to keep my ward safe, you realize. Because if word got out that Jimmy is a bastard, Jocelin would be ruined, and the boy would grow up with a stone about his neck."

"I suppose he would." Geoffrey searched his face. "But you seem far more concerned about Jocelin's and Jimmy's future prospects than Eliza's feelings for you."

"Is that what Eliza told you?"

Reluctantly, Geoffrey nodded. "She says you won't explain why. She says you claim it's only about your being Jocelin's guardian."

"It is." Not even Geoffrey could know the truth about *that*. "Trust me," he went on, "I always had Eliza's feelings in mind, too. How do you think she would have felt to learn that her husband had taken up with a girl of seventeen?"

"Wounded, I would imagine. But that's not why you didn't tell her. You were trying to keep her from knowing that you'd brought Jocelin to her door purposely, without considering what the truth might do to her."

"I didn't think she'd ever *learn* the truth, damn it!" He rubbed his bristly chin. He'd been up all night. He needed a shave *and* a bath. But what did any of that matter without

Eliza? "And I didn't expect to . . . come to care for her quite so much."

"Ah," Geoffrey said, as if he understood.

"Why do you think I wish to come to the bloody house party?" Nathaniel snapped. "So I can make amends. I haven't been able to do anything like that, because no one will *tell me where she is*!"

Geoffrey blinked. "Oh. I thought you knew. She's at Grenwood Lodge preparing for the house party."

Cursing under his breath, Nathaniel strode over to the fireplace. That made perfect sense. He should have realized it himself. He'd wondered if she might have gone to stay at one of Grenwood's properties, but he'd assumed it would be either Castle Grenwood in Yorkshire or the mansion near Hyde Park. The Richmond lodge hadn't occurred to him.

Nathaniel stared into the fire. "She's not the only one suffering, you know."

"You *do* look a fright, I confess."

Sparing a foul glance for Geoffrey, Nathaniel said, "And I never meant to hurt her, either. Indeed, that's one reason I hadn't told her the truth before this. I didn't want to trample her late husband's memory."

"I think he did that all by himself. Indeed, I've never had the impression she was mourning him all that much."

"She's a complicated woman, our Eliza. She mourned the loss of the man she'd thought she knew, not the one she really did."

"That's actually a pretty astute observation for a man who has merely 'come to care' for her." Geoffrey stared him down. "Do you love her?"

He'd been dancing around that question for days. "How the hell should I know?" he said hoarsely. "I've never been in love, not once. How would I even be able to recognize it?"

Geoffrey shrugged. "It's fairly simple really. If you love her, you'll fight for her. You'll tell her everything and put her needs above yours. If you don't love her, you won't."

"That's absurd. There are other matters at stake. It's not as simple as what you're making it seem."

"Ah, but it is. And she knows it. If this is a test, it's her testing you to make sure you're ready to be in a *good* marriage. Assuming you wish to marry her, that is."

"I do." The minute he said the words, he knew they were true. He didn't want a mistress. He wanted a wife, a partner, a companion. He wanted *Eliza*.

Geoffrey went on. "Because Eliza has already had a marriage where her husband kept secrets, and probably more than just the one, given that she didn't even know why he up and joined the army without apparent reason."

"She told you why?"

"No. But I know it was a concern of hers. Not that it would matter why, given the way her parents are. Her parents' marriage has already given her an idea of what a bad marriage is. So, for some time she's had two different perspectives of what bad marriages look like. And right now, she thinks yours would look like that, too. You have to show her it would look like something else, something she's never experienced before—real love and partnership, where the two of you confide in each other everything about your true selves."

"Yes, but how do I do that when she won't even see me?" he bit out.

Geoffrey scratched his chin, then fixed him with a long look. "I'm going to tell you something you have *not* heard from me, do you understand? Because Diana will have my hide if she knows I told you this."

"You have my word," Nathaniel said.

"Eliza is returning to Grosvenor Square this afternoon.

She said she needed a day to herself so she could prepare for the house party."

"Which begins day after tomorrow, right?"

"You can't come," Geoffrey said.

"Don't worry, I got that message." But by then it wouldn't matter. Because now that he knew exactly where Eliza would be today, he could woo her after all.

If she would allow him in. If she'd even talk to him.

"I have to go," Geoffrey said. "But if you need anything other than Eliza delivered up to you—"

"No, you have done more than enough." Because now he had a chance at regaining Eliza. "Go on—I understand. And I swear I won't show up at the house party."

As soon as Geoffrey left, he tossed the rest of his brandy into the fireplace and went in search of his butler.

Then he started spitting out orders. "Have one of the footmen bring me coffee, and lots of it. Then tell my valet to lay out my finest evening attire. Oh, and say I will need a shave and a bath."

In the bath, he would start thinking on how best to invade the inner sanctum. There must be a way. Although he didn't have much time to come up with one.

He spotted his sister. "Where's Jocelin?" The young lady might know exactly when Eliza would be arriving at Grosvenor Square. He might have to arrange his visit so he reached the place when *she* reached it. That might be his only way in.

Tess eyed him oddly. "She went shopping in Charlie Crowder's curricle. I-I thought you knew. I thought you approved."

"Why does everyone think I know everything when clearly I do not?" he grumbled.

"She *is* a widow, you know. And it's perfectly fine for

widows, even young ones, to ride with suitors in open curricles."

"Of course."

He wouldn't let this sour his mood. He was going to see Eliza. Finally. He would offer her marriage and promise to be a better husband than he'd been a lover.

His mind awhirl, he headed for the stairs. Damn. Did that mean he intended to tell Eliza the full truth about Jocelin?

What choice did he have? She would never accept his proposal of marriage if he didn't tell her, and she'd be wise not to. Because if he couldn't trust her to keep the secret, whom could he trust?

He still had to find a way to make her at least let him in the house to state his case. And since she learned from her mistakes, it was doubtful she would keep the lock to her bedroom window unlatched.

What did that leave? Jewelry? No. She didn't strike him as the sort of woman to be swayed by jewels. In any case, it had to be something that compelled her to open the door to him, even if just to reject him. Flowers? No. It couldn't be something Norris would just take from him and give to her. Besides, the last time he'd given her flowers, she had told him that if he had truly wished to buy her forgiveness . . .

That was it!

Making a quick turn about, he rushed out the door and down the steps, relieved to see that Geoffrey was just getting into his carriage.

"Geoffrey!" he cried as he ran up to his friend. "Do you happen to know where I could hire an orchestra?"

# Chapter 19

Eliza climbed the steps of her house alone, ridiculously happy that neither of her sisters were there, according to the groom. They weren't supposed to be, but they'd been pampering her for the past few days, so she wouldn't put it past them. Their coddling had begun to prey on her nerves. She was used to being the one who coddled people, not the other way around.

She was also happy she had dealt with Major Quinn for the final time before she'd left. He'd promised to keep quiet about Jocelin's past, but for Eliza's sake alone. After he'd said that, she'd been half-afraid he meant to offer for her, but thankfully he'd made no such remarks. He'd only said he was returning to the Peninsula shortly and hoped she'd permit him to write her. Of course she'd said he could. He *was* her cousin, after all.

As she entered the house, Norris approached to take her pelisse. "I thought you should know, madam, that Lord Foxstead has been here twice trying to find out where you went."

Her heart leapt. Even now, even after what had happened. Foolish heart. "What did you say?"

"I refused him entry and told him nothing, of course."

At least that explained why Nathaniel hadn't even

attempted to see her in Richmond. Not that she'd wanted him to. Really, she hadn't.

*Liar.* "That was very good of you, Norris, although you could have revealed where I was. I would have dealt with him."

"The duchess instructed me not to."

More coddling. Of course.

But once the house party began at Diana's, she would have to deal with Nathaniel. And if not then, eventually. She couldn't avoid him forever. She just wasn't sure what to say to him. *I'm in love with you? I want to be your wife?* Or rather, *I don't want to be your wife unless you're entirely honest with me*, which was true.

But what if he couldn't be? What then? She wanted desperately to be with him, yet she also wasn't sure she could endure more heartbreak stemming from his refusal to tell her the most important things in his life. Love wasn't always enough. Trust and truthfulness were important, too.

"I must say he was very irate," Norris said. "He even tried to bribe me. But I would never betray you for any amount of money. None of you."

She smiled at him. "That's because you're a good man, Norris. Hiring you was the wisest decision I ever made."

"Thank you, madam. I am glad I could be of service." The words were stiff and formal as usual, but Norris's ears betrayed his pleasure at the compliment, for they pinkened considerably. "Oh, and I should also mention that Mrs. March and Lieutenant Crowder are waiting for you in the drawing room."

That was curious. "Thank you, Norris." She headed up the stairs at once, tired as she was. She hadn't seen Jocelin since before she'd learned the truth about the woman's connection to Samuel. Indeed, that was one reason she'd fled to Grenwood Lodge. It had enabled her to avoid Jocelin.

But now, as she entered the drawing room, she realized she didn't care anymore that the young lady had lain with her late husband. She'd had five days to consider the fact that Jocelin had done her a favor—by showing her once and for all that her marital troubles could be laid at Samuel's door.

Mostly, anyway. *She* had been the one to choose him as a husband. Did she dare trust herself this time to choose the right man? She didn't want a marriage like her first one. Nor one like that of her parents.

Charlie, out of uniform for once, jumped to his feet as he spotted her, and Jocelin followed suit.

"Oh, please," Eliza said, sweeping her hand toward the settee they'd both been sitting on. "You know you needn't stand on ceremony with me."

Jocelin flashed her a wan smile. "I heard that you and his lordship quarreled, and I wasn't sure what it was over, so I didn't wish to overstep my bounds."

"He really didn't tell you why?" Eliza asked.

"He said it was private," Jocelin said.

"It was indeed," Eliza said, relieved that she didn't have to deal with that, too. "Please, do sit down."

They all took seats.

"To what do I owe this visit?" Eliza asked.

"Well," Charlie began, "I've asked Jocelin to be my bride, and she has agreed."

"Congratulations to both of you." Eliza was relieved that Jocelin had chosen the man who was fun and not too serious.

Oh dear, that now meant Eliza would have to test Charlie's mettle by telling him the truth about Jocelin. But she didn't want to.

"So," Charlie went on, "we were hoping you and your

sisters might be willing to have a small ceremony here in the next week, before I have to leave for my posting."

Several questions ran through her mind, but she began with only the one. "Wouldn't it be more appropriate for you to have it at Foxstead Place? Lord Foxstead *is* Jocelin's guardian, after all."

"Yes," Jocelin said, "but . . . well . . . Charlie hasn't asked the earl for my hand yet, and we want to be prepared in case he refuses."

"Why would he refuse?"

"I don't know," Jocelin said. "He seems to disapprove of me marrying a soldier."

Because Nathaniel didn't want Jocelin to carry Jimmy off to war. But Charlie *had* spoken as if he were going alone. Besides, did Eliza even have the right to question them further about their plans, given what had happened between her and Nathaniel?

Jocelin stared down at her hands. "Before we can even broach the subject with him, however, there is something I must tell you. Something I should have told you long ago. Given that you and your sisters have been so good to me, I feel it's only fair I tell you the truth about Jimmy's father."

Eliza blinked, her curiosity piqued. Did the woman actually mean to tell her about Samuel? In front of her soon-to-be husband? Surely not.

"If this is about Mr. March—" she began, hoping to spare Jocelin.

"There is no Mr. March," Jocelin said.

One look at Charlie's expression of loving concern told Eliza that he knew the truth already. "So this is about Samuel."

Clearly startled, Jocelin and Charlie exchanged glances. Then Jocelin said in a trembling voice, "You know?"

"Yes." And she wouldn't for the world tell Jocelin about

Major Quinn's petty revelations. "Nathaniel told me. Indeed, that's what we quarreled over—the fact that he kept it from me for so long."

"Ohh," Jocelin said, looking a bit anxious. "That explains why he's been so strange this past week."

Eliza stared at her. "Strange in what way?"

"He mopes about and snarls at everyone. Even Jimmy steers clear of him, and Jimmy *adores* him."

"Nathaniel adores Jimmy, too," Eliza said.

"He does." Jocelin swallowed. "Jimmy is very fond of you as well, you know."

Eliza couldn't hide her smile. "That's only fair since I'm quite fond of *him*. He's a sweet child."

Jocelin wouldn't meet her eyes. "Even though he's . . . well . . . your late husband's son with me? And a bastard?"

"Jimmy can't help who his father was," Eliza said softly. "It would hardly be fair to despise him for an accident of birth he had nothing whatsoever to do with."

At that, Jocelin burst into tears. "Oh, Mrs. Pierce . . . you are so good! I feel so ashamed . . . that I ever listened to . . . Samuel."

Oddly enough, it upset Eliza just to see Jocelin cry. Yes, the girl had been her husband's mistress or . . . or *something*, but . . . "It's all right, Jocelin, I have had nearly a week to reconcile myself to who you were to him."

"It's *not* all right," Jocelin sobbed. "Samuel said some . . . awful things about you—"

"Perhaps you shouldn't . . . um . . . mention that, my love," Charlie said while Eliza was still gaping at her. Charlie cast Eliza an apologetic look. "Forgive her, she is a bit overwhelmed."

"No, Charlie, I have to say it!" Taking out her handkerchief, Jocelin dabbed delicately at her nose and eyes. "None of what Samuel told me was true! You aren't the least bit cold or unfeeling. And I was such a . . . stupid little fool to believe . . . him. How could I have . . . done so?"

"You were young, my dear," Eliza said, not sure how else to answer what Jocelin didn't seem to realize was insulting.

"That's no excuse. You are the kindest, sweetest woman I have *ever* met," Jocelin gushed through her tears, "and I just feel . . . *awful* that I ever caused you any pain. I wish . . . I wish . . . I could go back and . . . and give him a piece of my mind for not appreciating you!"

Well, that was a sentiment Eliza certainly approved of. "I wish I could go back and do the same. But I was young, too, when I married, and no one had taught me it was fine for me to stand up to my husband."

That thought knocked her back on her heels. It was true. Mother had never stood up to Father, not directly. She had run away instead, when she couldn't take any more. And Father, like Samuel, had blamed her for the very things he'd done regularly.

So, when, at the beginning of their marriage, Samuel had argued with her at every turn, Eliza had learned not to say what she thought, not to risk having her husband go to other women . . . not to challenge him when he lied. It had taken Samuel running away to war for her to find herself again, and she *had*. How could she possibly blame Jocelin now for showing her just how far she had come?

What had Nathaniel said a few weeks ago? *I liked the old Eliza, but I like the new one better, the one who speaks her mind, who doesn't let anyone push her around.*

Jocelin wasn't the only one who'd shown her just how far she had come.

"Please, Eliza," Jocelin said, "don't let my foolishness keep you from marrying his lordship. He loves you."

She narrowed her gaze on Jocelin. "He told you that?"

"Well . . . no, but I can tell he does."

"Men who love you don't lie to you," Eliza said. At least Samuel had taught her *that* lesson.

"But . . . but he did that to protect me, you know. He was afraid the truth would get out, and Jimmy and I would be ruined."

"And he believed I'd reveal the truth?" Her throat tightened. "That doesn't speak well of his opinion of me."

"No . . . no, I'm saying this badly. He thought that if you championed me, then no one would ever question my right to be in society . . . even if the truth got out somehow. And I suppose he thought it might be easier for you to champion me if you didn't know of my connection to Samuel."

Eliza sighed. "Yes, he did tell me some of that. But he wouldn't say why it was so important to him that you succeed. I mean, I know he was close to your father, but his insistence on seeing you married speaks to a very close friendship indeed."

"It *is* curious, I'll admit," Jocelin said. "But even when he first came to the camp, when Papa introduced us, Lord Foxstead was kind to me. Not like other men were, always leering at me or flirting or such. He was just . . . nice. Like an uncle."

That gave her pause. He'd once said something along those lines, that she should think of Jocelin as a sister or niece or daughter to him. Like a female relation. But she couldn't figure out what relation that would be.

"And you have no idea why."

"I assumed he was like Papa, a true gentleman toward women, the way Charlie is, too." She sighed and took Charlie's hand in hers again. "Then when the earl was so upset over my . . . having Samuel's child, I'm ashamed to admit that I thought his concern for me was because he had taken a fancy to me—"

"As any sane man would," Charlie put in.

Jocelin's face positively glowed as she smiled up at him. Eliza was happy for her. But the sight of those two in love only widened the hole in her own heart.

"The thing is," Jocelin told Eliza, "he *never* looked at me the way he looks at you."

Her sisters had said much the same. But what if they were all merely seeing what they wanted to see? Lord knows she'd done that plenty enough with Samuel.

She was just about to ask Jocelin to elaborate, when the sound of instruments being played wafted up into the drawing room. *Several* instruments. She could hear woodwinds and drums and violins and . . . a harp? Could someone be holding an affair in the square that she didn't know about?

Charlie rose and walked over to the window that overlooked the square. "Someone's put an orchestra in the middle of the street, blocking a couple of carriages and horses from moving."

"Now why on earth would anyone . . ." Suddenly, she remembered what she'd said to Nathaniel on May Day after he'd given her that beautiful bouquet. Surely not. She couldn't imagine that he would . . .

She hurried to the window to look out, and just then Nathaniel went to stand in front of the same small orchestra she'd hired to perform at the house party. "I can't believe he actually did it."

"What?" Jocelin asked as she, too, rushed to the window. "Who?"

"Your guardian, that's who. I told him a few weeks ago that if he'd wished to buy my forgiveness, he should have presented me with a troubadour to serenade me. And he'd said next time he'd bring an entire orchestra to serenade me."

"And he did." Jocelin looked at her. "That's so sweet!"

Yes, it was, curse him. How could he manage to break

her heart in one moment and be so sweet the next? It was Samuel all over again.

She sighed. That wasn't true. Nathaniel had never made her think she was in the wrong even when she wasn't. Nathaniel had listened to her. Samuel hadn't cared enough to do that, to be sure.

Nathaniel's lies had partly stemmed from his attempts—wrong and foolish, but still attempts—to spare her feelings.

Then the sound of a man's voice, deep and strong and horribly off tune, sounded from below.

Charlie winced. "His lordship is singing."

"I wouldn't call that singing," she said, though she couldn't prevent a smile, remembering him saying he sang like a frog. "It's more like . . . caterwauling."

"I could have told you he couldn't sing," Jocelin said. "He used to try in the camp, and when the men mocked him for it, he did it louder just to annoy them."

"That does seem like something Nathaniel would do. Some part of him is definitely a rebel."

Then she realized what he was singing wasn't any song she'd ever heard. The tune was to a popular ballad she'd sung a time or two herself. But Nathaniel wasn't singing that, oh no. The words she *could* make out were different. And from the sounds of it, he was already on the second verse. Yet she still couldn't make out all the words.

Suddenly, it seemed very important for her to hear them. She opened the windows, but all she could hear up here were calls from her neighbors telling him to pipe down and crying out for the watch and all sorts of nonsense, not to mention a baying dog or two. That was probably precisely what he'd been hoping for—to make such a commotion that she'd be forced to let him in, if only to save her and her sisters embarrassment.

Still, he'd brought an *orchestra*, of all things. And she

had to know what he was singing, the daft fool. She could always kick him back out if this was just his sly way of getting her to allow him in without giving her what she really wanted.

So she rushed out to the stairs and fairly flew down them. Her servants were peering out the front windows as she hurried to the entrance. But as soon as she swung open the door, the singing stopped altogether, although the orchestra continued playing.

Then Nathaniel dropped to one knee at the bottom of the steps. And this time when he began to sing again, still badly, the orchestra played low enough so she could hear the words.

> *Let me feed you apples*
> *In the morning light*
> *After we've shared kisses*
> *All throughout the night.*
>
> *Let me wreathe you flowers*
> *For your golden hair*
> *So that you may smell them*
> *Through the day so fair.*
>
> *Let me sing you music*
> *Never sung before*
> *So that we might snuggle*
> *Till the light's no more.*
>
> *If you let me do these,*
> *I will make you mine.*
> *You will be my lady*
> *Till the end of time.*

Ignoring the imperfect rhyme at the end, she swallowed past the lump in her throat. "Where did you get that song?" she asked him.

"I wrote it. The words, anyway." He gestured behind him to the orchestra. "They provided the music."

"You wrote it?" she said skeptically.

"I told you I couldn't sing. I never said I couldn't write." He shrugged. "At Eton I was rather known for having a dab hand at verse." He rose, his face turning serious. "May I come in? I have something I desperately need to discuss with you."

When she hesitated, he turned to the orchestra and gave them the motion to continue.

"Oh, very well," she said calmly, though her heart was anything but calm. "You may come in. For a bit. Before you destroy the ears of everyone in Grosvenor Square and make all our neighbors hate us."

Still, she refused to make this too easy for him. If he offered marriage after his dramatic entrance but wouldn't tell her the only thing she wanted to know, then even his incredibly adorable lyrics meant nothing. Because if he couldn't talk to her, be open and honest with her, then their marriage would eventually end up the same as her parents'.

He followed her inside a bit warily, halting when he saw Charlie and Jocelin standing there. As the blood drained from his face, she realized she had the perfect way to either get the answers she deserved . . . or learn once and for all whether he ever meant to give them to her.

"Can we . . . speak privately?" he asked, turning his piercing gaze on her.

She waved a hand toward the entrance to the dining room, which was large enough that they could talk without being heard by anyone inside or out of the house. "Come,

Charlie, Jocelin. I should like to have some witnesses for this."

He was already in the dining room, but he whirled to look at her with something like panic in his face. "There's no need for—" he began.

"How odd that you should use that word," she said as she ushered the young couple in through the doors before entering and then shutting the doors behind her. "Everything you have done since you came here a month ago has been to help Jocelin. Indeed, you have always chosen your ward's *needs* over mine."

She approached him slowly. "And that was appropriate in the beginning. But once you professed to care for me . . . If you wish me to listen to anything you say now, Nathaniel, you'll have to choose my needs over hers for once. So tell me, why has Jocelin's future been so incredibly important to you that you would rather risk my future with you than risk hers and Jimmy's?"

# Chapter 20

God help him, but Eliza looked wonderful, even in her serviceable yellow gown, the practical one she wore when she had things to do. Nathaniel hadn't realized how starved he was for just the sight of her until she'd appeared in the doorway, shards of the dying afternoon sun glinting golden off her hair.

Even though the paleness of her cheeks and the doubts in her eyes showed how she'd suffered, she still looked absolutely beautiful to him. He just wanted to spend the rest of his life erasing that suffering, making her happy. He would cheerfully throw himself at her feet and beg her to marry him.

Because he loved her. He did. He couldn't imagine life without her irrepressible laugh, her tender kindnesses, her many different sorts of kisses.

But one look at Eliza's implacable expression told him that if he balked at telling her the full truth now, he would lose any chance at her. That had been the one true thing Samuel had ever said about her—she was stubborn. Like her father.

Like Nathaniel himself, to be honest.

So, if he wished to gain her heart, he had to reveal all. She'd already had one husband who was never honest with her. As Geoffrey had said, Nathaniel had to prove he could—*would*—be different.

And he had to prove it here. Where Jocelin could also hear it. He probably should have told Jocelin a long time ago, anyway. However . . . "Jocelin can stay, but Charlie cannot," he said firmly.

Charlie took Jocelin's hand. "Your ward has agreed to marry me, so I'm not leaving. Whatever concerns her concerns me, sir."

Damn. He should have realized that was why the two of them were here together, but once again he'd been caught by surprise. "Were you even planning on asking my permission to marry?"

"We were," Jocelin said. "After we . . . um . . . spoke to Eliza."

To ask *her* permission? What the devil?

"It seems that Charlie already knows the truth about the fictitious Mr. March," Eliza put in, her voice softening a fraction. "Apparently, Jocelin told Charlie about it when he offered for her."

Bloody hell. A lot had certainly happened before he'd arrived. So *that's* why they were all here. Was that good or bad?

Nathaniel stared Charlie down. "And you don't mind that Jocelin was . . . er . . ."

"Why should I mind?" Charlie asked. "When I met her, I was told she was a widow, so I already knew she wouldn't be a blushing, naïve bride. The fact that the scoundrel who took her innocence happened not to be her husband hardly matters to me."

"That's a very broad-minded opinion," Nathaniel said. One that Major Quinn obviously hadn't shared. Thank God she hadn't wished to marry *that* arse. Nathaniel would have been forced to call the man out.

"How can I have any other opinion? I love her." Charlie stared down at her with such adoration that Nathaniel couldn't doubt him. "And she loves me. So I am content."

"I, however, am not," Eliza said, crossing her arms over her chest. "Are you planning on answering my question? Or should I just leave the three of you to plan their wedding?"

She was growing impatient, and he couldn't really blame her. But he'd be risking a great deal to tell even *her* the truth. Because if she still didn't want him, she could destroy him with the new knowledge.

*She had a chance to destroy you this past five days, man, and she didn't take it. Can you really see this woman that you love ever purposely hurting someone?*

No, he could not.

"Sometimes, Nathaniel," she added, reading his fraught emotions in his expression as always, "you have to learn to trust people, especially those who are important to you. Because if you don't, eventually you find yourself all alone."

"I think I understand that better now." He tore his gaze from her. "You wanted to know why Jocelin's future is so important to me." He braced himself for any possible reaction. "It's because Jocelin is my sister."

A stunning silence met his pronouncement. As it continued longer than he knew how to handle, he nervously added, "Half sister, really. Which makes Jimmy my . . . er . . ."

"Half nephew?" Charlie said, the first to find his voice. "I don't know what you'd call it, actually."

"I believe it *is* half nephew, yes," Nathaniel said. When the two women just kept gaping at him, he said, rather inanely, "I've had a couple of years to think about it."

Eliza slowly sank into a dining room chair. He could see she was making connections, going back over conversations, trying to figure everything out.

Jocelin, however, was pale as death. "You . . . you mean, Mama and your father—"

"No, sweetheart, sorry. I should have clarified that it was *your* father and my mother. You and I share a father. And it happened long before Anson met your mother, so he never did anything wrong. I swear."

"Wh-Why didn't you tell me you're my *b-brother* before now?" Jocelin asked plaintively.

That was the hard part. "Because your father made me swear not to. He didn't want you to regard him differently. And after he died, I didn't want you to remember him differently."

He returned his gaze to Eliza. She still hadn't spoken, and she was the only one whose reaction he really cared about right now.

Then she lifted her eyes to his. "So . . . when you told me about your parents going to Italy to have you, that was another lie?"

Oh, God, so many little untruths. She was never going to forgive him, was she? "Not exactly. I mean, they did go to Italy. And the story I told you was the same as they told me when I was growing up. I believed it my whole life. Until right before I left for the Peninsula."

He threaded his fingers through his hair. "I told Mother I was considering buying a commission in the army. She tried to talk me out of it, and when I wouldn't let her, she said that if I insisted upon going, she could provide an introduction to a general who would make sure I was given a good posting."

"Papa," Jocelin interjected.

"Our father. Yes."

Jocelin frowned. "So you knew I was your half sister from the first time we met?"

He nodded, although this discussion was already starting

to get out of hand. "Look, I can explain all this in more detail later, but first you three must understand and accept that no one can know this. *Ever.* Not even Tess, since I've never told her and never will. She's my half-sister, too, after all, and I don't want her to look at our mother in the wrong light. She stayed with our grandmother the whole time we were in Italy and truly believes I am the child of both her parents."

"But . . . but *why* can't anyone know you're my brother?" Jocelin asked in a pleading tone. "And . . . and Jimmy's uncle, too?"

"Because if you tell anyone and it gets around," Eliza said softly, "Nathaniel's reputation in society will be harmed. People tolerate women in society bearing children who aren't their husband's—but not the heir. Never the heir. So he'll have a title people will feel he doesn't deserve, and they will gossip about him mercilessly."

Eliza understood, thank God.

"Worse yet," she went on, "anyone who thinks they should have received part of the unentailed inheritance of his fa— of the previous earl, like his disagreeable cousin, could argue that point in court. They probably wouldn't win, but by the time it was over, your brother and you and Jimmy—and Charlie now—would be dragged through the mud."

Nathaniel released a long-held breath. "Along with Tess and her husband and any children they might have."

"Damn, that's a lot of people," Charlie muttered.

"A lot of people I care deeply about." Nathaniel fixed Charlie with a steady look. "Including Jocelin and Jimmy. Because once the floodgates open on the gossip about me, others will start to explore whether Jimmy is a bastard. Promise me you will keep them safe from such a scandal. That you will never allow the truth to leave your lips, even around Jimmy. Or at least not until he's old enough to be relied upon to keep it secret."

Charlie straightened. "Of course. You can count on me, Lord Foxstead."

"Thank you." He stared at his precious sister, who seemed distracted. "Jocelin? Do you think you could keep quiet about it?"

"What? Oh, yes. I just don't know how you did it all this time."

"By never calling your father anything but General Anson, even in my head, or you as anything but my ward. Although I admit that sometimes it's hard not to think of Jimmy as anybody but my nephew."

That brought a smile to her lips, which was a relief to see.

He walked over to kiss Jocelin on the forehead. "I know that you, dear girl, probably have lots of questions. I'm happy to answer every one later back at Foxstead Place." He turned to shake Charlie's hand. "And tomorrow morning, I will expect you at the town house so we can discuss Jocelin's settlement and her dowry before you do anything rash like announce your engagement at the house party at Grenwood Lodge."

"Of course," Charlie said.

Nathaniel looked at Eliza again. "But right now, I have my own . . . future to sort out, so if you both wouldn't mind, I'd really like to speak to Eliza privately. Assuming she agrees."

The couple looked to her. He held his breath until she nodded.

Then she rose. "Let me just see them out and tell Norris not to worry and to leave us alone for a bit. I have lots of questions myself, after all."

"I'm not going anywhere unless you kick me out again," he said.

"You needn't worry about that," she said with a quick smile, giving him hope, for the first time in days, that he might actually have a chance of winning her.

Eliza repeated Nathaniel's warnings to Jocelin and Charlie before packing them off. Then she made sure that the orchestra knew they could leave and told Norris she and his lordship were *not* to be disturbed under any circumstances.

Finally, she stood outside the dining room door, taking deep breaths and letting everything sink in. Guilt tugged at her, making her wonder if she should have pressed him to reveal such a monumental secret in front of the young couple in the first place. Then again, if he and she were to marry—

Was that what she wanted, now that he'd revealed himself fully? To be his wife? Of course she did. But in the event that the truth got out, would he resent her for making him tell Jocelin? She hoped not.

And if he merely wanted a lover, she could do that, too, although it would never be enough for her. She knew that now. She loved him. She wanted everything.

Taking a deep breath, she opened the door to find him pacing the room impatiently. Then he whirled to face her.

"How is she?" he asked.

This time she could hardly resent the question. "She's fine. Or she will be once she grows used to the idea." She swallowed hard. "But I do wish you had told me she was your half sister before. If I'd known, I would *never* have put you in a position where you had to say all of it in front of Jocelin."

"I know," he said, with an endearing smile. "But you were right to do so. It was time for the secrets and parsing of the truth to end. And as you so astutely said, sometimes people need to trust the ones they care about."

He walked up to take her hands in his. "The ones they *love*. I love you so much, Eliza. If these past five miserable days have taught me anything, it was that. I love how you take people under your wing and help them be better. How you spread music and joy wherever you go."

The raw emotion in his face made her want to sing.

"And how can I not love the way you put up with me? According to Tess, it's fairly difficult."

"Not so difficult," she managed to choke out through all the happy tears pooling in her throat.

"Thank God." A sudden uncertainty crossed his face. "Do you think you could ever learn to trust *me* after all the secrets I kept from you for far too long? Do you think you could learn to love *me*, too?"

She gave a giddy laugh. "My dear Nathaniel, if you couldn't tell before this, I already love you. You're a much easier person to love than you apparently think. You're kind and generous, and you don't expect me to let you run everything." She paused. "Well, except in the matter of keeping secrets, which you are woefully stubborn about. Although I do understand a bit better now why you kept the one about Jocelin. Still, I need to know you will trust me from now on."

"I will, I promise." He squeezed her hands. "And anyway, there are no more secrets."

Thank heaven. "But I do still have many questions. Will you answer them?"

"Of course." He drew her to the dining table where they could both sit next to each other. "Ask whatever you wish, and I will answer. *If* I know the answer."

"Did your father . . . know about your mother's affair?"

He sighed. "Mother said it wasn't really an affair, or at

least not a love affair. But she said once Father realized that the fancy Italian doctor wouldn't be able to fix his . . ."

"Genitories?" she said, fighting a smile.

"Exactly," he said, flashing her a sardonic look. "He was determined to have an heir before it was too late to claim that the child was his."

"But your father couldn't have been sure your mother would bear him a son or even that she would become pregnant."

"I pointed that out, and Mother said they had realized that, but Father had wanted to try, in any case. Father handpicked Anson himself. At the time, Anson was a lowly soldier training in a Gloucestershire militia, which was how he met my father in the first place. Father offered to buy him a commission as an officer in one of Gloucestershire's actual regiments, and Anson jumped at the chance. That wouldn't have been a choice for him, given his background."

"What *was* his background?" Eliza asked. "You only told me his family was dead, and Jocelin never talked about him."

"As a youth, he was in an apprenticeship to a baker before joining the militia. So my father paid his way to Italy, paid for him to stay in my parents' hotel. Then Mother was able to go freely back and forth to Anson's room without much comment."

She stared at him, remembering something he'd told her when they'd first discussed his parents' trip to Italy. Then she rolled her eyes. "So you *weren't* actually small for your age."

He winced. "No. I was just small, period, because I was only a year old by the time we arrived in Gloucestershire. So they were forced to keep visitors away for a while.

Apparently, it had taken a couple of months for Mother to become enceinte, and then they had waited until I was born to be sure Father had his son, and after that, they waited another year to be make it easier to obscure my true age. If you'll recall, you weren't sure of Jimmy's age either."

"True." Eliza blinked. "Wait, does this mean you're even younger than you said?"

"Let's just say that my official birthdate is a fictional one."

She laughed. "What would they have done if you'd been a daughter?"

He shook his head. "Tried again, probably, and then 'claimed' that the doctor's 'treatments' had taken that long to work or some such nonsense."

"Good Lord, that was quite the plan."

"I know. And all so Father could have his heir."

"Didn't your mother find it humiliating?" Eliza asked.

"She didn't say. But I gather she wanted to make my Father happy." He shrugged. "Anson was fairly young when Father chose him—nineteen, I think? Mother said Father picked him for his apparent virility and attractive features."

Nathaniel glanced away. "Then Father resented my mother for going 'eagerly' to Anson's bed. Or so she assumed. She did say she and Father had been in love once. I confess I saw flashes of it now and again growing up. But she told me the whole experience changed their marriage irrevocably, and it was never quite the same."

"I would imagine so." Eliza shook her head. *Men.* She would never understand them. "Why didn't your father simply pass off some orphan infant as his heir?"

"And risk the child growing up to look like neither of them? Or worse yet"—he gave an exaggerated shudder— "have to raise a child with peasant blood as his own?

Horrors! At least if Mother bore the child, it would be half nobility."

The sarcasm in his voice masked a profound sadness. "Oh, Nathaniel, I'm so sorry." Then something occurred to her. "Wait, I thought your mother was born in Italy."

"She was. To an Italian count. Her blood might not have been English, but it was quite blue, I assure you. Didn't I mention that?"

"No, you did not. Among the many other things you didn't mention."

He sighed. "I know. I'm afraid my unusual family situation has made it hard for me to trust people. You have every right to feel betrayed. I should have told you sooner."

"At least you acknowledge that." She took a deep breath. "And in return, I will acknowledge that your mother's tale must have been hard for you to take."

"Actually, it was something of a relief." He flashed her a wan smile. "At last someone had explained why my father had never exactly warmed to me."

Her heart broke for him. "After your mother told you the truth, did you discuss any of this with your father before you went off to join the army?"

"Are you daft? I didn't want him to know I was going to war until I had already sailed for the Peninsula. He probably would have sent his own band of soldiers to try and bring me back."

"Who could blame him?"

"I suppose, although he couldn't have stopped me from going at that point. Once Mother had told me everything, I was determined to meet the man who'd sired me."

The truth hit her all at once. "Oh, that makes so much more sense than you running off to war just because you felt guilty over daring Samuel into joining the army."

"I did feel guilty. It's why I convinced Anson to make Sam his aide-de-camp. I figured Sam couldn't get himself killed in that situation." He shook his head. "Little did I know." He took her hand in his. "But you know what the worst part was?"

"That he got Jocelin with child?"

"Actually no, although that was awful, too. The worst part was having to tell you Sam was dead. Knowing that I had brought it about by daring him in the first place, and then by insisting we join the Twenty-Eighth Regiment so I could meet Anson. I felt enormous guilt over that. Still do."

"You shouldn't. It's not as if you killed him." She threaded her fingers through his. "I never blamed you for it, even after you told me about the dare." And the last thing she wanted to discuss right now was Samuel. "So you never did confirm with your father the truth of your mother's words?"

"I confirmed it with Anson. Besides, Father never discussed significant matters with his rapscallion of a son. Even if I'd attempted to talk to him about it, he would have told me he had no idea to what I was referring. Not that I would have tried. He'd already spent my entire life giving me hell for everything I did that he disapproved of—"

"And you responded by doing even more of those things." He narrowed his gaze on her. "How did you know?"

"Your reputation, of course. I daresay your father felt that only through his machinations did you even exist, and then you had the audacity to wish to live your own life. What madness!"

Nathaniel gave a rueful laugh. "That about sums him up."

"I have a similar sort of father," she said with a shrug. "I think it's endemic to men of a certain rank."

"Geoffrey's not like that, and he's a duke."

"Not your typical duke, you must admit."

"True."

"And he *can* be rather high-handed sometimes, trust me. Especially when he's discussing money."

Nathaniel grinned. "So *that's* why you were so scrupulous in discussing the bill for Jocelin with me."

"Oh, yes. Diana actually had to wrangle terms from Geoffrey when he first came to Elegant Occasions."

"Only because he wanted her in his bed, and he highly disapproved of that fact. Getting involved with a woman of her exalted standing was *not* in his plan." He sobered. "*You* were not in *my* plan. That is, I'd always found you attractive, but I never expected to fall so totally in love with you."

A lump caught in her throat. "Nor I with you." Then she drew herself up. "Although, let me tell you one thing, my darling. If I cannot bear you an heir except by sharing some other fellow's bed, you will not be having an heir. So you had best not get into any accidents involving reckless driving of a phaeton or the like."

He seemed startled by her words. Then his eyes gleamed at her. "I don't intend to. And I suppose that answers my question."

"What question?" she asked, truly perplexed.

"Whether you will marry me."

That was when she realized her statement had assumed they would have a life together as husband and wife. She blinked. "I-I wasn't hinting . . . I didn't mean . . ."

"Too late." He caught her hands in his, his face alight. "I've got you now, and I don't mean ever to let you go. Not for at least sixty years or so."

She arched one eyebrow. "I see you intend to be quite long-lived."

He chuckled. "Well, I do come from at least half-peasant stock, to my late father's way of thinking. It gives me an advantage over the usual doddering earls one encounters about London."

"Does it?" She walked her fingers up his starched cravat.

"I suspect your main advantage comes from the 'virility' of your peasant stock."

"Why, Eliza Harper, you little minx," he teased her, "are you by any chance trying to seduce me?"

"Is it working?" she asked, emboldened by his response.

"Of course." He leaned forward to kiss her sweetly on the lips, then gazed into her eyes with such earnestness that she knew it wasn't just passion he was feeling. "You know I can never resist you, my love."

# Epilogue

*August 1812*
*Castle Grenwood, Yorkshire*

Early in the evening, Eliza sat in the nursery at Geoffrey's Yorkshire estate, cooing at her new niece, Suzette Marie Brookhouse, as Verity sat next to her grinning at the child. Eliza had never seen a nursery so well appointed. In addition to the comfy sofa Eliza sat on, there were two rocking chairs, a couple of cribs, a bed for the nursemaid, and a temporary cot for Molly, who had come with her and Nathaniel to take care of Jimmy.

The boy leaned over to gaze in wonder at the two-week-old. "Pretty," he said. "Jimmy hold baby, Missis Pears."

Eliza had stopped reminding him she was now Lady Foxstead. To him, she would probably always be Missis Pears. "The baby is too small for you to hold yet," she said gently. "But perhaps in a few weeks, all right?"

Jimmy sighed. Eliza suspected he was a bit jealous of all the attention the chubby-cheeked baby was getting on the day of her christening. Then again, Suzette was indeed a very "pretty" child.

Molly walked over to take Jimmy by the hand. "Why don't we go down to the moat to feed the ducks?"

"Feed the ducks!" Just like that, Jimmy leapt off the sofa and was pulling on Molly's hand to make her go faster toward the door.

After they were gone, Eliza gazed over at Diana, who sat in the rocking chair opposite her. "I still can't believe you have a moat."

"I can't believe we do, either," Diana said. "Geoffrey is trying to figure out whether to fill it in or what."

"He could always build a skew bridge over it," Verity said.

The three of them laughed. Skew bridges seemed to be one of Geoffrey's favorite engineering feats.

Then Diana asked Eliza, "Have you heard from Jocelin and Charlie yet?"

"We just received our first letter from the Peninsula. I can't believe it's already been two months since they married."

"I can't believe you agreed to keep Jimmy for them until your wedding and then indefinitely afterward," Verity said. "That boy is adorable, but he's also a handful."

Eliza shrugged. "I know, but I wasn't going to let them take him on a transport to the Peninsula and raise him in an armed camp! He's only two and a half, for pity's sake."

"Still," Diana said, "you are the only woman I know who would take in the bastard son of your late husband."

Eliza couldn't say, of course, that Jimmy was also her nephew by marriage. Not even her sisters were privy to that knowledge. "Jocelin is still Nathaniel's ward, and by extension, so is Jimmy. Besides, it's not as if Nathaniel is poor. Foxstead Place alone is quite large."

"True." Diana gazed fondly at Suzette. "Although now that I'm a mother, I can't believe Jocelin could leave him behind so readily."

Privately, Eliza couldn't believe that either, despite *not* being a mother. Still . . . "She was very young when she had him, and she never had a chance at being in love before. I suspect what she felt for Samuel was a youthful infatuation. I gather that he showered her with compliments, made her feel like a real woman, seduced her into his bed, and then was either afraid to do more for fear her father would find out . . . or lost interest once he'd had her innocence."

Verity arched an eyebrow. "Either one seems equally likely to me. But I suppose you'll never know for certain."

"Especially since she's understandably a bit uncomfortable talking about it with his widow," Eliza said. "Although honestly, I never blamed her as much as I blamed him."

"I can understand that." Diana rocked a little. "Does Jimmy seem to miss her much?"

"Sometimes," Eliza said. "But honestly, even before she and Charlie left for the Peninsula, Jimmy spent most of his time with Molly."

Diana narrowed her gaze on Eliza. "I give you fair warning. I am seriously considering stealing Molly from you."

"If you do, you have to take Jimmy, too," she teased.

"Take Jimmy where?" Nathaniel asked from the nursery door.

"To raise," Eliza said. When he blinked, she added, "Diana wants to keep Molly."

"Ah." He went to sit beside Eliza on the other side from Verity. "No chance of that, Diana. Molly and Jimmy are permanently attached, as far as we're concerned. It's none or both. And I give you fair warning—that boy can run the hind legs off a hare."

"I've noticed." Diana made a face at him. "Very well. I suppose I'll—reluctantly, mind you—let you keep Molly."

"What's wrong with your nursemaid?" Eliza asked.

"I don't have one. We live in the wilds of Yorkshire now, you know. I shall have to go back to London to hire one, I fear." Diana arched an eyebrow. "We were so busy planning your wedding—and then the baby came early—that I hadn't looked for one yet."

"It was a lovely wedding, too, thank you," Eliza said. "Small but tasteful, in a quaint church with a delicious wedding breakfast. Oh, and the nearby dovecote was wonderful. I heard them cooing as we left."

"I didn't arrange that part," Diana said.

"I did," Verity said.

"Either way, it was a nice touch," Eliza said.

"The best part was that you ladies provided me with a wife for it," Nathaniel said. "I had no idea that Elegant Occasions offered such a service."

"Only for you, sir. We aim to please," Eliza said. Then she pressed a kiss to Suzette's brow. "But getting back to nursemaids, Diana, there has to be someone in the local village who would like to be in service at your castle."

"No doubt," Nathaniel said. "And if not, perhaps we could find one in Linden who would suit."

"I shall take care of that while I'm here," Eliza told her sister soothingly.

"Or I will," Verity said. "Especially since the Phantom Fellow isn't plaguing us anymore. He seems to be gone for good."

Nathaniel snorted. "How can you be sure?"

Verity tipped up her chin. "I haven't seen him anywhere since that May Day affair at the Crowders."

"And you still don't know why he was there?" Nathaniel asked.

"No," Verity said. "Or who he is. Even Monsieur Beaufort had no idea that he'd temporarily infiltrated the ranks of his kitchen staff."

Eliza sniffed. "Well, I say, good riddance to bad rubbish."

"We still don't know if he was rubbish," Verity pointed out. When Nathaniel looked skeptical, Eliza explained. "For all his secrecy, the man was good-looking, or so Verity says. I think she fancies him."

Coloring deeply, Verity jumped to her feet. "Don't be ridiculous. I don't even know the man's name." She headed for the door. "And I must make sure dinner is going smoothly."

With that, she was gone.

"Verity doesn't like it when we tease her about the Phantom Fellow," Eliza said with a laugh.

"Which only means we tease her more," Diana said.

Suzette started fussing, but Eliza managed to soothe her with a few soft words and some swaying in place. Then she looked at Diana. "Getting back to the nursemaid issue, I meant it about finding you one while I'm here."

"That would be *wonderful,* thank you," Diana gushed. "Although whatever you do, don't tell Mama I'm looking. She'll try to force some ghastly, prune-faced chit like Miss Grimes on me. I want my child to grow up with loving care, not constant judgment."

"Don't worry," Eliza assured her. "Miss Grimes will never darken any of our doors. Besides, didn't Mama and Lord Rumridge leave right after the christening?"

"Oh! Yes." Diana let out a relieved breath. "I completely forgot. Of course, that means we now have Papa for the next two days."

"That's someone who will never darken *my* door," Eliza muttered.

Nathaniel chuckled beside her. He'd heard her rail against her father more than once.

"He would have barged in regardless," Diana said. "But it was rather inspired of you to suggest that one couple come in advance of the christening, and the other come after, so that their only interaction was during the service itself. They could hardly kill each other in a church. It would be very bad form."

"I'm not so sure," Nathaniel said. "If looks could slay . . ." When both ladies looked at him, he said, "What? Did neither of you notice your parents glowering at each other the whole time?"

"I was too busy trying to keep Suzette from crying while it was going on," Diana said.

Eliza nudged him. "And I was too busy admiring my handsome husband as Suzette's godfather."

Little Suzette began to fuss again, and Diana held out her arms. "Give her to me. It's time for her to be fed."

Nathaniel got a strained look on his face and jumped to his feet. "Um, I may be her godfather, but I draw the line at some things. So that's my cue to leave."

Eliza laughed. "Diana won't do it in front of *you*, silly man." Still holding the baby, she rose to hand Suzette to her mother. "Besides, shouldn't it be nearly time for dinner?"

"Wine and punch first," he said. "I came up here to fetch you."

When Eliza looked at Diana, her sister said, "I'll be downstairs in time for dinner. Go on, you two."

They hurried from the room.


As they headed for the stairs, Nathaniel gazed down at his wife, pleased that he'd managed the hard part, which was to get her out of the nursery in enough time to do as he'd planned.

"I should warn you," he said. "Jimmy is annoyed there are no soldiers guarding the moat. He has requested that he and I march beside it all night. I've informed him you would get lonely without me."

"I would, too." She shook her head. "That poor lad does love his soldiers, doesn't he?"

"Perhaps it's in his blood. His grandfather was General Anson, after all, and we both know who his father was."

"Excellent point."

Sobering, he lowered his voice. "Are you sure you don't mind raising Sam's son?"

"Isn't it a bit late to be asking?" she said, then laughed. "Of course I don't mind. He's also your half nephew, after all. Besides, I adore Jimmy."

"You don't mind *now*." He thought of how sweet she'd looked caring for Suzette. "But when we have children . . . assuming you want children . . ."

"I absolutely want children. If I'm not too old, that is, to have any."

Nathaniel shook his head. "You're twenty-seven, for God's sake. That's not too old for anything."

"Well, then. It's settled. And no, it will not bother me in the least to have Jimmy acting as an older brother to our children. Besides, you never know when Jocelin and Charlie may choose to return."

"We can only hope."

They had descended to the floor where their room was when he stopped her. "I have a confession to make. I did *not* go up to fetch you down to dinner. That's not for another hour."

She arched an eyebrow. "Oh? Then where are we going?"

"I want to show you something." He tugged her down the hall to their room, which was conveniently far away from those of the other guests. God bless Diana. "Actually, it's a gift for you—to mark the two-month anniversary of when we agreed to marry."

As soon as they were inside, he pulled out a framed

copy of the song he'd written for her, penned in Verity's flowing hand. Once he'd learned that Verity wrote out all of Elegant Occasions' invitations, he'd enlisted her for the task.

Eliza beamed up at him as she looked it over. "Oh, it's so lovely. And much nicer than the scribbled version you left for me that night when we parted." Setting it on a nearby table, she said, "Now, wait here and I'll be back shortly."

Startled, he took a seat on the end of the bed and tried to think what she was up to. He'd hoped to seduce her after she saw his gift, but now that she'd disappeared—

"I'm back," she said in a sultry voice.

He turned his head, and his pulse jumped into triple time. Before him was his seductress wife, wearing the flimsiest shift he'd ever seen . . . and naught else. With the setting sun streaming through the window behind her, he could see right through the thing, not that he minded.

Already his trousers were constricting certain parts of his anatomy. Then he caught sight of her knowing smile and got suspicious. "You *knew* about my surprise."

She laughed. "Verity let it slip."

He groaned. "Your sister is the worst secret keeper I know."

"I could have told you that. Woe be unto the 'Phantom Fellow' if she ever learns who he is. His secret will be out everywhere." She came slowly toward Nathaniel. "Now I have a surprise for *you*. One I was wise enough not to tell my sister about."

She began to sing in her pure, melodic voice, coming closer with every note.

*As the daylight's waning*
*And we are alone,*
*Let me give you kisses*
*And songs of my own.*

*Then I'll share my body,*
*And you'll warm me through.*
*Let me show you, darling,*
*How much I love you.*

*When the morning greets us*
*With its fiery kiss.*
*Let me hold you closer*
*In our marriage bliss.*

*If you let me do this,*
*I will make you mine.*
*And you'll be my husband*
*Till the end of time.*

"You changed the words," Nathaniel said softly as she untied his cravat.

"Most of them," she murmured while he shrugged off his coat. "Not because there was anything wrong with yours, mind you, but because I wished to write a version for *you* to have."

"I can hardly fault you for that, especially when you sing so much better than I." As she dispensed with his waistcoat, he filled his hands with her luscious breasts. "Not to mention, you look so much better while doing it, too."

"I beg to differ," she said as she unbuttoned his trousers and drawers. "I am quite pleased with my virile husband."

"Glad to hear it." He got rid of the rest of his clothes with great haste, then tumbled her back onto the bed. "Because I don't think we're going to make it to dinner after all."

*Watch for Verity's story in early 2024!*

Visit our website at
**KensingtonBooks.com**
to sign up for our newsletters, read
more from your favorite authors, see
books by series, view reading group
guides, and more!

Become a Part of Our
**Between the Chapters Book Club**
Community and Join the Conversation

Betweenthechapters.net